A Knock on the Door

Each breath was a blast of frost shooting straight into Falco's lungs. He knew he'd suffer frostbite on his face in a few minutes if he didn't protect his skin, but that was the least of his problems. He crawled to a vantage point between a couple of square-topped rocks and snapped another full magazine, his second to last, into his G15. The pursuers were ▓▓▓ning out as they moved down th▓ ▓▓▓▓▓, ▓▓▓ ▓▓ ▓▓▓ second he lowered hi▓ ▓▓▓▓▓▓▓▓ ▓▓▓ ▓▓▓ ark 30 Hammer rifle.

At less than 2▓▓ ▓▓▓▓▓ ▓▓▓▓▓ ▓▓ ▓▓ ▓▓ ▓▓▓ ▓ay he could miss, and ▓▓▓ ▓▓ ▓▓▓▓ ▓▓ ▓▓▓ ▓▓eezed off six rounds, killi▓▓ ▓▓ ▓▓▓▓▓▓ an equal number of the enemy. LaRue snapped off controlled bursts, the 6.8-mm slugs churning the snow around the pursuing soldiers, dropping several of them onto their faces. The SEALS could see several places where the pristine white snow was being stained a shocking bright red.

They heard it before they saw it: a grinding engine, treads crunching the snow. It loomed suddenly on the crest of the ridge like some arctic-equipped Abrams tank, rumbling up the crest and immediately toppling over to descend the near slope. Snow flew from the churning treads as the second snow tank came into view, veering and juking wildly so as to present a difficult target. The barrel in a low, flat turret was aimed toward the SEALS' position, and it immediately spit a gout of flame. A high-explosive round smashed into the rocks before them, sending both men tumbling backward.

Also by Kevin Dockery and Douglas Niles

STARSTRIKE: TASK FORCE MARS

STARSTRIKE

OPERATION
ORION

Kevin Dockery and Douglas Niles

BALLANTINE BOOKS • NEW YORK

A Del Rey Books Mass Market Original

Copyright © 2008 by Bill Fawcett and Associates

Published in the United States by Del Rey Books, an imprint of The Random House Publishing Group, a division of Random House, Inc., New York.

DEL REY is a registered trademark and the Del Rey colophon is a trademark of Random House, Inc.

ISBN 978-0-345-49042-1

Printed in the United States of America

www.delreybooks.com

OPM   9   8   7   6   5   4   3

In Memoriam: Hank Reinhardt
Swordsman, Smith, Author, Businessman
He lived life to the fullest,
a Renaissance man who thrived in our time,
and would have thrived then as well.

One: Envoys to the Stars

The ship was a silver giant: a long, sleek cylinder with four massive engines arrayed at the stern and docking pods for as many as six shuttles at a time jutting from various spots along the otherwise sleek hull. Rows of bright portholes allowed passengers and crew to gape at the vastness of space in all directions. Three Plexiglas domed observation pods—very high-tech cocktail lounges, each offering the occupants an unprecedented view through a full 180-degree sweep—sprouted from the hull near the bow. The entire vessel spanned a length equal to two football fields. Her name was *Pangaea,* and she was the first internationally commissioned spaceship built by humans—and the largest spacefaring vessel ever to call Earth her home. Her captain, and much of his staff, was a United States Navy officer, and the rest of the command group included members of the Chinese, British, Russian, French, and Indian navies, though the vessel herself flew the flag of no country.

She was crewed by some forty men and women, with another fifty staff aboard to tend to the needs of the passengers. Although she could be configured to haul cargo, there was little of that on the current mission. Instead, she carried an official embassy party of some 100 dignitaries. Those luminaries had been boarding over the last three days, rocketing upward from planet Earth aboard a succession of shuttles while the *Pangaea* orbited the globe and her crew finalized the preparations for an interstellar jump.

Unlike the two United States Navy frigates (space) that made up her escort, *Pangaea* was unarmed. Her mission, symbolized by the United Nations emblem emblazoned on her hull, was peaceful. In the main, she would be used to carry cargo and passengers from one star system to another, jumping through the interstellar void with the aid of the faster-than-light technology that had been brought to Earth by the Shamani some five years earlier. Now, however, with one test jump behind her, the *Pangaea* was ready to embark on a mission that held great promise—and unknown but very real danger—for all the humans of planet Earth.

On this particular voyage she would carry very important passengers indeed. From the point of view of USN Lieutenant Thomas (Stonewall) Jackson, his fellow travelers belonged in an orbit worlds, if not galaxies, above the circles in which he usually dwelled. Merely in making the journey from his "cabin"—actually a tube barely long enough to allow him to roll over in his sleep—to the mess hall, he had encountered a four-star general, the ambassador from China, the Secretary General of the United Nations, and lastly the Chief of Naval Operations (CNO) himself, Admiral Brian "Ball-Breaker" Ballard.

"So you're Jackson?" the admiral queried casually, taking his time looking the lieutenant up and down. The two officers stood on the deck just outside one of *Pangaea*'s elegantly appointed lounges. For the moment, they were alone.

"Yes, sir," Jackson replied. "U.S. Navy SEALS, sir."

"I know you're the SEAL—excuse me, SEALS," the admiral retorted with more than a touch of sarcasm. "I suppose you think that extra 'S' on the term stands for 'Special Privileges'?"

Jackson stood at attention but made no reply. The admiral

knew as well as anyone that the SEALS classification was an elite status, indicating a SEAL who was qualified not only for Sea, Air, and Land operations but for Space as well. He was proud of his Team and it was galling to listen to the admiral's unpleasant tone, but there was nothing to be gained by arguing. He wondered where this was going and tried to suppress a longing for the safe and secure, if claustrophobic, confines of his sleeping tube.

Ballard nodded at the ribbon signifying the Silver Star that emblazoned the decorations on the breast of Jackson's dress uniform. Jackson was justifiably proud of his decoration, the third highest given for valor in the United States military. Originally, he had been nominated for the Navy Cross for his actions in leading his contingent of SEALS in action against a hostile enemy force consisting of an entire planet of aliens who had wanted to kill or capture the SEALS. But politics had reduced the award received by Jackson to the Silver Star, with the SEALS he had brought home all receiving a Bronze Star for their part in the action. There had been some in the military command structure as well as politicians who had felt that Jackson and his men deserved courts-martial rather than decorations for their actions, the least of which had been the unauthorized release of nuclear weapons. Right now Jackson had a pretty good idea of just where the CNO might have stood on that issue.

"I know about your little escapade back in '50. You probably think you're some kind of Buck Rogers space cowboy, don't you?"

"Sir, no sir, I do not," Jackson replied stiffly.

"Well, I want you to remember that on this mission, sailor! This is a diplomatic embassy, with nothing less than the future of your country—of your whole goddamn planet!—at stake."

"Yes, sir. I understand, Admiral."

"Make sure you do!" The statement was like a broadside

from an *Iowa*-class battleship of a hundred years earlier. "Because what I mean by that is that you and your men are along on this embassy *not* because you have a mission but merely as a precaution. Powers that dwell on a much higher plane than myself"—Jackson was surprised to realize that there could be such powers!—"deemed it appropriate that we have a small military component to our ambassadorial team. But you are not to advertise your presence in any way!

"What I wanted to accompany this mission was a traditional detachment of marine embassy guards. They have the special training to deal with this kind of diplomatic environment. Instead, I had you and your Team thrust on me supposedly because you and the rest of your SEALS are the only troops around who have direct extraterrestrial combat experience—which is *not* something a diplomatic mission is supposed to require in its military contingent! You special operations types seem to give your loyalties to the Special Operations Command rather than your original service branches. That is not a fault I can place on the marines, who remember that they're a part of the navy. But it seems that the Shamani think a great deal of you and your men, so I was overruled by the UN, the president, and the chief of staff in my recommendation for a marine contingent. And that is not a position I care to be put in, understand, Lieutenant?"

"Yes, sir. I think I understand, sir," Jackson said tightly. He was more than a little offended by the admiral's words. It was a studied insult for the naval officer to voice a preference for marines to Navy SEALs or SEALS, no matter what the mission. But Jackson was not going to say anything more no matter what the provocation.

"Do you? That means you are not to be seen, not to be heard! I don't want to hear so much as a single question among these diplomats as to who you are or why you are here!"

"Yes, sir." Jackson stood at rigid attention, unsure of what else he could say, not that there weren't a few old-sailor phrases he *wanted* to utter. His temper was surging dangerously, but he forced himself to draw a slow, calming breath. *Don't do anything stupid, Stonewall,* he reminded himself.

"That being the case, what in the name of hell are you doing on this ship, right out where you'll practically fall over those same diplomats and ambassadors?" the admiral demanded, his voice dropping in volume if not in menace.

"Following orders, sir," Jackson replied. "My Team is aboard the *Pegasus,* and I thought I'd be traveling there, too, until I got word back on SATSTAR1 to board *Pangaea.* Sir, I request permission to transfer to the frigate at the earliest opportunity."

In truth, Jackson didn't know why he had been directed to travel aboard the civilian ship. The orders had come directly from the Special Operations Command at Tampa, Florida, and he had known better than to argue. But neither was he going to throw anyone at SOCOM under Ball-Breaker's bus. In any event, Ballard didn't seem interested in following up on where the orders had come from. He clearly wanted to get this lowly SEALS officer out of his sight.

"Dammit, man, we're going to jump in six hours, and we're accelerating under full power. You won't be able to transfer till we come out in the Centauri system. Until then, you stay out of sight! Do you read me?"

"Loud and clear, Admiral!"

"Then what are you waiting for? Dismissed!" Ballard snapped.

Jackson came to a crisp, Naval Academy–style stance of attention, knowing that the admiral would continue with his dressing-down if Jackson snapped up a salute while they were in the corridors of the ship. The SEALS officer then turned on his heel and marched back toward his cabin. He was relieved to get away from the fire-breathing admiral until he reached the hatch to his quarters and remembered exactly how unappealing they were.

He stepped from the corridor into the dressing area, which was a closet-size alcove where two adults possibly could stand at the same time if they were prepared to be very close to each other. A total of nine small hatches in stacks of three faced into the central compartment. Each of the hatches was one passenger's sleeping compartment, a flat-bottomed cylinder a little more than two and a half meters long and one meter in diameter. It was comfortable enough for sleeping and was equipped with variable lighting, a keyboard, and a vidscreen so that the occupant could read, work, or watch while lying on his back. But that was about it.

Jackson was contemplating with little enthusiasm the prospect of sliding into his cocoon and riding out the journey in seclusion, when he was startled by a buzz from the outer corridor: Someone was at the hatch.

"Please," Jackson muttered as his shoulders slumped at the thought of a battle he knew he couldn't win, "don't let it be Ball-Breaker again."

He pushed a button to open the hatch and was pleasantly surprised to see Doctor Irina Sulati, the petite, attractive physician he had first met on Mars more than a year earlier. She smiled, her white teeth dazzling against her chocolate skin and ink-black hair.

"Stonewall Jackson!" she declared with a laugh, grinning as she looked up and down his dress tunic. "I thought that was you—and I must say, you clean up very well!"

"Irina!" Jackson replied, giving her a hug and an affectionate kiss. "Fancy meeting you here!" He blushed, suddenly uncomfortable, and looked around at the tight confines of the dressing alcove. "I'd invite you in, but as you can see, I'd have to leave just to make room for you."

"Never mind," she said, taking his hand. "Come with

me—there's a little more space on the medical deck. We can sit down and get caught up. It's so nice to see you again!"

Jackson was pleased at the encounter, as well. He had said goodbye to Irina only reluctantly when *Pegasus* had returned to SATSTAR1. She had embarked for her position on Mars, where she led the medical team on the most important research station, while Jackson had dropped back to Earth for a well-deserved leave. In the months after that he had been reassembling his Team, training the new men, and preparing for the next mission.

"I'd love to come with you," he replied, knowing the transport tube hatch was only a few paces away. Certainly Ballard would never find him on the medical deck.

"But first, have a look around for me," he suggested, nodding toward the passageway. "You don't see any admirals out there, do you?"

"Congratulations, *Lieutenant* Sanders," Captain Carstairs said to the beaming young man. He nodded at the silver bar on the other officer's collar. "It's a well-deserved promotion."

Newly minted Lieutenant (j.g.) Dennis Sanders couldn't help smiling broadly. "Thank you, sir. It means a lot to me to hear you say it."

"Nonsense. What you SEALS accomplished last year will go into the annals of the U.S. Navy as one of the finest military actions in this nation's history, not to mention the *first* action outside of our own atmosphere."

"I expect this mission will be a lot smoother," Sanders suggested.

"We can only hope," the CO of the *Pegasus* replied.

The two officers occupied the observation dome in the bow of the frigate. They stood firmly on the circular deck, oriented so that the top of the dome—the very prow of the spaceship—was directly overhead. The gravity holding them in place was provided by the ship's steady acceleration, muted by the inertial dampening system that prevented them from being squashed flat under what was in reality more than 10 Gs of artificial but potentially crushing gravity.

To one side they saw the speck of light that was the *Pangaea* accelerating in formation some ten kilometers away; the second frigate of the escort, the *Troy,* was barely visible another ten klicks beyond the civilian ship. The sun was directly astern, invisible from their position, though Sanders knew that it would have been the brightest thing in space if they had been in the aft observation platform, looking "down" through the deck at the life-giving orb. In fact, he had been on L Deck just an hour before and had been surprised at how small the sun already looked. The little fleet was moving toward deep space at a phenomenal speed, still accelerating, and already had passed outside the orbit of Mars.

"How long until we make the jump?" asked the recently promoted lieutenant.

Carstairs checked his watch. "A little over two hours," he replied. "Is your Team all settled in?"

"Yes, sir. They know the drill—all except the new men, of course."

"Ah, right," the captain replied. For a moment both men were silent, remembering the four Teammates who had died on Mars during the SEALS' first mission.

"That tall Minnesotan—Robinson, right?—looks like he made a good recovery," Carstairs suggested. "Your medic did a hell of a job bringing him off Batuun in one piece."

"Yes, sir. Six months of rehab in Coronado, and Smokey couldn't wait to blast off with the rest of us," Sanders acknowledged. "And the new men fit right in. If only we had the LT on board, we'd have all sixteen of the platoon together."

"He's no doubt hobnobbing with the high brass and the diplomat corps," the CO said, not unkindly. They both looked at the speck of the *Pangaea,* apparently motionless in space despite her tremendous acceleration.

"This will be the first jump for the *Troy,* won't it, sir?" Sanders knew that the other frigate was only the second spacefaring vessel of the United States Navy and that she had been commissioned only a few months earlier.

"Yes. She made the usual local runs, out to the moon, down for a circuit around Mercury. But she hasn't left the solar system yet."

"Have you been aboard her, sir?"

Carstairs nodded. "Skip Kilkenny was a classmate of mine—he's her captain—and he gave me the nickel tour. She's the same class as the *Pegasus* but a little longer, with a larger hold and two shuttles bigger than your drop boats. Word is, she'll eventually carry a company of marines, but for the time being you SEALS are still the only off-planet combat troops we have."

"Well, it doesn't seem likely that we'll have any shooting on this trip. We're just an escort, right?" Sanders asked.

"Yes. The real action is going to happen on *Pangaea,* and when the diplomatic party lands in the Darius system—that's one of the stars we see, located right in Orion's belt when you look at the sky from Earth—we'll see how our people stack up against the negotiators from across the galaxy. First, we're going to stage through Alpha Centauri—the system, not the star itself—to get a better bearing on the jump to Arcton."

The thought did not inspire extreme confidence, but Sanders was a natural optimist. "They're supposed to be the best and brightest in the world, those folks on the *Pangaea.* I have to like our chances."

Carstairs laughed, though not with a lot of humor. "Have you seen the lounges in those observation pods?" he asked, nodding toward the massive passenger ship. "I guess it's probably cocktail hour right about now."

"Well," Sanders said wistfully, "I hope the LT is having enough for all of us."

Six decks below, it was cocktail hour on the *Pegasus,* though her captain at least pretended to be unaware of the fact. In the sacrosanct cabin area known as the goat locker, the domain of the chief petty officer of the ship's crew, the chief of the boat (COB), Master Chief Bosun's Mate Curt Swanson, was holding court with two of his crewmates— both petty officers—and two of the SEALS. Master Chief Rafael Ruiz and Chief Bosun's Mate Fred Harris were happy to enjoy the COB's hospitality and were trading speculation about the nature of their current mission.

"I think they're sending us SEALS along to make sure the alien women are duly impressed with humankind," Ruiz suggested, taking a sip from the tin cup Swanson had given him. The clear liquid seared his throat and almost brought tears to his eyes. "You know, in case you swabbies give 'em the wrong impression." He nodded at the lone female, a navy petty officer, in the group. "With all respect, ma'am," he added.

"My guess is they hope you SEALS pick up some civilized traits after hanging out with us prime specimens in the U.S. Navy," CPO Amy McClellan retorted, shaking her head to clear the zing from the alcohol from her tongue.

"No doubt," Swanson opined. Hoisting his cup in a toast, he carefully extended his little finger. "This is the way we do it in high so—SI—ity," he enunciated before tossing back the entire contents of the drink.

The other four whistled, impressed, as the COB smiled broadly. "Now, kiddies, I suggest we see that all of our charges are properly tucked in. Can't have them asking for a glass of water just as we make the jump, can we?"

The other NCOs agreed. The ship's petty officers left to check on the crew, and the two SEALS descended the transport shaft to H Deck, the compartment where the Team was stationed.

There were a dozen men sprawled about the surprisingly spacious area. Eight were veterans of the first mission, the job that had taken them to Mars and then, unexpectedly, had vaulted them as captives through hyperspace to the star system known as Batuu. There, they had turned the tables on their captors, the Eluoi, managing to disrupt the operations of a major interstellar slave merchant known as Tezlac Catal. Enlisting the aid of another alien warrior, the Assarn pilot Olin Parvik, the SEALS had raised considerable havoc in the Eluoi city before escaping from the planet in a stolen shuttle to rendezvous with the *Pegasus* as the frigate made the interstellar jump to rescue them.

Four new men, each an accomplished SEAL operator, had passed the rigorous training regimen—including stints at McMurdo Station in Antarctica and final commissioning aboard the space station known as SATSTAR1—and earned the rocket fins of the elite of the elite: They were now SEALS. Baxter and Keast each possessed a steady eye and were deadly shots with any firearm. Corpsman Mirowski and Electrician's Mate James Schroeder also were assets to the SEALS. The big blond Pole was an inveterate jokester, and "Schrade" brought some excellent technical expertise into the Team. All the new men had been assigned to a veteran to make up a shooter pair while they developed their experience in operating with the unique unit. All in all, they were a group of men to be extremely proud of, as both Master Chief Ruiz and Chief Harris well knew.

"All right, you SEALS," Chief Harris said cheerfully. "This old boat is about to go very, very fast. I need you to strap everything down—including yourselves—and be ready to do a little traveling."

The men moved to obey, and in surprisingly short order

the collective chaos of the compartment had been squared away.

An hour later the little fleet reached jump speed. Now far astern, the sun flickered and, from the point of view of all three ships, abruptly disappeared.

Jackson and Doctor Sulati buckled themselves to a comfortable lounge seat as the ships jumped from the solar system to the star known to the people of Earth as Alpha Centauri. As usual, the jump passed almost instantaneously, with just a flicker of lights and a sensation of a rather sharp jolt, hence the requirement that everyone and everything be strapped down. For a short time they were weightless as the ship pivoted to bring her stern in line with the destination. Then the engines fired at full power, and the sensation of gravity—now the result of deceleration—returned.

As soon as the ships completed the jump, Jackson turned back to Doctor Sulati. The pair settled into their comfortable seat in a lounge next to the *Pangaea*'s medical compartment, secure from the prying eyes of officious admirals and dutiful diplomats. They had spent several congenial hours getting reacquainted, but their conversation naturally turned to the mission and the unknown destination before them.

"The conference will be held on one of the moons in the Centauri system. It orbits a gas giant, but I understand the star is intense enough to keep the temperature around zero," the doctor noted.

"I hope you brought your mittens," quipped Jackson.

Sulati chuckled. "I don't think I'm getting off this ship. They have me doing twelve-hour shifts in the clinic, just making sure that none of the ambassadors gets so much as a runny nose."

"What do they think they can accomplish?" the lieutenant asked, turning serious. He was voicing a question that many military personnel had pondered: Why would the governments of Earth send so many valuable leaders into what could be nothing more than an interplanetary trap?

"Well, the Shamani have guaranteed our safety," the doctor noted, referring to the first of the three empires to have contacted Earth, back in 2047. The Shamani had provided the initial technology to allow humankind to reach the stars, and in those initial explorations, men—most notably, the SEALS—had come into contact with both the Eluoi and the Assarn, the other two empires, each of which spanned hundreds or even thousands of star systems within the galaxy. The Shamani had become important trading partners with Earth even as they worked to keep humankind separate from the other empires. The Eluoi, whom Jackson knew to be slavers and worse, were fanatically loyal to their rulers, called savants. They already had attempted aggressive action in the solar system with an attack on the human-manned research stations on Mars. The Assarn, in the lieutenant's limited experience, seemed to be rough and ready space pirates, ready to make a profit or pick a fight wherever the opportunity presented. The SEALS had rescued, and been in turn carried to safety, by a cocky Assarn pilot named Olin Parvik.

"And it seems true that treaties can be arranged that are binding among all three governments. It does make sense for us to have a presence, at least a voice, in some of these negotiations. The Eluoi, for example, bear watching."

"I couldn't agree more. I still get a headache when I think about that savant Tezlac Catal. Just hearing him talk was enough to knock my feet out from under me."

"I never had the pleasure of meeting him," Sulati said. "But I remember your description. Do you think he has some kind of psychic power?"

"That's what it seemed like, but I've never been much for that brain wave stuff. It certainly felt like a physical attack."

"Maybe it's some sort of electrical impulse," the doctor suggested. "You know, a negative charge, perhaps, that disrupts the normal functioning of your brain. Something that he can trigger with his own mind."

"That makes as much sense as anything," Jackson agreed. "I just hope I never have to hear that SOB talk again."

"He's going to be at this conference. Did you know that?" she said. "He's the chief of the Eluoi delegation."

"Great," the SEALS officer said bitterly. "At least I have an excuse to make myself scarce."

"So do I," Sulati said with a quiet chuckle before she again grew serious. "But don't you think it's a good thing that our governments are involved, sending representatives to meet with the three empires?"

"I suppose so," Jackson allowed. "But I'm not sure it makes sense to deliver a hundred high-value hostages into Eluoi hands. I know these bastards—they can't be trusted."

"Well, doesn't it help that both the Assarn and the Shamani will have representatives there? This is supposed to be neutral ground, isn't it?"

The SEALS officer shrugged. "I'm just not sure. The site is supposed to be nonaligned, but the Shamani ambassador admits it used to be an Eluoi stronghold."

"They yielded it in a treaty," Sulati replied. "I guess it all comes down to taking a chance, trying to work out some kind of official status for Earth in the middle of three powerful empires."

"You're right: We have to try," Jackson admitted. He knew that any one of the triumvirate had the capability to conquer, subjugate, and quite probably destroy the home planet of humankind. He pictured the ambassadors, the professors and philosophers, and the soldiers of the embassy mission.

He could only hope they were up to the task.

Two: SOS

Doctor Sulati turned down the lights in the small lounge compartment while Jackson bought a bottle of wine from the nearby bar. Naturally, his personal comset went off three seconds after he had, with considerable panache, removed the cork.

"Damn," he muttered. "I have to take this."

"Of course," Sulati replied.

The SEALS officer flipped open the compact device. "Jackson here."

"Lieutenant Thomas Jackson?" came the tinny, officious inquiry.

Jackson glanced at the bottle, which had cost him a little more than 200 credits—some three days' pay—and sighed. "Speaking."

"Orders from Captain Carstairs, sir. You're to return to the *Pegasus* immediately. You have Priority One; there's a shuttle waiting for you on the hangar deck."

"I'm on my way," he said, pausing only long enough for a brief and most unsatisfying goodbye kiss. "Savor every drop of that," he said with a nod at the wine.

"I'm putting the cork back in as soon as you go," she said firmly. "We'll drink it together."

He didn't take time to thank her as he jogged toward the transport tube, puzzling over the orders. Orders from Admiral Ballard he would have understood, even expected. But why would Carstairs be calling him back to the frigate?

He found out less than an hour later as he pulled himself through the air lock in the *Pegasus*. The ship and the docked shuttle drifted in zero-G condition—that is, the engines were neither accelerating nor decelerating—while the transfer was made.

"We've picked up a distress signal from a Shamani ship," Captain Carstairs informed Jackson when the SEALS leader pulled himself by handrails into the frigate's combat information center. The CIC, a windowless and well-armored compartment, was located on C Deck. Now the crowded room was abuzz with activity. A half-dozen sailors—four male and two female—sat at consoles, consulting an array of information gained from radar, energy, and radiation detection, real imagery—pictures captured by nanotechnology lenses capable of nearly 100,000-power magnification—and a host of other sensors. The frigate's main weaponry also was controlled from there and included four turrets, two each for the rail guns and missile launchers, and, most recently, after the engineers had finished examining it, a tail gun assembly where the particle beam cannon was mounted. That unique, long-range, and powerful energy weapon had been salvaged from their Assarn ally's, the pilot Olin Parvik, wrecked destroyer. Parvik had given it to Captain Carstairs and, by extension, the U.S. Navy as a token of appreciation and respect after the Assarn's harrowing adventures with the SEALS.

Even as the lieutenant looked at the operations screen—the monitor that displayed significant features across the breadth of a single star system—Jackson heard the triple pinging of the klaxon. Knowing the ship was about to get under way, he swung his feet "downward" toward the deck. Carstairs and the two other officers in the CIC did the same thing; the sailors, strapped into chairs, continued to monitor their electronics.

Immediately the engines surged, causing a quiet hum to permeate the ship. As always, Jackson deemed it something one felt more than heard. At the same time, the gravitational effect occurred. His feet contacted the deck lightly, as if he were being lowered gently to the ground. Swiftly the pressure built until he was standing comfortably at the equivalent of Terran gravity.

Jackson looked at the chart of the star system. He correctly identified a flashing green blip as the location of the Shamani ship. The radiant swath of Alpha Centauri itself washed out the image at the top of the screen. To Jackson, it looked like the stricken vessel was about half the distance to the star from the current position of the *Pegasus*.

"What do you know about this SOS?" the SEALS officer asked.

"It was pretty cryptic," Carstairs replied. "But I gathered that they were in bad shape. It was an emergency broadcast in their own language, but the translating program allowed us to pick up the coordinates. They went off the air right quick, though. No details as to the nature of the problem. It came from a ship called the *Lotus*."

The captain pointed to an adjacent screen, where Jackson saw a schematic outline of a large spaceship. Six engines were mounted in two sets of three around the outside of the hull, and the interior seemed to include a mix of cargo holds and passenger compartments. "That's her. At least, she's listed as the *Lotus* in our ship identifier catalog."

Jackson knew about the SIC: It was an encyclopedic database about the known types of spacefaring vessels, sort of a *Jane's Fighting Ships* for space. Because humans had interacted with the Shamani for the last five years and maintained good trading and diplomatic relations with that exotic culture, the Shamani fleet was well represented in the SIC. The

Eluoi, with their many classes of warships, had been analyzed and cataloged from Shamani sources. Little was
known about the Assarn combat vessels, however. The single
entry in the SIC was based on the inspection of a derelict destroyer by the crew of the *Pegasus* just a year earlier.

"The *Lotus* is in this star system, I take it."

"Yes, on the near side of the star. We've plotted as close to
a straight line as we dare, but it'll take us a few hours to get
there, and we'll have to decelerate into the site in order to at-
tain a stationary orbit relative to the *Lotus*. The *Troy* is keeping watch on the *Pangaea,* and the Secretary General himself
suggested it would be good if we could do the Shamani a
favor on the way to the conference. So we're authorized to
embark on a rescue mission." The captain rubbed a hand
across his forehead and then looked frankly at Jackson. "I've
got a knotty feeling about this one, Tom. I think your Team
should be ready to take to the boats if it comes to that."

"Aye, aye, sir. I'll go down to the hold and spread the
word."

The lieutenant found his second in command, Sanders, in
the officers' wardroom. Together they descended the five
decks to the hold where the Team bunked and trained. Jackson found his men sharp and edgy after the slightly unsettling experience of the jump.

"Any prospects of action, sir?" asked Master Chief Rafael
Ruiz. "The men are getting a bit of cabin fever."

"As a matter of fact, Chief, you'll need to have the boys
get their play clothes on. There's a good chance we'll need to
drop in about three hours."

"Hot damn!" crowed Mirowski, slapping the G-Man and
Harry Teal on their sturdy shoulders. "Now you guys can
show a newbie how it's done."

"Just keep your eyes open, Grasshopper—you'll learn a
lot," the massive LaRue growled. The G-Man already was

inspecting "Baby," his massive rail gun. "Permission to take an extra case of ammo, sir?" he asked the lieutenant.

"Rack it up for this one, LaRue. You're going to be packing enough with the breacher's gear. Master Chief, I want a zero-G close-quarters battle loadout made ready." The close-quarters battle (CQB) routine meant leaving most of the heavy and long-range weapons behind, selecting grenade ordnance for stunning blasts rather than frag or incendiary, and so forth. "Prep for shipboard CQB. This may be a rescue op, but there's no reason not to be ready for the worst. I'll get back to you with a clearer picture of the action when we get a little closer."

"Aye, sir," Master Chief Ruiz answered in a clear voice.

The men knew what to do without having been told by either their officers or their chiefs. Everyone had a job to do and set to work preparing the Team's gear as well as his own. Extensive training had instilled knowledge of what had to be done even in the new men.

Sanders stayed with the Team to coordinate the preparations: The men would embark in the pressurized yet flexible suits that protected them against the vacuum of space. These were the Mark IV models, the next generation from the suits they had worn on the first mission. In addition to an improved self-sealing capacity that allowed them to repair small punctures such as bullet holes quickly, they were made of a tough interwoven fiber that added some significant protection against abrasions, cuts, projectiles, and blast effects. Like the earlier versions, the suits included complete life support and communication systems for the wearer.

For normal combat operations, the SEALS carried an astonishing amount of firepower for such a small group of men. The standard shoulder weapon was the G15 assault rifle, a compact rifle that fired 6.8-mm caseless ammunition from a magazine that lay horizontally across the top of the receiver, just underneath the aiming module. The top-mounted magazine allowed the SEALS to reload the G15 quickly and watch what they were doing by just lifting the weapon to their sight line. New men didn't think that was such a big deal until they found out that one couldn't bend one's head downward while wearing a hard vacuum suit.

For the possibility of close-quarters battle in a zero-G environment, even the low recoil of the 6.8-mm caseless rounds off the G15 could throw one of the SEALS spinning off into space. But the weapon was designed for that possibility. By stripping out the standard barrel, installing a special new one, and changing some of the operating settings, a SEALS could use the G15 to fire the very exotic 7.62-mm rocket round. Operating normally, the G15 would fire the 7.62-mm rockets from their own magazine, feeding them through the mechanism and launching them at a rate of up to 650 rounds per minute on full automatic. The entire body of the rocket round would be launched from the G15 without any recoil to throw off the firer. The little rockets were precisely made and hideously expensive compared with other cartridges, but only the SEALS used them and they didn't waste ammunition. Anticipating zero G for this mission, Jackson ordered his men to swap out the standard barrels and load up with the new rocket rounds.

Each man would have his standard firearm—the G15 assault rifle in most cases—as well as a sidearm and some kind of bladed weapon. G-Man LaRue, of course, would have Baby; Derek Falco, the sniper, would take his "squirrel gun"; and Rocky Rodale would have his M76 handheld missile launcher. When they opened up with everything, the SEALS could put out a volume of fire that would have stricken awe into the hearts of any World War II battalion.

Chiefs Harris and Ruiz went with the coxswains to check out the two drop boats. Those small shuttles carried eight men—that is, half the Team—in each one, as well as a great deal of equipment and ammunition. With a crew of three, the drop boats were armed with a single turret-mounted chain gun and several missiles, including two Mark 90 tactical nuclear devices. Named *Tommy* and *Mikey* after legendary SEALs, the boats had rocket engines that allowed them to maneuver in space and set down on a planet with up to twice the equivalent of Earth's gravity. They were capable of taking off only from low-gravity bodies, but the primary mission of the drop boats was to get the SEALS into position. The details of extracting the Team sometimes had to be worked out later.

While the men's preparations went on, Jackson returned to the CIC and followed the painfully slow data collection process.

"She seems to be in orbit around the star," Carstairs noted, reading out the course they had plotted for the blinking green blip. "No sign of engine power."

The *Pegasus* still was decelerating under high power, but the crew stood comfortably on the deck because the inertial dampening system (IDS) limited the gravitation effect to a single G. This meant that they were essentially "backing" toward the target, but that was not a significant disadvantage.

"One reason I'm glad we mounted that particle cannon in the stern," the captain allowed, acutely conscious of the unknown presence out there in space, trying to anticipate any eventuality. "We'll go in with our eyes open and our fingers on the trigger."

"Captain. We're getting a clearer picture," said one of the sailors at the vidscreens. "I think the *Lotus* might have broken in two, sir."

Jackson saw immediately that the green blip had separated into two spots, with the increased resolution no doubt the result of the frigate's steadily closing range to target. Carstairs scrutinized the image, shifting to a filter that emphasized the infrared (IR) emissions of the target. As the blips gained more definition, they took on long, slender shapes suggestive of a spaceship—or *two* spaceships.

"I think the *Lotus* has some unwelcome company," Carstairs said. He turned to one of his com specialists. "Send a message to Admiral Ballard on the *Pangaea*. Tell him we're still investigating; we'll report more detail as it becomes available."

"Yes, sir." The technician started typing the message. Jackson was impressed by the dearth of information in the communication; he agreed that for now, Admiral Ballard didn't need to be told anything more than what was absolutely necessary.

Captain Carstairs glanced at the chronometer and turned his attention to the SEALS officer. "Fifty-five minutes until we're on station. You'd better mount up your men, Tom."

Jackson nodded. The familiar tingle of adrenaline was kicking in. "Each drop boat has a full vidscreen array, just installed," the captain continued. "We'll send you real-time updates as we get the images. Good luck."

For only the second time in history, the U.S. Navy SEALS got ready to drop from the frigate on a combat mission. It took less than thirty minutes for the Team to deploy into the two drop boats. The navy coxswains and a pilot and a copilot, as well as a gunner, would operate the craft while the SEALS got ready for full-vacuum environment. Jackson commanded the Teammates aboard *Mikey* with Master Chief Ruiz as senior NCO; Sanders and Harris fulfilled those roles on *Tommy.*

Jackson turned on his screen and looked at the images and readouts pouring directly from the CIC's main computer. They were approaching two spaceships, it was clear. One of them was a large vessel matching the image of the *Lotus* he had seen earlier; the other was a much smaller ship with two massive engine pods.

"We're picking up energy weapon discharges from the

smaller ship," Carstairs was explaining in the lieutenant's earphones. "There's an IR thumbprint in the stern half of the *Lotus*. Her forward quarter is as dark and cold as space itself."

"She's under attack, then," Jackson deduced.

"Yes. I want your Team to stay put until we get a little closer. The range is eight thousand klicks and closing fast."

"Aye, aye, sir. Can you download the deck plan schematics for the *Lotus* into *Mikey*'s computer?"

"Good idea. I'll have it done," the frigate's skipper responded.

Jackson was examining the blueprints, finely detailed, that displayed the various passages, compartments, holds, and machinery of the *Lotus* when the *Pegasus* was rocked by a powerful jolt. The SEALS, each man strapped in, felt the lurch but maintained position. The lieutenant's earphones crackled into life.

"Drop boats! Away all boarders!" Carstairs barked. "Make for the Shamani ship. We're taking fire from the bogey, and I'm going to bring all hell down on that buccaneer."

Immediately the hangar doors slid open, revealing the fiery bulk of Alpha Centauri. The star appeared to be unsettlingly close to them, though it was still many millions of kilometers away. The launch rockets exploded, propelling the two drop boats away from the frigate, and immediately the engines blasted, guiding the two small craft straight toward the star. With his visor down, Jackson saw their target, a slim outline of shadow against the brightness of the flaming thermonuclear surface. The filters in the canopy and hull of the boats kept the temperature at a tolerable level, but even so Jackson could feel the warmth on his face.

The other ship was nearby, and as they flew closer, he saw specks of light blinking from the hull. With a sick churn of his stomach, he realized that he was observing the blasts of an energy weapon, probably the thing that had given the frigate such a blast. If a beam from that caught one of the little boats, his Team could vanish in an instant. The sense that he had utterly no control over this part of the mission tossed his guts into an acidic lake. If only he could *do* something!

He saw sparks of light astern and saw that the rapidly receding *Pegasus* was blasting away with the particle cannon. The eerie green beam flickered in his eyes, but he knew it was a constant barrage, like a stream of water moving at the speed of light. The smaller ship—he had come to accept Carstairs's assessment of it as a buccaneer—moved away from the *Lotus,* engines blazing. The energy weapon on the pirate ship flashed again, but Jackson sensed that it was firing wildly now.

The Shamani ship was expanding to fill their field of view, fortunately blocking out some of the intense radiance of the star. Jackson recognized it from the image in the SIC but saw immediately that the forward hull section had been riddled with violent impacts. Dark, airless holes gaped along that section of the ship, and in places he could see all the way through the shattered hull to the star blazing millions of kilometers away.

The after section had avoided visible damage except where two of the engines had been blown away, leaving struts blackened and charred like the branches of a dead tree. As the coxswains slowed the boats by reversing the thrust of the rocket engines, Jackson studied the massive hull, knowing he had only seconds to choose a point of attack.

"There," he said, pointing over the coxswain's shoulder at the wide slash of a shuttle hangar. The hangar door was open and was more than wide enough to allow the two drop boats to enter. The navy pilots did their job well, and the two small vessels coasted to a halt just as they entered the large, well-illuminated hangar space. *Tommy* and *Mikey* floated weightlessly, as the coxswains matched the regal tumble of the *Lotus*'s orbit.

Open to space, the hangar was hard vacuum, utterly airless. Jackson saw signs of battle there: Two small shuttles had been peppered by some kind of projectile weapon and were clearly out of service. Several air locks led to the interior of the ship, and one of them had been blasted open. The entrance gaped dark, obviously exposed to the vacuum of space. The SEALS couldn't see how far they might have to go before reaching a secure air lock.

Then the coxswain cursed, and Jackson felt the drop boat shudder. He recognized it at once:

They were under attack.

Three: The *Lotus*

Mikey's gunner opened up with the chain gun in its bow-mounted turret. A stream of depleted-uranium slugs chewed across the hangar floor, tearing up a bank of metal cabinets and perforating the body of the hidden shooter just beyond that cover. The barrage of fire was strangely soundless in the vacuum of space, but Jackson could feel the stuttering vibration—more of a *zip* than a chatter because of the high rate of fire—through the drop boat's hull. The body of the target floated into view, a torn space suit leaking crimson-tinted vapor from a number of obviously lethal bullet holes. An ugly-looking firearm floated out of his lifeless hands.

At the same time, the overhead Plexiglas hatches swished backward on each drop boat, and the SEALS sprang upward and away from the landing craft. Each man used the mobility jets on his suit to guide his trajectory, and so the eight SEALS emerging from each of the drop boats scattered in a haphazard and unpredictable pattern. Fortunately, the chain gun seemed to have dealt with the initial threat.

The Teammates took cover at various places in the hangar without drawing any more fire. Exploiting the lack of gravity, four men—one complete fire team—took shelter between the overhead bulkheads of the large compartment. Others moved toward one of the disabled shuttles parked near the drop boat. The alien craft was strapped down to the deck, though a halo of debris—bits of metal and plastic, some stuffing that looked like it might have been part of a seat—floated in space all around the perforated craft.

From his position below and behind the chain gun turret at the chin position of the drop boat, Jackson took stock of their initial deployment. His men had remained together in pairs, each shooter pair and fire team intact and ready. Rodale and LaRue had their heavy weapons up, and the gunners on the two drop boats continued to swivel the bow turrets, the multibarreled chain guns pointing around the hangar with dull menace. The two scouts, Sanchez and Marannis, jetted across the deck to a large workbench, positioning themselves back to back as they scrutinized the corners of the vast, shadowy space.

"LT, over here, sir—take a look." It was one of the new men, Keast, and he gestured to Jackson from his position near the ruptured air lock the officer had noticed earlier. Charring blast damage scoured the steel of the bulkhead, and the air lock hatch itself—about the size of the door of a single-car garage—floated incongruously sideways, attached to the ship only by a thin strip of metal, all that remained of a shattered hinge.

Keast gestured toward the far end of the hangar, beyond the two destroyed shuttles. There were other vehicles over there, the lieutenant saw: low and sleek, with outboard engines and bubble canopies. At least three of those canopies were open, and Jackson allowed himself to drift upward to get a better view over the wrecked transport ships. These aircraft were scuffed, stained, and dented; they looked nothing like the sleek boats used by the Shamani. Jackson guessed they had carried the pirates aboard the large alien ship.

He was still studying the small shuttles when he saw movement, and then observed another canopy popping open. Three manlike figures wearing supple space suits and carrying small assault guns flew upward from the cockpit and immediately opened fire. Tracers zipped through the hangar, terrifyingly close, even as the recoil from their weapons sent the ambushing pirates tumbling backward.

Jackson squeezed off a burst from his G15 at the same time a dozen other SEALS opened fire. The rocket slugs fired straight and true, each round sizzling through the vacuum, trailing fire and smoke. Almost instantly the three attackers were killed, their bodies twisting and tumbling crazily as the pressurized suits vented freely from the many bullet holes. Unlike their enemies, the SEALS, with their recoil-free ammunition, had no difficulty holding their weapons ready, seeking new targets. The firefight occurred in silence, with the vacuum snuffing out any suggestion of sound, though the officer's breathing was loud in his earpiece as the lieutenant caught his breath and looked around for additional threats.

"Anybody hit?" Jackson asked over the local communicator. He was relieved as all his men checked in; no one had so much as a tear in his pressure suit. "All right. In pairs, let's secure this hangar before we move into the ship," he ordered.

The men moved like the precision-trained commandos they were. As half the SEALS started out, one moving along each wall and several checking the ceiling or poking around behind the hulks of the battered shuttles, the other member of each shooter pair kept his weapon ready and his eyes open, watching for any threat. When the first group had moved halfway across the hangar, which was large enough to hold three or four good-sized jetliners, they halted and took up firing positions so that the second member of each pair could advance.

"Got a varmint runnin' over here!" barked Gunner's Mate Dobson, his thick Alabama accent unmistakable over the comlink. The SEALS snapped off a shot at a suited figure who dived between a pair of metal crates, but the slugs skipped off the cover in a shower of sparks. Dobson kept his weapon sighted on the spot while Keast and his partner,

Robinson, shot past the crates, weapons trained on the place where the pirate had disappeared. With a push of his long legs, the lanky Alabaman followed his fellow SEALS to investigate.

"Damn, skipper. Sumbitch made it through the air lock!" Dobson declared in a disgusted tone.

"Well, we know where they are, then," Jackson noted, using his jets to propel him over to the fire team. He saw the secured hatch, smaller than some of the other passages out of the hangar, leading toward the interior of the ship. It was a personnel access hatch, about the size of a small door. Of course, there was no way to tell how many bad guys were on the other side of that barrier or what kind of reception they were arranging for the SEALS.

"Want me to blow the door, LT?" asked Harry Teal, who, despite his medical skills as a corpsman, was also a whiz at just about every kind of explosive. "We could make it pretty hot for them."

"I know," Jackson replied, thinking. He looked to the right, where the gaping black hole of the blasted air lock provided another way into the ship. Below the awkwardly floating hatch itself, which no doubt possessed several tons of mass, he could make out smaller pieces of debris, probably the residue of the initial blast. But there was plenty of space for his Team to move through the opening. He knew that within that dark chamber they eventually would come up against some kind of closed hatch, but he was considering the possibility of taking those fellows by surprise.

"Tell you what, Harry. Why don't you rig a charge. Set it for remote detonation so you can set it off with your clicker. The rest of you men, regroup over here."

The corpsman set to work preparing a breaching explosive for remote detonation while the Team formed up outside the blasted air lock. The two scouts, Sanchez and Marannis, probed into the shadowy confines, and Harry Teal set his

C-6 charge. The corpsman drifted over to the CO after two minutes, holding a small detonator in his hand. "I can set it off from up to a kilometer away, LT," he said.

"Good." Jackson kept one eye on his men while he analyzed the entry and formulated a plan. He activated his microphone and spoke to Coxswain Grafton, the pilot of *Mikey*. "Grafty, can you download those deck plans into my computer? I want to check out what's behind door number three here."

"No problem, sir." In a few seconds, the boat's computer had spit the high-density data stream into Jackson's wrist-mounted computer. He projected the results as a heads-up display, examining the deck plan of the *Lotus* as a HUD projected onto the inside of his helmet's face shield. The results were encouraging, suggesting that the adjacent smaller passageway ran roughly parallel to this larger cargo hall.

By that time Sanchez had glided back out of the air lock to make his report. "Got a short corridor inside. It T's after about twelve meters. The branches go twenty or thirty meters right and left. Each ends in another air lock, closed and secured. There's also a hatch just at the base of the T. That one's open. The control panel looks dark. I think it's disabled, skipper."

"All right. Harry, keep a finger on your clicker. The rest of you, move out, standard penetration drill."

Still moving in combat formation, half the men stationary to cover their companions who were moving, the Team moved through the blasted hatch. The metal of the framework was peeled and twisted, indicating that considerable force had been used in the entry. Fortunately, the inner lock, though currently open, did not look to have been twisted out of alignment.

As Sanchez had described, there was a second, undamaged air lock hatch a short distance inside the blasted barrier. The hatch was open, but if they could seal it, they would secure this T-shaped corridor section from the vacuum of the hangar deck and outer space beyond.

Jackson gestured to Baxter, who in his short time with the Team had displayed a remarkable skill with mechanics and electronics. "Fritz, see if you can get that air lock operable."

"Aye, aye, sir. It's just a matter of hooking up a power source," Baxter reported. He shrugged out of the ungainly battery pack he wore on his back and pulled out a pair of wires tipped with alligator clips. With a quick slice of a hand torch, he cut away the faceplate of the hatch control panel. In a few seconds, he identified a pair of contacts and affixed the stout terminals of his Mark 21 battery pack. Jackson knew that the compact unit could generate enough electricity to run a small office building if necessary. It shouldn't take that much to close and seal the air lock.

And it didn't. Fritz fiddled with the controls, adjusted the output of his power source, and waited for Jackson's signal. The lieutenant checked to see that his entire Team was positioned inside the corridors and then gave the thumbs-up. Baxter pushed the button, and the door slid down and nested into its gasket with a smooth, soundless glide. Of course, the corridor they occupied was still in a vacuum state, but now that vacuum wasn't connected to the whole gulf of space outside.

"The rest of you, follow me."

It was time to move. Jackson found Teal and Harris near the front of the formation. Calling up the schematic of the deck plan onto his HUD again, the officer studied the shape of the corridor and tried to picture the adjacent air lock where the lone surviving pirate had escaped from the hangar.

"I want another C-6 charge on the bulkhead, right here," he ordered. "Set it to go off ten seconds after the first one."

"Gotcha, LT," Harry Teal replied. In less than a minute he had affixed a small packet of plastic explosive to the wall Jackson had indicated.

The Team backed into the other dead-end corridor, as far away from the explosive as they could get and out of the direct line of the blast effect. Jackson didn't need to explain the plan in any more detail. Each man understood that the first blast, on the outer air lock, was intended to distract the enemy. The second explosion would blast in the side wall of the hostiles' position and, they hoped, create the breach for the Team's attack. Teal held his clicker at the ready, watching Jackson, and finally the officer nodded his go-ahead.

The first blast was a distant *crump,* barely felt through the metal of the surrounding bulkheads. The small hatch connecting the hangar to the ship's interior should have been blown off its hinges by the charge, but of course they couldn't see that. The ten seconds seemed to last for half an hour, but when the nearer explosive blasted, it sent a flash of light and debris through the corridor where the SEALS were waiting. Smoke churned through the air, and bits of metal and plastic bounced from the walls and decks, creating a small hailstorm of tiny high-speed fragments. Fortunately, the Mark IV suits were tough enough to withstand the bombardments of ricochets.

"Go! Go! Go!" Jackson shouted the unnecessary encouragement as his men, using their jets to move through the weightless environment, started for the breach torn by Teal's second explosion. The first men, Marannis and Sanchez, were blown back by a gust of air—they obviously had tapped into a pressurized compartment—but almost immediately the pressure equalized because the T-shaped corridor had been sealed off from space and quickly filled with the air spilling in through the breach. The first two SEALS tumbled through, snapping off shots against vaguely seen targets in the murky interior. Two by two, the rest of the Team followed.

"Damn!" Falco snapped, dropping his long sniper rifle and tumbling backward, head over heels. Jackson saw a jet of air puffing from his shoulder where his suit had been punctured, but the quickly equalized atmosphere served to stop the leak. The lieutenant was relieved to see no sign of blood emerging from the tear in the suit, and the self-sealing material already was closing over the breach.

Meanwhile, the SEALS took the adjacent corridor by storm. Bodies floated: pirates who were bleeding and motionless where the initial bursts of fire had caught them. One, presumably killed by the initial blast, was twisted around so violently that his suit had torn; the man's torso and head faced one way while his legs and feet were oriented the other way. Jackson saw three men slumped over a heavy machine gun, the weapon propped behind a half-bulkhead and trained toward the air lock where the first blast had occurred. There was an interior hatch behind the first, and the pirates had been covering that entry with a dozen weapons. Clearly the diversion had worked. The enemy had expected a frontal attack, but the Team had taken them in the flank.

With devastating effects, the CO saw as he powered himself forward through the debris of the brief, violent clash. At least a dozen pirates, all of them in space suits and armed with a miscellany of very deadly looking weaponry, had been prepared to defend against the breaching of the air lock. Some of them had been blasted by the force of the breaching charge, and the others had been too stunned to aim when the SEALS had come pouring through the hole.

"A few of 'em got away," Sanchez reported. "They were heading farther into the ship."

"Let's not let them catch their breath," Jackson admonished. "Full pursuit, Team."

Even in their haste, the men did not forget their training or their partners. Two shooter pairs—Sanchez with Marannis and Keast with Robinson—probed the corridor in a coordinated advance, one man covering while his partner moved. Sanders took several men down a side passage, and Rafe

Ruiz and one of the new men, Fritz Baxter, settled in to guard the rear.

"Permission to take off the helmets, LT?" Chief Harris asked as he and Harry Teal accompanied Jackson deeper into the ship. The two SEALS were propelling themselves along near the upper deck while the officer flew steadily forward just above the "floor."

"Denied, Chief. There are too many ways these bastards could surprise us," replied the CO. He checked the readout on the interior of his Plexiglas faceplate, confirming that the air in the corridor was in fact quite breathable. Even so, he worried about a sudden breach, accidental or planned, that could result in an almost immediate vacuum. Nor could he afford to ignore the threats of poison or disabling gas, which he had learned was a common tactic in sealed operations.

A burst of gunfire ripped out before him, silent but bright with muzzle flashes and tracer rounds. Marannis sprayed a juncture in the corridor before them, and Sanchez lobbed a grenade from his underbarrel launcher. The device exploded twenty meters ahead, concussion and flash punching through the compartment where the enemy seemed to be making a stand. The rocket rounds of the SEALS' G15s sputtered and spit down the corridor, but the enemy was ensconced behind steel bulkheads to either side of the hatchway and for the moment seemed to be protected against the fire.

"I got six or eight hostiles up here, LT," reported one of his point men. "They got cover and don't look to be backing up anymore."

As if to punctuate the point, a barrage of tracer fire erupted from the large compartment ahead of the SEALS. Immediately the Teammates flowed toward the edges of the corridor, taking cover behind arches and chairs and within the closed doorways that dotted the bulkheads. They returned fire, adding a few more grenades to the party, but even after the explosions the enemy returned a heavy volley, keeping the Team pinned in place.

"Sanders, do you copy?" Jackson barked into his helmet mike. He knew that his subordinate had embarked down a side corridor twenty meters back from their position.

"Loud and clear, boss," came the junior lieutenant's reply.

"See if you can take a right turn. We've got a tough nut in front of us and could use a little flank support."

"Aye, aye, sir."

More fire spit from the large compartment before them. Through the smoke Jackson could make out a collection of tables and chairs, like a mess hall. He couldn't see how wide the space was, but from the firepower a good number of hostiles were forted up there.

"Grenade!" someone shouted, and the men instinctively pulled flat against the walls or hunkered deeper into their doorway niches. Jackson saw the flash and felt the explosion at the same time, the blast knocking him hard against the floor. A number of red lights flashed on his HUD, and he knew his suit had been breached, but when he pushed himself up again, he was pretty sure he hadn't taken any significant wounds.

"We're going in, LT." It was Sanders's voice, sounding very confident. Abruptly Jackson saw the rocket tracers of his men's counterattack, the rounds streaking sideways across his field of view into the compartment. His junior officer had found a perfectly located side door, and his men looked to be opening up with everything they had.

"Take it to the bastards!" the officer shouted, activating his jets and shooting forward along the floor. Guns blazing, the rest of the SEALS attacked as well, spilling through the hatch.

They were indeed in a large mess hall with signs of damage—broken chairs and tables, soot-blackened bulkheads and decks—all around. The furniture was anchored to the floor, with many broken parts floating in the weightless space of the large compartment. Several pirates were shooting at Sanders and his men, and Jackson drew a bead and fired a sizzling burst of rocket-propelled rounds, shattering the helmet—and head—of one of the shooters. The enemy's suits looked as shabby as its shuttles, dirty and patched together. They moved now in sheer terror, trying to flee into a corridor to the right. Their weapons fired wildly, the powerful recoil sending them rolling and tumbling away. The SEALS, by contrast, were able to hold position and fire with deadly accuracy.

Abruptly, a blast of gunfire erupted from the corridor of retreat, and the fleeing pirates were shredded by the new attack. Two bodies drifted forward, blood trailing from the lethal wounds that had been inflicted on their backs. More fighters, carrying assault rifles and wearing bright white space suits trimmed with red braid, came charging in from that direction.

"Wait—don't shoot!" Jackson shouted as chaotic bursts of fire ripped into the compartment where the pirates were holed up. With Sanders and the LT attacking from two sides and an unknown ally firing from the third, the enemy didn't have a chance. The shooters were new arrivals—not SEALS, but they seemed to have the same enemy.

The surviving pirates in their redoubt were shooting wildly now, under attack from three directions. Jackson saw a burst of some kind of energy weapon—definitely not Terran in origin—tear through one of the hostiles, cutting his body almost in half. The riddled corpse drifted grotesquely through the air as the SEALS punched home their attack, six or eight Teammates tumbling into the large compartment at once.

Marannis had his small breaching ax out and used it to crack the helmet—and the skull—of one struggling pirate. Another was hit while he was trying to shoot and tumbled over like a child's toy, drifting eerily. A third fired, his slugs sparking off a metal table as the recoil forced him back. Ruiz fired one round right through the center of the shooter's face-plate, and the pirate immediately went limp, his gun drifting out of his lifeless hands.

The two attacking forces converged in the large compartment, and Jackson identified the white and red suits of their allies as Shamani. He guessed, correctly as it turned out, that these were some of the original crew of the *Lotus* who impulsively had joined the attack to reclaim their ship.

In less than a minute the firefight was over. Several of the white-suited crewmen saluted the wary SEALS, and Jackson returned the gesture, encouraged by the discipline displayed by his men.

"We got one prisoner, skipper," Smokey Robinson reported as he and his partner, Keast, held the arms of a pirate behind his back.

"Take off his helmet," Jackson ordered, gliding up to have a look at the fellow.

The man's face was swarthy, needing a shave. His eyes were too dark to determine which of the three empires he belonged to. He glowered at the lieutenant as Jackson halted and stared at him.

"Does he have a translator in his ear?" the officer asked. His suit contained software that could translate any known language into his earpiece, but he wouldn't be able to communicate with the prisoner unless the fellow was wearing a device of his own. Fortunately the translators had proved to be very common among space travelers, and Keast quickly confirmed that the pirate was wearing one.

"Your ship is gone," the lieutenant declared bluntly. "We chased it off, and they left you and your comrades behind to die."

The pirate merely smirked. "We're all going to die," he spit after a second.

Abruptly he convulsed, his eyes rolling back in his head. White foam drifted from his clenched jaws, and by the time Baxter pressed a hand to the man's neck, there was no pulse to be found.

"He suicided, LT," the electrician's mate declared grimly. "Musta had some secrets he didn't want to share."

Only then did Jackson turn his attention to the Shamani crewmen who were drifting through the compartment, checking the bodies of the slain pirates. The newcomers abruptly parted, moving to open a path and saluting a new arrival, an officer who came gliding into the increasingly crowded compartment.

From the alluring outline of that person's suit, Jackson guessed her to be female. Even so, he was shocked when she removed her helmet to reveal an attractive, olive-skinned face with startling—and unforgettable—crimson eyes.

"Consul Char-Kane!" Jackson declared. "This is a surprise!"

"No less for me, Lieutenant," said the Shamani Consul de Campe. It made sense for a diplomat to be on the ship, of course, but the SEALS officer was startled to recognize the alien official who had been their companion for so much of their first mission. "This vessel was my transport. When we were attacked by these pirates, I feared we were doomed."

"Are you on your way to the Orion conference?" he asked.

"I was," she said. "But we have more pressing problems right now." Jackson gestured for her to go on, and she continued. "I heard what that prisoner said, and I know what he means."

"What," he asked.

"These pirates—they have occupied the hold of this ship for several hours. There are no survivors, but I am certain they have left a powerful bomb on board. It could detonate at any time."

Four: Defusing

"Can you get your people off this ship? How many of you are there?" asked Jackson, wondering about the presence of the bomb. Was there even time for an evacuation? He reasoned that they must have a few minutes or more because the pirates hadn't been preparing to depart when the SEALS had arrived. He guessed that they would have set the timer for some time after they were well removed from the ship.

Still, Char-Kane seemed very certain that some sort of charge had been set, and he knew her well enough not to allow himself much skepticism on that point.

Char-Kane shook her head in response to his questions. "I know of at least three hundred survivors in the main passenger compartments. And others, no doubt, are trapped here and there in the ship, wherever they could take shelter when the pirates attacked. Some of them will be running short of air by now. The ship's central life support systems have been disabled, and damage has affected many of the compartments that are remote from this intact stern section. Unfortunately, I believe all of our shuttles were disabled in the attack; we have no way to move people off the ship except for the boats that brought you and your Team to our rescue."

"Well, we have the two drop boats, but there's precious little room on the frigate," the SEALS officer reflected, thinking out loud. "Even if we could get them there in the drop boats." He remembered, too, that the last time he had heard from the *Pegasus,* Captain Carstairs had been running in pursuit of the fleeing pirate ship. He could be a very long way away from them by now.

"The attack was sudden and very violent," the Shamani woman commented. "We were badly damaged."

"I could see on the approach that your ship took some hard hits," the officer noted grimly.

"Yes. The pirates had many weapons. They caught us in a barrage right after we made the jump into this system. The captain died at the bridge. He managed to get enough power out of our failing engines to put us into orbit around the star rather than tumble so close to it that we burned up."

"All right." Jackson knew that the drop boats could shuttle only a couple of dozen people, at the most, off the derelict *Lotus.* "Get your people looking for the bomb. My men will help. You said they were in the main hold?"

"Yes. This way." Char-Kane blinked suddenly, and Jackson had the unsettling impression that the aloof diplomat was trying not to blush. "Hello, Chief Harris," she said as the SEALS NCO came up to them.

"Lady Consul!" Harris declared as Jackson remembered that the two of them had developed a rather strong friendship, or even more, when they all had come back together from the Batuu system. "I didn't think I'd ever see—that is, you're looking mighty fine."

"And you, too, Sir Chief. But before we speak more, there is an emergency."

Jackson quickly briefed his Team on the threat of a bomb. He thought briefly of pulling his men out of there in the drop boats but discarded the notion almost immediately. The Shamani were allies, and this ship included an important diplomatic mission. They would do everything they could to see that the explosion never happened.

"Okay," the lieutenant said decisively. "We'll join the search for the bomb." He switched on his communicator.

"SEALS, we have a presumed explosive device equipped with an unknown time delay somewhere aboard this vessel. Most probable site is the main hold. Spread out in fire teams and shooter pairs and see what you can find."

Each member of the Team was equipped with significant detection equipment as part of his space suit. Geiger counters, thermal detectors, sniffers, and other devices gave them considerably more search power than a simple eyeball. He could only hope it would be enough.

"Grafty?" he said next, contacting the coxswain who had remained in the drop boat in the main shuttle hangar.

"Right here, Lieutenant," came the reply.

"Have you been in touch with our mother ship? Is she anywhere in our neighborhood? And can you patch me through to the captain?"

"Your wish is my command, sir," the pilot replied. "The *Pegasus* just pulled up next door in the last few minutes. Give me a moment to establish a comlink."

As soon as the search parties had been deployed, Jackson was in contact with the CIC of the frigate, and he broadcast a message to Carstairs. The captain of the *Pegasus* came back on the line immediately.

"We have the ship secured, sir. You were right: They were pirates. But there's a wrinkle. Consul Char-Kane is here, and she's pretty certain the pirates would have left some kind of bomb on board. We're conducting a search right now, but I suggest you stand off with the frigate a good safe distance. You know, in case . . ."

"I understand, Tom," the navy captain replied. "We're about a hundred klicks off now, which should be safe. I'll hold on station until we get the all-clear from you."

"Good, sir. Thanks. About that pirate ship?"

"She made a getaway, diving close to the star and then shooting out into the system. We chased her for a ways and we're still tracking her, but I didn't want to leave you fellows behind."

"And thank you for that, too, sir. I'll be in touch. Over."

Char-Kane led the lieutenant toward the main hold while his men spread out, joining the Shamani crew on the search. Accompanied by Char-Kane, Jackson made his way through the ship, at least the stern half, which was still relatively intact. He passed large carpeted compartments and lounges that made him think of the luxury accommodations on a cruise ship. They soon gave way to a network of smaller passages with tiny sleeping berths that were more reminiscent of his sleeping tube aboard the *Pangaea*. Since they remained weightless, they propelled themselves by releasing jets of air from their suits' mobility nozzles, and Jackson was grateful that he wasn't walking; it seemed that the tight corridors were only about a meter and a half from floor to ceiling.

Finally, they emerged into a reactor room where several Shamani engineers were busily trying to keep one of the cores operational. Reports from the searchers, both SEALS and Shamani, came in steadily as they cleared one compartment after another without finding a sign of any explosive device.

As they were approaching the hatch at the far end, it was the new guy, Mirowski, whose voice crackled into Jackson's earpiece with the welcome news. "We've got a nasty-looking package here in the main hold, LT. It's causing all sorts of funny sounds on the rad meter. No doubt about it: We've got a nuke ticking away down here. It doesn't have one of those little red timers like you see in all the spy movies, though. I thought that was required."

The officer had to suppress a chuckle. He was impressed with Mirowski's aplomb. "Good work," Jackson replied. "Baxter, Teal, do you read me?"

"Aye, aye, sir," came the double reply.

"Make tracks to the main hold. Get to Mirowski and see what you can do about disabling that bomb."

He turned to Char-Kane. "Why would they go to the trouble—and risk—of booby-trapping a ship they had all but captured?"

"I have been wondering that myself. It would not be to destroy the ambassadorial mission; pirates would have no interest in that. But there is something else . . ." Her voice trailed off, her prim mouth creasing in alarm.

"Tell me," Jackson urged, trying to hold his impatience in check. These Shamani were just too damned deliberate!

"We are carrying the prototype of a new type of defensive technology. It is a shield, an energy barrier that can be used to protect a ship from various kinds of attacks such as laser and particle beam weapons. Our cargo does not include the entire device, but from what I understand, our engineers have installed the main driver mechanism for the shield. It is only lacking in the application software."

"You mean, like a bulletproof vest for a space ship?" Jackson asked, amazed. It didn't take a lot of imagination to see how useful such potentially lifesaving technology could prove to be.

"Yes. Only it will not stop physical devices such as projectiles. It is designed to deflect all wave spectra. I am wondering if the pirates might have been after that device. If so, they may have intended the bomb to cover their tracks, as you say. To remove the evidence of their theft."

"Makes sense," Jackson agreed. "They can probably sell it for a pretty penny at some kind of alien market. Can you show me this device?"

"Come with me. We will see it after your men have deactivated the bomb."

She spoke as if success were automatic. Jackson was grateful for her confidence in his Team, even though he wasn't enough of an optimist to be totally certain the bomb could be stopped.

They continued through a double air lock, floating into the massive cargo compartment in the belly of the great ship. The after hold of the *Lotus* was large enough to hold a football field, including the end zones. Like the rest of the habitable parts of the ship, it was pressurized, but it currently lacked any gravitational pull since the ship still was drifting. Rows and rows of crates, most of them identical, were stacked in rows and columns, fastened down by their own latches so that nothing drifted freely.

It wasn't hard to spot the bomb: It was a much smaller box than the cargo crates and had been nestled in a gap between two rows of cargo. Knowing it was a nuke, Jackson understood that it didn't matter where they were on the ship or even in nearby space. If the thing exploded, they were all dead, so he might as well move in for a closer look.

Jackson and the consul slowly approached the device where Baxter and Teal were working to defuse it. The officer and the Shamani diplomat drifted soundlessly nearby, careful to make no sound or movement that would distract the two men.

The two SEALS used a variety of small low-tech tools, including pliers, screwdrivers, and wedges. They also had several miniature computers hooked up to the control panel via a tangled nest of wires. For several minutes they consulted dials and probed at contact points; then they finally zeroed in on a small button. Baxter took off the housing around the knob, and Teal extended a needle-nose pliers, firmly grasping at a wire and decisively plucking it free.

"Got it, sir," the corpsman said after consulting all of his dials and meters. "She's dead as a doornail now."

"Good work, SEALS," Jackson said, slowly exhaling and wondering just how long he'd been holding his breath. Char-Kane looked at him in palpable relief.

"Now, where's this shield device you were talking about?" asked the officer.

"This way," the Shamani consul said, jetting up and over a rack of containers. "The shield driver is in a long rectangular crate. I would guess that it is about four of your meters long, one meter wide, and one meter tall."

Jackson followed, and when Char-Kane went suddenly rigid, he got a very bad feeling in the pit of his stomach.

"It was right between these rows," the consul said, looking around frantically. "But it's not there anymore! The shield machinery," Char-Kane said in shock. "It's gone!"

"I want to talk to Lieutenant Jackson."

Admiral Ballard's voice, even over the communicator receiving his broadcast from the *Pangaea* half a million kilometers away, carried an ominous undertone of menace. Given the delay in radio traffic, the SEALS officer had to sit and squirm for several seconds before the confirmation of his presence reached the *Pangaea* and the response could be broadcast back.

He had brought Char-Kane and several injured Shamani crew members with him when the drop boats had returned the SEALS to the frigate. Now Jackson and Carstairs were in the CIC, and the captain finally had put through the call to the admiral. He had explained in terse and unheroic language the rescue mission and the detour that had carried the *Pegasus* so far away from the other two Terran ships.

"This is Lieutenant Jackson, sir," the officer reported. He waited for the message, traveling at the speed of light, to reach the larger ship in the outer reaches of the star system. The reply came back all too quickly for his taste.

"I thought I made myself clear, mister!" Ball-Breaker snapped. "You and your men were to stay out of sight and out of mind. From what I hear, you've been shooting up the whole star system on a peripheral mission when you were supposed to sit in the background." The tone sharpened, heavy with sarcasm. "Maybe you think you should put out a press release: The SEALS are here. To hell with the rest of the planet."

The admiral paused to catch his breath, but Jackson knew better than to reply to the rhetorical questions. It took too long to hold a conversation at those distances. There was nothing for it but to sit there and take the rebuke.

"Now see here," Ballard began again. "I have already spoken to Captain Carstairs; he's as much to blame as you! You're a couple of goddamn space cowboys is what you are! And that kind of behavior is not tolerated in this man's navy!"

"Excuse me, sir. I have a message for the American admiral." It was Consul de Campe Char-Kane, who had entered the wardroom quietly while the lecture was in progress. Jackson felt the first flush of embarrassment. How much of the rebuke had she seen?

Ballard continued his harangue, but Carstairs flashed Jackson a sly look and then pressed the transmit button and nodded to the Shamani diplomat, encouraging her to speak.

"Greetings Admiral Ballard of America. I am Consul de Campe Shastana fu Char-Kane of the empire of the Shamani."

She paused while the message was sent through space. Given the time lapse, the admiral was able to touch on several points, including courts-martial, painting the decks of rusty destroyers in the South China Sea, various brigs, and hard labor at Leavenworth, before he got the communication from the Shamani woman. When he did, he suddenly halted his harangue, startled almost to speechlessness by the interruption.

Char-Kane already had continued her statement. "I wish to thank you and all the heroic members of the United States Navy," she stated calmly. "These men, the SEALS and the crew of the *Pegasus,* have saved an entire diplomatic mission: the Shamani delegation to the same conference you yourself are about to attend. You know, the meeting at Orion, I believe they are calling it on your world.

"At great risk to their personal safety, displaying the kind of courage humans of America are so famed for, they drove off a pirate ship that had disabled our transport. My delegation and I were at the point of surrender when the SEALS came aboard, destroyed the pirates, and brought us all to safety."

Char-Kane drew a breath and continued to speak very calmly. Jackson amused himself by trying to picture the exact color of the admiral's face. Even so, he remained silent and allowed her to speak.

"I wish to express the gratitude not only of myself and my delegation but of the whole Shamani Empire. These men are an example to all the races, and I am proud to call them my saviors."

"Well, thank you, Madame Consul. Thank you very much," Ballard said gruffly. "Rest assured that we will do whatever we can to help a ship and a crew in distress."

"I am very glad to hear that, Sir Admiral," she replied. "The pirates have stolen a very valuable piece of technology from us. It is a military device that could be of great use to humans as well as to the Shamani. Your heroic sailors and SEALS are in position to try to retrieve this device, but they are reluctant to do so without orders from a higher authority. An authority, Sir Admiral, such as yourself."

"I see," Ballard said, sounding like he didn't see at all. "Let me talk to the captain and the lieutenant again, would you, please, Madame Consul."

"Of course, Sir Admiral."

Carstairs and Jackson each picked up a headset and mike. "What the hell is she talking about?" Ball-Breaker demanded.

"Some kind of defensive shield, sir," Jackson explained. "It's new and revolutionary. Very high tech. She indicated the Shamani might be willing to share some of the secrets with us if they can only get it back."

"Damn it to hell! We're on a mission here!" The transmission went silent, and the two officers looked at each other, wondering if Ballard had gone off the air. "All right," he barked after the long pause. "I'll authorize twenty-four hours. See what you can find out. But by God, don't waste another second and make the jump to the fleet so you can meet us in the Arcton system."

"Aye, aye, sir. Message received and understood," Carstairs replied.

"All right. Jackson, Carstairs. That will be all. Over and out."

"Aye, aye, sir," the two officers said in unison. Carstairs again pushed the transmit button and then turned the device off before any follow-up message could be received.

"We've got a reading on that pirate ship," Carstairs reported to Jackson a few hours later. "Seems they veered away from the star far enough that we could pick them up. They were making a course for these asteroids, about three hundred million klicks out from the star."

"Any idea where in the asteroid belt they went?" Jackson asked, intrigued. He had told Carstairs about the shield technology that had been removed from the Shamani ship, and he knew the naval officer was as eager as he was to have a look at it.

"As a matter of fact, we have a pretty good idea," the captain replied. "There's one rock out there about ten times larger than any of the rest of them—large enough to have some gravity even, maybe point one G."

"Do you want to go there and have a look?" Jackson asked.

"Well, it's practically on the way back to the *Pangaea*," the captain replied. "So I've had the course already plotted."

"Good idea, sir. Er . . ." Jackson let the pause grow long. "Have you talked to the admiral?"

Carstairs grinned, looking a bit like a buccaneer himself. "What he doesn't know won't hurt him," he said.

Five: Kicking Asteroid

Despite his protestations about the pirate base being "practically on the way" to the *Pangaea,* Captain Carstairs elected to take an oblique approach, guiding the frigate toward the target while using the asteroids themselves as cover. A burst of acceleration propelled the *Pegasus* away from the massive star, and then the ship reversed orientation and decelerated hard as she approached the asteroid belt. She was moving relatively slowly, with the crew in a zero-G state, as she slipped into the belt of drifting rock in orbit around Alpha Centauri.

Like a submarine moving silently through shallow waters, she relied mainly on passive detection systems to avoid the hazardous planetoids drifting to all sides. Her crew primarily employed high-resolution camera images, pictures collected by nanotech lenses and magnified to a power of 100,000 or more, to pick a path, backing up the visuals with low-power radar signals. Steering rockets burned briefly, easing the silver spaceship past one obstacle after another as she closed steadily on the target Captain Carstairs had identified.

"Fortunately, these asteroids aren't quite as densely packed as those in our own system," the captain remarked to Jackson. "But any one of the damned things could do us a world of hurt."

The SEALS lieutenant could only nod, marveling at Carstairs's calm while his own hands were clenched into white-knuckled fists and he pictured, at any moment, a jagged and lethal chunk of ice-crusted rock smashing through the hull and ending their mission and their lives in an instant.

Still, he knew there was a logical reason for their divergent emotions: Carstairs was in his element here, commanding a fleet ship of war, making way toward a target, while he, Jackson, could only stand around and twiddle his thumbs. No doubt their stress levels would reverse when the SEALS went into action and the frigate had to wait around to pick them up again.

"That's the target," Carstairs said, taking pity on his fellow officer and pointing out their destination on the screen. Even in the blurry image, Jackson could discern the large oblong shape of the asteroid. It was far bigger than any of the other celestial bodies tumbling around them.

"We picked up some emissions here"—Carstairs indicated a depression on the far side of the asteroid—"including both light and heat. There's something there for certain. And that looks to be where the pirate ship ended up. So you can do the math as well as I can. Those are the raiders that hit the *Lotus,* and that's their base of operations."

Jackson nodded. "Nice work, sir. I think you've tracked the *Jolly Roger* to her lair."

The picture was less detailed than they were used to because many of the frigate's detection systems, most significantly the long-range radar, were turned off to avoid sending a definite signal of their presence in the asteroid belt. Floating just above the deck in zero G, the two officers held their positions by grasping railings; the seated crew members, of course, were strapped into their chairs.

The engines pulsed infrequently, but they couldn't be shut down entirely. The captain hoped that the IR shielding on the powerful rockets would mask the signal from any kind of heat detection systems that the pirates might possess, but there was no way to mask the signature when the rockets had to fire forward to provide steering. Still, they were approaching the asteroid from the opposite side of the spot where Carstairs had identified the emissions, so they could hope that the pirates were not sufficiently organized to have global detection systems. If they were not scrutinizing approaches to their asteroid from a full 360-degree arc, there was at least the prospect of making a surprise attack.

"We're an hour out now," the captain declared a short time later.

Jackson nodded and pulled himself to the transport shaft to ride the lift in a quick descent to H Deck. There he was not surprised to see that the Team was ready to go. All the men had seen the damage done to the *Lotus,* and there was an unambiguous sense of purpose: They were going after some real bad guys. LaRue was giving the electrical connections on the capacitors of his rail gun a final polish while Teal considered an assortment of breaching charges in addition to the six or eight he already had attached to the torso of his suit. All the SEALS were bulky with spare ammunition magazines stuck to the fasteners on hips, belly, and thighs.

"We're going to drop on the far side of the asteroid from the enemy base," Jackson explained tersely. "We'll come in low and touch down about fifteen klicks out. The approach will be overland. We'll have about point one G—enough to hold us to the ground, but it shouldn't slow us down much."

The men already had been briefed about the latter point.

Once again the SEALS took up positions in the drop boats, filing through the entry hatches with quiet determination. Fully armed and loaded, they waited silently while Jackson and Sanders followed the frigate's progress on their viewscreens. The asteroid now filled more than half the screen, and the tension in Jackson's body was building to a nearly unbearable level.

Finally they got the word: "Time to go. Good luck, SEALS," Carstairs's voice crackled tautly in the earphones.

Immediately Jackson's tension dissipated. He could almost picture it flowing to the captain, who now could do little more than wait. The drop boats, propelled by the release of pressurized air, blasted outward from the frigate's hold. Immediately the rockets fired, and the little shuttles flew toward the looming rock of the asteroid.

From there, the target looked pretty much like a planet: It filled the entire view before them, and they could see only a small fraction of the surface as they zoomed closer. The coxswains had the coordinates, and Jackson left it to them to plot the course. The boats cruised straight down toward the surface of the asteroid. Finally, at an altitude of about a kilometer, the rockets fired a prolonged burst, and they gradually switched to a horizontal flight path, following the very irregular surface of the planetoid as they cruised toward the suspected pirate base.

Gradually the boats dropped even lower until they were following the irregularities in terrain, barely a hundred meters above the surface. They scooted up till they were practically grazing the top of a jagged outcropping, then dropped suddenly to cruise along the base of a wide crater. The tug of the asteroid's gravity was barely perceptible but present: a gentle pull that held the men in their seats and added a sense of lightness when the boats suddenly dived.

Side by side, *Tommy* and *Mikey* came to rest on a relatively smooth patch of stone just beyond the large crater. The upper hatches slid back, and the SEALS popped out, weapons ready. Almost floating, the men came down in a defensive perimeter around the landing zone.

"We'll wait here for orders, Lieutenant," Coxswain Grafton said on the short-range transmitter. "Good luck, sir."

Jackson gave a thumbs-up in thanks and turned his attention to the Team. The heavily laden SEALS formed up in two files about a hundred meters apart. Marannis and Sanchez, as usual, took the lead, one man on point for each file. Unique among the SEALS, the scouts wore camouflaging ghillie cloaks, filmy covers over their pressure suits with a nearly magical ability to mimic the background color and texture of their environment. When the two scouts moved off by themselves, they were almost impossible to see.

Naturally, the men had loaded up on ordnance, taking advantage of the low gravity even as they remembered the lessons they had learned on Mars: Just because you could *lift* a small truck, that didn't make it any easier to *stop* once that small truck got moving forward. Once more they had fitted the vented barrels onto the weapons and carried the recoilless rocket rounds for the G15s. Each man had breaching charges, spare magazines, extra grenades, and other toys attached to every spare inch of the outer surface of his pressure suit. They looked almost robotic as they lunged along, the shape of the human inside the suit distorted by the helmet, the multiple packages attached, and the bulky backpack that was the suit's life support module, providing air, water, and heat against the harsh, hard vacuum of space.

Advancing in long strides, they made good time over the initially flat terrain of the LZ. Soon they came to a jagged ridge of rock where the terrain soared upward in a virtual cliff. Despite the light gravity, the SEALS had to work hard to climb the steep slope, using hands as well as feet for purchase. Jackson's breathing came as a steady rasp in his earphones, but he didn't want to risk even a low-power transmission as they drew closer to the target. He simply trusted his men to remember their training and recognize the peril of a slip or a fall: As with forward momentum, the kinetic energy of a tumbling heavily loaded man would be very difficult to reverse if one of them lost his balance.

But they made it to the crest in formation, and Jackson instinctively lowered himself to the rock as he crept up beside the prone figure of the scout Sanchez. He could see, barely a kilometer away, the outline of several manufactured domes.

Just beyond, jutting up from the surface of the asteroid like a needle pointed at space, was the sleek, powerful shape of the pirate ship that nearly had destroyed the *Lotus*.

They had reached the target, and the presence of the ship confirmed beyond doubt that they had found the pirate base. The Team, separated into the first and second squads, deployed along the crest of the ridge, every man visually inspecting the objective. No one activated his communicator, and Jackson would give his orders by sign language.

For a few minutes he scrutinized the base and its environs. The installation itself consisted of a large dome with two smaller domes attached at right angles, as if in an east and north orientation to the base. He saw an air lock on the face of the large dome; no other points of access were visible from their current position. The pirate ship, resting on its stern in the low-G environment, stood just beyond the north dome. For a long time those were the only features Jackson discerned. He turned the magnification feature of his faceplate on, creating an effect similar to 15× binoculars, and patiently swept the surroundings.

Finally he saw the external turret. Camouflaged with the natural rock surface of the asteroid, it was distinguished by a pair of slender dark barrels barely emerging from narrow slits in the surface. It was some two hundred meters from the main dome of the base. He saw the G-Man looking at him and indicated the gun; LaRue nodded, signaling that he had spotted it, too. He laid Baby on the rocks before him, the two-meter-long barrel perched on its folding ground mount, a round ready in the chamber of the powerful gun, and drew a bead while he waited for the order to fire.

Next Jackson found Sanders and, again using signs, ordered the junior lieutenant to take the second squad around to the rear of the east dome. They were to break in through an air lock if they found one or else use a breaching charge to go directly through the side of the dome. Sanders organized his seven men into fire teams and shooter pairs and, with the confirmation of an attack in fifteen minutes, moved out below the crest of the ridge, beyond the line of sight—theoretically, at least—of the objective.

Finally, Jackson arrayed the first squad to make a frontal attack against the air lock. Deployed into the two fire teams, with Jackson, Dobson, Robinson, and Keast to the left and Chief Harris, Teal, Falco, and the G-Man on the right, they gathered themselves, checking weapons and still studying the objective, as the LT kept his eye on the clock. He allowed eleven minutes to pass, then gave the thumbs-up to LaRue, who had been watching his CO carefully.

The G-Man sighted the long barrel of his rail gun onto the external turret and fired. A blast of fire and smoke billowed from the back of the big weapon, an effect that canceled about 80 percent of the gun's powerful recoil as the copper-jacketed slug with its core of depleted uranium accelerated down the four rails of the track. In milliseconds the round was traveling faster than a World War II–era antitank shell. LaRue's aim was dead-on, and the missile penetrated the rocky shell of the gun turret with a greenish surge of flame, the color being caused by the incineration of the copper. The explosion continued out the other side of the lumpy gun emplacement as the superheated metal fiercely ripped through the works.

At the same instant, Jackson waved his men forward, and the eight SEALS of the first squad sprang over the crest of the ridge and started toward the domed installation in long, loping strides. They had a kilometer to cover, and the blast of the rail gun presumably had provided the enemy with a warning that they were under attack. It was the LT's intent to close on the base so quickly that the warning could not be translated into defensive action. Each man ran in a series of long jumps, covering ten or fifteen meters with each stride, concentrating, as they had been trained to do, on pushing forward rather than up with each springing step.

In less than a minute they passed the camouflaged turret, from which sparks and puffs of smoke were emerging. The twin barrels were askew, and there was no sign of movement within the shattered shell. Approaching the air lock on the large dome and mindful of the effects of the mass of their heavy loads, the SEALS began to slow down, shortening their steps, digging in their feet, taking care not to let their heavy packs push them down.

As they came up to the dome, Chief Harris and Harry Teal each pulled a breaching charge from his belly clip. Leaving their G15 carbines hanging by the straps, they slapped the two charges to either side of the round hatch of the air lock. Splitting into their fire teams, the eight SEALS pressed tightly to the surface of the dome, four on each side of the entry. The charges, set by prearrangement to five seconds, detonated with perfect synchronization, sending a soundless blast of flame and debris shooting outward from the entry-way to the dome.

The time for radio silence was past. "Go!" Jackson barked to Chief Harris, who led the second fire team around the side of the shattered hatch.

"Got an inner door, LT—closed and sealed!" the chief said.

"LaRue. Take it out," the lieutenant ordered.

Mindful of Baby's backblast, which spumed into a wide fan some twenty-five meters long, the other Teammates ducked to the side as the G-Man raised his rail gun and in rapid succession sent three blisteringly hot rounds against the inner air lock door. Air billowed out of the holes, a mist of smoke and water vapor and miscellaneous debris erupting as the dome depressurized. But the hatch, punctured and mangled, did not break away.

"Harris! Teal! Two more charges," Jackson commanded,

and his two breachers snatched up their C-6 charges and pushed against the blast of air, forcing themselves into the air lock, where they clapped the charges against the hinges of the second hatch.

"Grenade launchers!" the LT ordered the rest of his men, snapping one of the explosive missiles under the barrel of his G15.

The second round of breaching charges did the trick, blasting the hatch off its hinges. The Teammates stayed back, out of the blast effect, and watched as the heavy steel door tumbled past, expelled from its frame by the continuing blast of depressurization. Fighting the flow, which was like a powerful gust of wind, Jackson leaned around the outer air lock and fired his grenade into the installation. Several other SEALS did the same thing, ducking back out of the way as a satisfying series of flashes indicated the detonations somewhere within the pirate base.

By then the flow of escaping vapors had settled to a brisk breeze, and Chief Harris, with Teal, Robinson, and Keast following closely, charged into the installation. Each man fired another grenade as he came through the door, the first two shooting forward and the next two lobbing their missiles to the left and right, respectively.

Jackson and his fire team came after them to find that the SEALS' attack had wreaked utter havoc in a functional but fairly large utility chamber. A large hatch, currently open, led deeper into the pirate installation; smaller hatches to the right and left were closed and, to judge from the lack of leaking atmosphere, sealed. The multiple grenades had killed five or six men in the room and had blasted racks containing space suits—now thoroughly punctured—as well as a weapons cabinet, a tool bench, and bare, functional tables, chairs, and benches.

At a word from Jackson, Harris and Teal took breaching

charges to the two side hatches, while Jackson led his men straight through the entry chamber into the passageway through the open doorway. Keenly aware of their advantage—his men were wearing pressure suits whereas the occupants of the base presumably were not—the LT was eager to wreak as much havoc as possible in the first minutes of the attack. They passed several sliding doors, now shut, and he gestured to Robinson and Keast to blast them with breaching charges as he and Dobson continued deeper into the installation.

Soon the pair of them came up against another secure door and set charges of their own even as the two men behind them blew open the doors. The LT and his shooting partner withdrew to discover that the other two men had blasted their way into a computer room to the left and a storage locker to the right. A pair of computer operators, as scruffy and unshaven as the pirates they had fought aboard the *Lotus,* were in the process of dying from the sudden lack of air. Jackson gave them only a brief glance as he strode to the bank of equipment.

At the same time, the charges he and Dobson had set erupted at the end of the corridor. "Keep going!" he ordered, and the chief led the other two SEALS forward. Jackson paused long enough to drop a couple of grenades onto the main computer consoles, ducking out of the room just before their explosion shook the deck under his feet.

"We got company, LT—from the left of the front door," Harris's voice crackled in Jackson's earphones.

"Can you hold them up?" he asked.

"For the time being, sure. They're suited up, but Falco poked holes in the first two with his squirrel gun. The rest seem a little reluctant to come up and get acquainted."

"Good." Jackson knew that the sniper's squirrel gun, the Mark 30 Hammer sniper rifle, could send a high-velocity 10.2-mm caseless slug through just about any level of body armor or personal protection. He hoped his lethal shooting

would give the attackers enough pause for the LT to get a
better view of the situation.

To that end, he bounded down the corridor in two long
strides, coming up to the hatch he and Dobson had just
blown. Following his men through, he found that they stood
atop a surprisingly deep pit, a stone-lined depression that apparently had been excavated within an existing crater on the
asteroid's surface. A metal catwalk circled like a balcony
around the rim of the pit, and multiple layers of concentric
decks dropped into the depths below him. Because of the numerous breaches caused by the SEALS' attacks, the whole
area was depressurized, and the sight of a dozen pirate bodies sprawled on the stairs and decks indicated that the sudden
loss of air had come as a shock.

"Shit!" Dobson cursed, and tumbled backward, falling in
slow motion toward the floor. "Hostiles at twelve o'clock!"
he shouted, bouncing onto his back and, in the low gravity,
propelling himself to a sitting position by flexing his back
and legs. "Sumbitch creased my helmet, LT," he added, to
Jackson's considerable relief.

The officer already had spotted the shooters: Nearly a
dozen men in pressure suits carrying assault rifles had appeared across the wide atrium of the crater. They shot at the
SEALS from the cover of a long bank of equipment, popping up to squeeze off short bursts, then dropping from sight
again. Slugs sparked off the gridwork of the catwalk, and
Jackson felt the impacts through his feet; the Teammates
could see that the enemy shooters were being forced back by
the recoil of their weapons.

Robinson and Keast returned fire, spraying long, carefully
aimed bursts of rocket rounds from their G15s. Unaffected
by recoil, the double barrage chewed along the top of the
consoles behind which the pirates hid. One raised his head at
the wrong time, and a number of rounds shattered the faceplate of his helmet and the skull behind the Plexiglas barrier.

With his launcher still attached, Jackson pump-cocked a grenade into firing position and launched the missile against the far wall of the large compartment. It burst against the stone barrier, spraying fragments, he hoped, against a few of the enemy shooters that were out of the SEALS' line of sight. Another man popped into view, spraying a round, and the LT was knocked backward by the force of a slug punching into his shoulder. Fortunately, the flexible armor of his suit absorbed the impact without rupture, but even so, he dived for cover behind a table Robinson had toppled over, cursing the low gravity that made it seem like forever before he dropped behind the barrier.

The four SEALS of Jackson's fire team held a position on the inside of the upper level of the crater. They had a good view of the opposite side of the depression, including several of the lower levels, though the farther down they tried to look, the more of the opposing decks were covered by the overhang of the upper floors. Quick bursts from the G15s kept the pirates down, but they could see hostiles starting to work their way around the circle in both directions. The only connection between the decks in the crater seemed to be an exposed stairway, an open gridwork of metal that spiraled from their level down into the crater not far from where the four SEALS had forted up.

"Skipper, we're getting heat from both sides now," Harris reported, his voice calm despite the deteriorating situation. "A lotta cross fire."

Damn, Jackson cursed silently and then forced his voice to remain as calm as the chief's when he replied. "Copy. Pull your men out of the entryway, into the passage behind us. See if you can hold them from there," the lieutenant ordered.

And pray that the second squad has a little more luck than we did. He thought the words but once again kept them to himself.

Six: Saga of the
Second Squad

Lieutenant (j.g.) Sanders led his men on a fast flanking maneuver, running in the long strides the men had perfected for the low-G environment. They stayed below the horizon of the ridge crest from which they first had observed the pirate base, but the young officer was pleased to see that the elevation curved in the direction in which they needed to go. When, after more than a kilometer of travel, he signaled a halt and again climbed to the top for a look, he saw why: The ridge was actually the rim of a crater, and the target installation was situated in the center of the circular depression. As a result, their distance to the objective was about the same as it had been when they first had spotted the base: about one klick.

He checked his watch and saw that they had about one more minute before the skipper and the first squad moved out. He waved his men up to the crest, where they all took up concealed observing positions in time to see the backblast of LaRue's rail gun signal the start of the attack.

As ordered, Sanders waited another four minutes to move out, all the while studying the triple-domed pirate base. He could discern nothing that looked like an air lock or any other point of access on the side of the east dome that previously had been out of view. With a shrug, he gestured to Sanchez and Marannis, the scouts, that they should prepare breaching charges.

At the appointed second, the eight SEALS of the second squad hopped over the ridge and sprinted toward the objective. In the airless silence there was nothing to indicate the progress of their comrades' attack, but that was only to be expected. The men raced forward, carrying their heavy loads in long, springing steps, slowing only as they approached the wall of the dome.

Moving quickly and surely, the two scouts affixed their charges, allowing several seconds' delay to their Teammates to clear the blast zone; there was no alcove such as the air lock that shielded the first squad from the nearby explosions. The blasts went off in sequence, and Sanders looked up to see the gush of steamy air that indicated the dome's wall had been breached.

By then Jackson had broken radio silence, and the men of the second squad were able to follow to some extent the progress of their Teammates as the LT ordered them through the air lock and deployed them within the entryway. They heard the order to go in behind a volley of grenades and followed the calm, professional voices of their fellow SEALS discussing matters of life and death as they searched through the first rooms of the pirate base. Uncertain if the enemy was tracking with radio direction finders, Sanders held up a finger, admonishing his men to stay off the air for the time being.

The hurricane-like decompression lasted for nearly half a minute, but as soon as the stream of air eased to the force of a strong wind, Sanders gestured for his two scouts to lead the way inside. The junior lieutenant and Schroeder came next, G15s at the ready, and the four men of the second fire team followed immediately—three with their carbines at the ready and Rocky Rodale following with a missile readied in his M76 Wasp launcher.

Immediately the men spread out, the four shooter pairs moving through the large, dark chamber. It was clear that this auxiliary dome was some sort of storage chamber: They encountered several small rover-type vehicles, six-wheeled, with pressurized passenger compartments large enough for only a couple of passengers. There were banks of shelves, many of them containing sealed crates; others were open, stacked with suits, oxygen bottles, fresh water, and other miscellaneous stores. They didn't encounter any pirates in the storage chamber.

Remembering the objective of their mission, Sanders broke radio silence just long enough to order his men to make a quick search, seeking the torpedo-shaped crate containing the shield driver that Consul Char-Kane had described. A few hasty minutes of scanning up and down the rows of shelves revealed nothing promising; by then the chatter in their ears indicated that Jackson's squad was running into some resistance, so Sanders decided to postpone the search.

Their reconnaissance had revealed the presence of a large air lock on the far side of the circular chamber, and Sanders guessed with a high degree of confidence that this was the passage connecting the storage dome to the rest of the pirate installation. Baxter went to work on it with his battery-powered access computer and swiftly found the code that would open it.

"Seems to be vacuum on the other side, sir," he reported, consulting one of his meters.

"Okay. See if you can pop it open," the young officer ordered.

"Righto, sir."

As Baxter went to work, Sanders picked up another transmission, a message from his commanding officer. "Sandy, we're in a tight spot here. Any chance the cavalry is coming over the hill?" Jackson's voice crackled with perfect timing.

"On our way, sir," Sanders reported, signaling to Baxter that he should open the hatch. "Can you give me a sitrep?"

"We're on the top floor of a large crater ringed with decks. Some hostiles are directly across from us; others are on the lower levels."

Even as the LT was describing the situation, the electrician's mate released the electronic lock—his computer had broken the code easily—and spun the wheel that would open the first hatch. It swung wide to reveal a small air lock, and when the hatch on the far side of that passage proved to be unsecured, Baxter went ahead and pushed that one open as well. Because both sides of the hatch were currently in a vacuum state, no depressurization occurred when the hatch was forced.

Following his electrician's mate, Sanders immediately spotted a half dozen pirates. They were hunkered down behind a bank of computer equipment, and the SEALS of the second squad had surprised them by approaching from their left rear quarter. Sanders, Baxter, and Ruiz opened up with their G15s, the rocket rounds raking through the surprised—and doomed—hostiles. The sputtering bullets chewed through the pirates' space suits, helmets, and life support modules, along with the equipment behind which they had sought shelter. In less than two seconds all six of them had been cut down.

Sanders and Schroeder charged through the air lock door, ducking to the right and looking for other targets. Baxter and Master Chief Ruiz came next, moving to the left, circling around the ring of deck that surrounded the crater. Moving against the compartment wall, the SEALS were still unable to see very far down into that depression, but they spotted their Teammates of the first squad on the other side of the ring-shaped deck and saw Jackson indicating the deck immediately underneath them, a clear statement that more of the bad guys were lurking down there. There were a couple of other SEALS over there with the LT, but he guessed that at least one whole fire team remained in the outer corridor, protecting the first squad against the attackers approaching from behind.

Sanders spotted the metal stairway spiraling down from this, the top level of the stacked rings, not far from Jackson's position. The metal steps looked very unappealing as a route into the crater, at least if there were other hostiles below, as the officer suspected. He immediately began looking around for another path downward.

Meanwhile, his men were inspecting the bodies of the pirates they had killed in their attack, making sure that none of the hostiles was playing possum. Sanders studied the outer wall surrounding the upper ring and was discouraged by the impression that they were within a circle of solid rock. He approached the inner edge of the ringed deck where it dropped away into the interior of the crater and caught a glimpse of at least four more decks, all arrayed in a ring that allowed the deep center of the crater to plunge into the unseen darkness below.

Sanders activated his communicator. "Can you give me an estimate of the enemy position, LT?" he asked.

"Pretty much directly under you, Sandy," replied Jackson.

The junior officer studied the deck. It was metal, but he reasoned that it wouldn't need to be terribly heavy or thick in the asteroid's very light gravity. "Sir, I suggest my squad play Santa Claus. We'll make our own chimney."

"Good idea," the CO said. "We'll try to keep their attention focused on us over here." To underscore his point, the lieutenant popped up from behind the table he'd been using for cover and sprayed a burst of rocket rounds into the unseen compartment directly under Sanders's position.

"Mirowski, Schrade," the junior officer called. "Plant a couple of breaching charges right on the deck here. We're going to fall on these assholes' heads."

The big Pole grinned wickedly at the suggestion, and the two men immediately affixed their C-6 charges to the deck, placing them several meters apart. Sanders's squad separated into fire teams, and four men prepared to advance on each hole, though they backed away from the charges before the blasts. He gave Jackson the thumbs-up and signaled his men to start their timers.

At the same time, the SEALS of the first squad opened up with their carbines, spitting a spray of rocket rounds into the deck underneath Sanders's men. The hissing, self-propelled rounds crackled through the compartment, filling the deep atrium with tracers of smoke and vapor. The junior officer saw the searing red beam of an energy weapon flash toward his Teammates, but the shot was wide and brief; the shooter presumably had been driven back into cover by the aggressive shooting of Jackson's fire team.

Then the breaching charges went off. Flames burst upward, but because of the nature of the charges and the way they were affixed to their target, the great bulk of the blasts was directed downward. Each explosion blasted a hole more than a meter wide through the metal deck and scattered the lower level with razor-sharp shards of steel and the crushing force of the blast.

Sanchez and Marannis jumped one after the other through the nearest hole while Ruiz and Baxter led the way through the second aperture. In the low G they dropped slowly, firing on the way down. By the time Sanders followed his scouts, the first four SEALS had taken out five hostiles and were bounding around the lower deck, seeking more of the enemy.

A bolt of energy exploded from an alcove in the wall, sending the two scouts diving for cover. Sanchez grasped his arm, and the officer saw a film of red-tinged mist erupting from the rip in his suit. Sanders saw a pirate just beyond, suited and carrying one of the battery-powered weapons the Team had encountered on Batuun. That smoldering barrel was swinging toward Sanders as he snapped off a burst, centering his rocket rounds in the neat circle of the pirate's faceplate. The impact knocked the shooter backward into the stone wall, with a burst of blood and air erupting from the shattered helmet. He slumped to the deck with an almost graceful slow-motion collapse.

"Second deck secured, sir," Ruiz reported as Sanders went to check on Sanchez.

The scout lay on his back, his face locked in a grimace of pain. The beam had cut through his suit just below the left shoulder, but the officer saw with considerable relief that the self-sealing material had patched the cut quickly before catastrophic depressurization had claimed the SEALS' life.

"Just a scratch, sir," the scout grunted. "Bastard got the drop on me, but I'll be okay."

"Well, that was the last shot he'll ever take," Sanders said grimly. "Can you use the arm?"

Sanchez stretched out the limb and winced. "No problem," he said, though his expression belied the assertion.

"Take it easy for a few minutes," the officer said, acutely aware that there was no way to treat the wound in the airless vacuum of the pirate base.

By that time, Lieutenant Jackson had dropped down from the upper level, sliding quickly along the spiral steps to join his executive officer. Sanders reported on Sanchez's status and learned that Keast had taken a hit in the leg that might have broken his tibia.

"Damn," he commiserated. "What about the hostiles behind your position up there?"

"Chief Harris has six men with him. He decided that was enough to make a counterattack, and the last word I had was that he'd cornered one survivor in the head. He was in negotiations over the translator, asking the fellow if he wanted to give up or take a dozen rounds up his ass. I don't think the chief cared much either way."

Sanders snorted at the dark humor even as Harris's voice

came over the comlink, reporting that one pirate indeed had been captured.

More of the Team were continuing down into the depths of the crater, one member of a shooter pair covering his partner as they slipped down the stairway, checking on the third and then fourth levels. Both proved to have rows of bunks, with a mess hall on the lower level. The fifth, bottom deck was the actual stone floor of the crater.

"There's an air lock down here," Ruiz reported grimly. "It was closing as I came down the last steps. I'm guessing some hostiles got away. The door looks pretty heavy-duty, too. It'll take us some work to smash through it."

"What's the orientation of the escape route?" Jackson asked immediately.

"Looks like due north of the central chamber," the master chief informed him.

"Damn, they're making for the ship," the LT cursed.

"Sir, request permission to put a firecracker up their tail if they take off," Rodale said, cradling his M76 rocket launcher.

Jackson looked at his junior officer. "No sign of that shield driver, I don't suppose."

"Negative, sir. It didn't seem to be in the storage module, though we didn't take time for a careful search."

"Well, if it's still on that ship, I don't want it getting off this asteroid. Rocky, permission granted. G-Man, see if you can also punch a few holes in their escape plans."

"Aye, aye, sir!" the two SEALS replied in unison. They started upward in long bounds, each carrying one of the Team's heavy weapons.

"Sandy, you follow along, will you? See that the boys don't get into any more trouble than they absolutely have to."

"Gotcha, skipper," Sanders said. Schroeder and Mirowski came with him as they chased the two gunner's mates up to the top level and out through the breach in the wall of the storage chamber.

Once they were back out onto the cold, dark stone of the asteroid, the silver dart of the pirate ship loomed above them like a deadly dagger. Even as they watched, the twin engines at the stern, rocket muzzles perched just above the rocky surface, pulsed with an eerie glow of ignition.

"The LT says he doesn't want that thing to get away," Sanders said drolly, addressing Rodale and LaRue, both of whom had raised their heavy weapons to their shoulders. "You fellows think you can make the skipper happy?"

"I can damn sure try," Rodale said. "I'll take the starboard engine, G-Man, if that's all right with you."

"By all means, Rock," LaRue agreed graciously. He sighted his rail gun on the port rocket.

The ship's engines pulsed again, thrumming with an energy that the SEALS could feel through the rock beneath their feet. The eerie glow brightened to a white fire, surging flames pressing downward, starting the ship upward through the light gravity.

The two SEALS fired at the same time. The slug from the rail gun, traveling at extreme velocity, punched through the housing of the port engine, and that pod immediately was engulfed by flame. Rodale's rocket, flying straight and true in the airless vacuum, caught the starboard engine near the nacelle. The explosion was smaller than that caused by the rail gun, but the ship already was veering off its course. Twisting crazily, the pirate vessel corkscrewed away from the asteroid, rising and turning like a deranged bird.

When it was ten or fifteen kilometers away, the rocket ship vanished in a vast explosion, a searing circle of flame brightening the darkness of space for just an instant before the vacuum snuffed out the flames.

The asteroid's gravity was so low that most of the pieces didn't come down.

Seven: Cold and Lonely

By the time the low hatch was breached, Ruiz and Baxter had completed an inspection of the ship's launching site. It proved to be connected by an underground tunnel to the crater in the middle of the pirate base, but all the hostiles who had escaped through that passage apparently had boarded the ship for the short one-way flight to oblivion.

"The installation is secure, LT," Master Chief Ruiz reported.

Jackson immediately activated the medium-range communicator. "Grafty?" he called, seeking the drop boat's coxswain.

"Thank God, Lieutenant," the petty officer replied with palpable relief. "We saw a pretty big flash over there and were prepared for the worst."

"That was the *Jolly Roger*'s going-out-of-business celebration," Jackson replied. "I do have two men wounded, though. Can you get the boats over here ASAP?"

"We're on the way, sir."

Ruiz had brought the battery pack and energy weapon he had picked up from the dead pirate. "Permission to try a few practice shots, LT?" he asked.

"Sure, Rafe. Just don't point it at anything *too* important."

The master chief, together with Electrician's Mate Baxter, went out through the breached air lock to check out the captured device on the surface of the asteroid. At the same time,

Chief Harris and Harry Teal brought the sole surviving pirate up to Jackson, who was supervising operations from the upper deck of the central crater. The prisoner was sullen but seemed to have no fighting spirit left. His face was downcast, and through the faceplate of his visor the officer could see that he was gaunt and unshaven.

"Look at me," Jackson snapped, presuming that the fellow's comlink contained a translator program—if he didn't have one implanted in his skull, which was a common practice throughout the galaxy.

Indeed, the prisoner raised his face, and the LT found himself looking into eyes of a full, startling green. "So you're an Eluoi?" he began, speaking conversationally. "Where is your home?"

The pirate flinched at the first words but then seemed to relax a bit. His eyes glanced this way and that as if he couldn't believe he wasn't going to be summarily executed.

"I come from the Arakest system, near the center of the galaxy," he said. The words in Jackson's earpiece were tinny and flat, as the man's voice was changed by the SEALS' translation program. Even so, he detected that the fellow was sincerely proud of his home world.

"There was a piece of cargo on that ship, something stolen from the Shamani ship near the star in this system. I know it was removed from the ship and brought into this station." Jackson was bluffing; he knew no such thing. "If you tell me where we can find it, things will go easy for you. We'll see that you're fed and taken off this rock when we leave."

"I know nothing about that!" the pirate said. "I worked in the atmosphere module. I don't know what happened outside of my own compartment."

"Did you know when the ship arrived back here?" Jackson probed.

The man looked away briefly, then met the officer's eyes. "Yes," he admitted. "We had to pressurize the connecting tunnel from the ship dock to the installation. It was no more than twelve hours before you bandits attacked us." The pirate managed to convey a little hostile bravado in the last remark.

The LT snorted with laughter, a bark of contempt. "I will ask you again: Where did they take the object that came off the ship? Answer me, or I might just decide that you're a waste of valuable air."

"I tell you, I don't know where they took it!" the pirate snapped. He immediately grimaced, apparently understanding that he had said too much. Jackson nodded and waved the man away. "Lock him in a closet somewhere," he told Harris.

At least the prisoner's answer had confirmed that something had been taken off the pirate ship. That allowed some hope that they might be able to find it somewhere on the asteroid if only they had enough time.

Ruiz's voice crackled in his earpiece. "LT, I see *Tommy* and *Mikey* coming in for a landing."

"Thanks, Master Chief. Attention, SEALS. Make ready to evacuate the wounded." Jackson made his way out the blasted air lock in time to see the two drop boats, flying in horizontal orientation, come to rest like a pair of flying PT boats on the rocky flat just outside the pirate base. Each boat rested on four ski-like skids, and in that low-G environment, the LT understood that they would be able to lift off again.

Sanchez, resisting attempts by his fellow SEALS to help him walk, made his way out to the landing zone. Keast, with an apparently broken leg, was borne along by leaning on Smokey Robinson's sturdy shoulder and eased by the gravity that caused him to weigh something like twenty pounds. In both cases, Jackson observed with relief, the self-sealing features of their pressure suits had patched the punctures immediately, saving the lives of the wounded men.

"Grafty, can you take these men back to the frigate? I want *Mikey* to stay here while we finish our search."

"Sure thing, Lieutenant," the coxswain said.

While they were carefully loaded aboard *Tommy*, Jackson used the drop boat's stronger radio to raise the frigate. "Captain Carstairs?"

"How'd it go, Stonewall?" the CO asked from the frigate. The planet-to-orbiter comlink delayed the sound slightly, but the sound was as clear as a digital soundtrack despite the fact that nearby space was littered with asteroids.

"Successful so far, Captain. The enemy is neutralized. But we haven't had any luck locating the shield driver. I'm sending Coxswain Grafton and *Tommy* back up with two wounded men. If you'll allow it, I'd like him to bring Consul Char-Kane down to help us in our search. She's the only one along who's familiar with what we're looking for."

"She's right here, Tom." Jackson waited through a brief pause. "She's willing to come down. I'll get her outfitted with a suit so she can depart as soon as Grafton gets here."

"Thank you, sir. *Tommy* will be on its way momentarily." Jackson took a few seconds to talk to his wounded men, neither of whom wanted to be evacuated, to assure them that the entire Team would assemble aboard the frigate in a matter of hours. After that, he jumped down from the open cockpit and took a couple of long, leaping strides to carry him away from the danger zone.

With a blast of four evenly spaced rockets, the drop boat lifted off the asteroid and quickly flashed into space. Jackson watched the flare of the engines for half a minute until they were swallowed by the distance and then turned to matters on the ground.

Most of his men were still busily searching every nook and cranny of the captured installation, but he saw Ruiz and Baxter nearby with the captured energy gun. He bounced over to see what they had discovered.

"It's like a combination laser and cutting torch," the master chief explained, showing Jackson the device. The weapon was like a long rifle with a series of rings surrounding a barrel that looked like clear glass. The battery pack was connected to the gun with a pair of stout cables and displayed a series of dials and switches that were marked with symbols Jackson had come to know as Eluoi hieroglyphics.

"No way to tell for sure how much juice it has left," Baxter noted. "But the master chief took three or four practice shots, and this little dial here moved over a bit each time. If I had to guess, I'd say it still has half power remaining. And this knob here, on the barrel, seems to control the strength of the blast. It was only at about 20 percent while the shooter was using it. I wonder what kind of range and killing power it has at 100 percent."

"Nice work," Jackson said. "But belay the experiment for now. We'll take it aboard the frigate and see what Carstairs's engineers can learn. For the time being, you can join the search parties. I want this station covered with a fine-tooth comb."

But they could discover nothing suggestive of the presence of the shield driver. Finally, about four hours later, *Tommy* returned to land beside its sister ship, and the Shamani woman stepped out of the rugged drop boat just outside the pirate station. She bounced easily out of the boat when the hatch opened; Chief Harris was standing by to steady her as she came down onto the asteroid's surface.

"Takes a little getting used to," he said, holding her a little more firmly than was strictly necessary. "There's just enough gravity to allow a person to fall."

"Thank you," she replied demurely.

Jackson found himself surprisingly glad to see her. "We've been through their warehouse and depot areas but haven't found anything that matches the description and picture you provided. We're hoping you might have some ideas."

She shook her head, then blinked. "I understand that the pirate ship was destroyed in attempting to leave the asteroid. Could the device have been lost with the ship?"

"Possibly, but I don't think so. We have a prisoner, and he admitted that something had been removed from the ship. But we have no idea where they might have hidden it. It doesn't seem to be in the installation, and from what you've described—it's a crate four meters long—they couldn't have just hidden it in a drawer somewhere."

"I have one suggestion," the Shamani woman said deliberately. "I know that the key piece of the shield activation is magnetic. I'm not certain, but it seems that the device would have some kind of magnetic signature, a way that you could possibly locate it."

"Better than nothing," Jackson allowed. He turned to Harris. "Chief, have the men activate the magnetometer function on their detection packets. Let see if we can't get a reading."

The SEALS continued to move through the ruined pirate base, still protected by their pressure suits. Jackson made no attempt to restore the atmosphere. For one thing, their attack had seriously disrupted the station's air lock integrity. For another, he didn't intend to stay there any longer than the time required to find the stolen shield device. He didn't even want to think about his explanation to Admiral Ballard if it turned out that they were on some kind of a wild-goose chase.

It was Mirowski who spoke over the communicator with a promising announcement. "I've got some fluctuations in the surrounding magnetic field, LT. I'm outside the landing pad, above some deep crevasses. These cuts run right across the surface of the asteroid, but the disruption is really local, just where I'm standing right here."

"Hang on, Ski. SEALS, let's all gather around our Polish comrade in arms."

"Polish-American, with all due respect, sir," Mirowski responded.

Within ten minutes the Teammates who had remained on the asteroid, as well as Consul Char-Kane, had emerged from the interior of the base to see that Mirowski had spoken aptly. He stood at the brink of a wide, lightless crack that descended into invisible depths. Across a gap of five or six meters—an easy enough jump in the low gravity—the opposite side of the chasm was as sharp-edged and smooth as the cliff below them. Several men played the beams of their helmet lamps into the crevasse, but the light was swallowed up by the distance before they could see a bottom.

"Like some giant took an ax and tried to chop this rock in two," Ruiz noted.

"Damn near succeeded, too," Dobson allowed. "Who knows if this hole don't come right out the other side?"

Jackson was consulting the magnetometer on his own instrument array. "I see what you mean, Ski. There's something down there that's making the magnetic field go all wacky on us."

"Sir?" Mirowski's cheerful, boyish face was surprisingly serious. "Request permission to go down and have a look."

The officer didn't have to think about it. "Granted. Chief, let's get him snapped to a cable so we can haul him back out of there."

Each SEALS had a 200-meter cable spooled around his waist. They uncoiled and linked together the cables from four men, latching one end to Mirowski's chest strap. Chief Harris would hold the belay while a couple of men helped brace him in place. In the light gravity, it was hard for a man to feel like he really had his feet planted on the ground.

"Lower away," Mirowski called, stepping backward off the ledge and leaning out to brace his feet on the cliff wall. With remarkable ease he twisted around and started to sidle sideways down the precipice, the beam of his lamp flickering back and forth between the two dark walls.

Farther and farther he dropped, with Harris calling out each hundred-meter increment of cable. By 700 meters, the light cast by the descending SEALS was a small beacon in the distance.

"Still going down, Ski?" the LT asked. "Or can you see some sign of the bottom?"

"Nothing but shadows, skipper," the corpsman replied. "I've got a lot of room to maneuver, though. I can go a long way yet. And the magnetometer likes whatever it's hearing down here."

"All right. Hold up a second; we'll give you a little more line."

Harris braced the line while the cables from four more SEALS were added, bringing the total length to 1,600 meters. When he finally started to lower the man again, the flickering glow of his lamp continued to grow more faint. As he passed 1,200 meters, the men on the top of the precipice barely could make out where he was.

All the way down Mirowski's commentary—"Still dark." "Damn, this thing is deep." "You guys still up there?"— provided a reassuring sense that things were under control.

Sometime after 1,400 meters, the tone of Mirowski's voice changed. "The walls are closing in a bit. I can reach the far side with my feet still touching the near wall. Wait, here's a rock. Looks like it fell from up above and got wedged in place here."

"Steer clear of any obstacles!" Jackson barked, his sudden concern harshening his voice. "We don't want to pull a thousand tons of boulder out of the way to get you out!"

"Aye, aye, sir. Hold on—I see something promising. There's a bottom down here, where the two walls kind of pinch together. And I see a long crate resting there. Holy shit—excuse my language, sir—all my dials are spinning. This has got to be it!"

"Good job. Fix your cable to it and trail it behind you as you come out," the lieutenant ordered.

"Can do, sir." The communicator was silent, except for the clear rasp of Mirowski's breathing over the next minute or so. "Got it, LT," the SEALS reported. "Haul away, men!"

Harris used the small motor in his cable spool so that they didn't have to hoist him hand over hand, but even so it took a good five minutes to lift Mirowski out of the crevasse. A minute later they had the crate, positively ID'd by Char-Kane as the shield driver, outside the crevasse. As she had described, it was in a nondescript rectangular crate some four meters long by one meter wide and one high.

Only twelve minutes after that the SEALS, the Shamani woman, and their high-tech prize were aboard the two drop boats. The prisoner was there, too, strapped in tightly and under the watchful eye of LaRue. Since his partner, Falco, had suffered the most serious wound of the fight, the G-Man was in no mood to grant the captive any favors.

A minute later the whole Team was strapped in. The coxswains closed the hatches and fired up the rockets, and *Tommy* and *Mikey* blasted off on a course for the nearby frigate.

The two little shuttles eased into the twin docking ports on the frigate's hangar deck. The coxswains, each a veteran of more than two years of training and experience, expertly steered the boats toward the ventral and dorsal docks. With a final push of the rockets, the boats connected to the air locks and the docking clamps snapped home. Even as the frigate's hangar doors closed over the upper Plexiglas hatches of the two boats, the SEALS and their Shamani passenger were debarking through the deck hatches, swimming along weightlessly into the transport shaft of the *Pegasus*.

LaRue turned the prisoner over to the chief of the boat, Swanson, who in turn designated two sailors to escort the Eluoi to the small brig nestled between the engines on K Deck.

Ruiz, Baxter, and Mirowski came last, hauling the long rectangular case of the shield driver between them. They detoured down to J Deck, where the device would be studied and stored for the duration of the voyage.

"Get that thing secured and then strap yourselves in," Sanders ordered. "Come up to SEALS country once we're under way."

"Aye, aye, sir," the master chief replied, as he and the electrician's mate gingerly propelled the long, awkward shape through the transport hatch toward the stern.

The rest of the Team moved smoothly in the other direction, a maneuver they had practiced many times, until they had filed up to H Deck, the large compartment that was SEALS country. One after the other the men shifted position until the formerly spacious hold was crowded with men and equipment.

The executive officer of the *Pegasus,* Lieutenant Commander Pat Seghers, greeted the Team and Consul Char-Kane as they snapped open their helmets and started to drop their gear, each piece of which drifted around the compartment until it was snapped, belted, or strapped down.

"We're getting under way immediately," the XO said. Seghers was a gray-haired veteran of the "wet" navy but had really found his home in the spacefaring fleet. He was best known for playing his harmonica in the officers' wardroom, occasionally piping the music through the ship's intercom for the amusement and edification of the crew. "The captain would like you all to prepare for one G; he's waiting for me to give him the word to go."

"Chief? Master Chief?" Jackson asked Harris and Ruiz. "How long will that take?"

"Make fast, SEALS!" Harris barked. "Sixty seconds until we move out!"

"What about my wounded?" the LT asked Seghers.

"They're in the infirmary up on D Deck. I understand they didn't want sedation, but Lieutenant Alderson pulled rank on them and made them take the shots. She put a splint on Keast's leg and dressed the wounds. They're resting comfortably now."

"Good for her," Jackson said approvingly. He knew that the frigate's short, sturdy medical officer was a no-nonsense kind of woman. "I'll check on them once we're under way."

The SEALS wasted no time fastening the rest of their gear, shrugging out of their suits, or simply settling into the seats while they still wore parts of their gear. They knew there would be time for more permanent stowing once the ship was moving and artificial gravity was restored.

Seghers, the two SEALS lieutenants, and Consul Char-Kane took the four seats nearest the transport hatch. The XO pushed the button on his communicator. "We're all fastened in down here, sir," he reported.

Almost immediately the *Pegasus* surged, her engines almost soundless but undeniably powerful as they pushed the frigate into steady acceleration. As soon as the jolt of sudden gravity passed and the captain ordered the all-clear klaxon, indicating that the inertial dampening system was functioning normally, the officers and the Shamani woman started for the CIC.

"Nice work," Carstairs said, as they arrived. "Mister Dawson can't wait to have a look at that piece of equipment. A shield that can protect a ship in space? That would be quite a find."

"It's still a prototype," Char-Kane explained. "But our scientists seem to feel it has a lot of potential." She hesitated. "It would have been disastrous if the pirates had held control of it. They could have sold it to any bidder, and I have no doubt that the Eluoi would have been exceptionally anxious to get their hands on it."

"Well, now it's a bargaining chip in our own corner. I'll brief Admiral Ballard as soon as we link up with the rest of the fleet."

"How far behind are we?" Jackson asked, wincing at the memory of the fire-breathing admiral.

"Better than twenty-four hours by the time we make the jump," Carstairs noted seriously. "We'll need to accelerate at top power for the next eight hours just to be ready to make the jump. It's a bit of a navigation nightmare, as a matter of fact."

"Where are we headed, sir?" Jackson asked.

"This will be the longest jump we've ever made. Something over a thousand light-years. We're meeting the *Pangaea* and the *Troy* at a star called Arcton. It's not visible from our solar sytem. And it's a lot farther from the center of the galaxy than any place humans have visited before."

Eight: Rendezvous
with Nothing

The *Pegasus* vaulted out of the Alpha Centauri system almost twenty-four hours after the SEALS and their prize had come back aboard. Captain Carstairs had plotted as direct a course as possible, but their beginning position in the star's asteroid belt required some nifty maneuvering before he could unleash the full power of the engines. Furthermore, since the jump required the ship to be accelerating directly away from the star, the frigate had been forced to spend more than a day simply racing in an orbital pattern around the star. Only when her position was oriented with the direction of the jump had she been able to kick in the full power of the engines and streak toward the launching point for the interstellar vault.

The next destination on the path to the Orion conference was a star named Arcton. It was a remote body, well out near the rim of the galaxy, though not as far away as the constellation itself. Humans never had visited it before, but it was well cataloged in the galactic directory that the Shamani had provided to humankind shortly after they first had established contact with the peoples of Earth.

After the brief period of weightless limbo that was the jump itself, the ship emerged into the Arcton system, exactly as the captain and his navigational computers had plotted her course. Swiftly she pivoted into a stern-first orientation, and then once again the powerful engines fired. The massive deceleration provided a solid sense of gravity as the ship "backed" toward another fiery star.

Jackson, Consul Char-Kane, and Sanders were standing on the viewing deck in the after con, looking "down" through the Plexiglas surface under their feet, watching the star called Arcton. The SEALS' commanding officer already had researched the system on the ship's encyclopedic directory of the galaxy. It was a common jump junction for travel around the rim of the galaxy, with a variety of outposts controlled by all three empires and the thriving free trade city called Arcton V.

It was a large star, some five times more powerful than the Earth's sun, and even at this great distance—they were the equivalent of Neptune's orbit away from the fiery body— the immense energy radiated by Arcton was apparent to both men. The effect was amplified by the relative dearth of stars beyond the gas giant. From there, even farther toward the rim of the galaxy than Earth's own position, they were looking at a few sparse stars and then the whole vastness of intergalactic space, the void so big and so deep that no ship, not Shamani, Eluoi, Assarn, or human, ever had made the jump to the next massive cluster of stars.

"You see those seven stars arrayed in a twisting line beyond Arcton?" Consul Char-Kane asked. "That is the constellation known as the Winged Serpent, a creature rather like your humankind's dragons, which I understand are mythical, though in fact such animals actually exist on several planets. But the constellation is visible only from a very few stars in this remote corner of the galaxy."

To Jackson the stars didn't look anything like a dragon, but then, he'd never been able to spot the bears in Ursa Major and Ursa Minor when he'd been stargazing back on his home planet, so that wasn't particularly surprising. As to the fact that such creatures actually existed on some planets, he fervently hoped those worlds weren't on the itinerary of this or any other mission.

"There are several planets orbiting Arcton," Jackson reminded his junior officer. "None of them are habitable—they have something like ten or twelve Gs of pressure—but apparently each has a few moons. These have been developed for colonies and, at least in the case of Arcton V, as a diplomatic free city. There are bases held by the Eluoi, the Assarn, and the Shamani on different moons within the system."

"I see at least one of the planets from here," Sanders noted, nodding to a bright speck—brighter than any star except for Arcton—that was nearly perpendicular to their course.

Before the SEALS CO could reply, they were interrupted by a crackling message over the speaker: "Lieutenant Jackson to the CIC. Requesting the presence of Consul Char-Kane, as well."

"We're on our way," the lieutenant replied as soon as he saw the Shamani woman nod her agreement. They immediately entered the transport hatch, the small lift cage gliding swiftly upward from L Deck all the way to the combat information center on C Deck.

"What's up, Captain?" Jackson asked as soon as he entered, with Char-Kane right behind him.

"Nothing, and that worries me," Carstairs replied. "We've been broadcasting a call sign since we came out of the jump. Either the *Pangaea* or the *Troy*, most likely both of them, should be able to answer our hail, but there's no sign of either of them anywhere in this system."

Jackson felt a prickle of alarm. "Is it possible we've jumped to the wrong star system?" Suddenly the galaxy felt like a very large place.

But Carstairs shook his head with reassuring confidence. "Not only did we triple-check all the coordinates—and they all confirm our course—but we've located the three gas giant planets that orbit Arcton. It would take one hell of a coincidence to end up in a system that matched our destination so perfectly."

"You are not mistaken, Captain," said the Shamani woman. "My own memories of this place are strong, and I recognized several constellations from the viewing deck. This is indeed the Arcton system."

"So these planets—well, the moons, anyway—have colonies on them, I understand," the SEALS officer said. "Are you getting some electronic transmissions? Some sigint that confirms the population centers?"

"Yes. This is a lot busier system than, for example, our own. There are no fewer than four moons that are broadcasting on all frequencies. Each of them seems nearly as populous as Earth, at least to judge by the signal intelligence."

"I see, sir. But no sign of our ships." Jackson was thinking aloud. "Could they be oriented behind one of those gas giants? That would block communication pretty thoroughly, wouldn't it?"

"Yes. They could even be on the far side of the star, and we'd have no way of knowing. But I doubt they could have made it that far this soon after making the jump. They'd have come into the system on the same orientation we did, after all, and they must have arrived within the last thirty-six or forty hours, maximum. But you're right about the planets, too. I've ordered a full orbital search of the nearest one. We'll check them all if necessary."

"Yes, sir. Any orders for my Team?"

"Take the time to get some rest for your men. The coxswains and my crew are seeing to the drop boats; both of them are low on fuel and life support. They should be ready to go again in ten hours if necessary. It will take about that long to get to the nearest planet—Arcton II—and set up a search orbit."

"Very good, sir. Do you want me standing by in the CIC?"

"No, Tom, that won't be necessary. You get some rest, too. You men have done a helluva lot of good work in the last forty hours. And I'm not sure that we won't be needing you again."

"Of course. Good luck, sir."

"Um, Madame Consul?" the captain asked.

"Yes?" she replied.

"Would you mind keeping us company here in the CIC for a few hours? To help us get a handle on the layout of this system. The charts show us who owns what, of course, but a hands-on lesson would be very helpful."

"Of course, Captain."

"If you don't mind, sir, I'd like to hang out and pay attention for a while. Get the lay of the land, so to speak," Jackson said. After the SEALS officer promised to get some shut-eye in the very near future, Carstairs assented, and Char-Kane went to the large vidscreen and began to explain.

"This planet you correctly identified as Arcton II—or Arc 2, for short—is the largest planet in the sysem, with no fewer than four habitable moons. One of the moons is a large Eluoi trading and manufacturing center serving much the same role as the planet Batuu where the SEALS were in action previously."

"Do you mean they move slaves through there like they were doing on Batuu?" Jackson asked, bristling at the memory.

She nodded without apparent emotion. "The Eluoi operate slaving businesses everywhere they control. They dismiss any moral concerns by claiming that it is a standard tenet of their religion. Those who do not follow the savants are deemed unworthy of independence. Of course, they make exceptions for those strong enough to resist through military might."

"What about the other moons around Arc 2?" Carstairs asked.

"One hosts a small military command center of my own culture," Char-Kane explained. "Not nearly so numerous in population as the Eluoi center but very well defended. It is also a spaceport capable of servicing our largest star cruisers, and we make sure that there is always a substantial fleet on hand."

"That must drive the Eluoi crazy," Carstairs noted approvingly. "Having a potential enemy force right in the same neighborhood."

Char-Kane allowed herself the slightest hint of a smile. "It helps to maintain the peace," she allowed.

"And the other two moons?" Jackson pressed.

"Well, one of them—categorized as Arc 2C—is barely habitable," the Shamani woman said, amending her earlier statement. "That is, the air contains some oxygen, but it is only about what you would encounter in your own planet's atmosphere above the elevation of some six or eight thousand meters. Furthermore, the mean temperature is far below zero on your Celsius scale."

"So it's about as balmy as the top of Mount Everest," Jackson summarized.

"Perhaps. I recall learning about that very tall mountain," she replied. "And as for the fourth moon, Arc 2D, it is not the property of any of the three empires. It is extremely rich in minerals, especially heavy metals, and there are a number of independent mining operations centered there. Its orbit keeps it on the star side of the planet—unlike Arc 2C—so that the temperature is very hot. Liquid water is common, and there is a great deal of conflict on the surface. For the most part, this conflict has avoided extension into space, since all sides seem to agree that it could spiral too easily out of control."

"And the conference is to be held on one of the moons orbiting Arcton V. Is that correct?" Carstairs asked.

"Yes. That planet is farther from the star, and the moon orbits it relatively smoothly. It has fluctuations of temperature—it grows quite cold for the three-month time period when the moon is in the planet's shadow—but even so the climate remains survivable. And the free city, of course, is mostly enclosed so that the population—at least that part of the population with money and power—is little exposed to the elements."

"Not too different from Earth in that respect," Captain Carstairs said thoughtfully.

Any further comment was precluded by one of the sailors at the com center, a young African American woman with a calm but clipped voice. "Captain! We're picking up a transmission—garbled, but it's bracketed in the *Troy*'s call sign!"

"Originating where?" the CO demanded, crossing the CIC in two long strides. Jackson followed.

"From the vicinity of that large planet, the one we're marking a course toward." The sailor checked her plot. "That would be Arcton II, sir."

"Good work. See if you can slow it down and pull some of the meaning out of it. Put it over the speakers."

"Yes, sir." The sailor rotated a dial and typed quickly on her keyboard. In moments the sounds of static crackled into the room.

Jackson strained to hear. The origin—"USSS *Troy*"—came through several times. There were other sounds, half words, but nothing that made much sense.

"Just a second, sir. I'm working on a text transmission," the sailor replied. If she was nervous about the command attention or the degree of importance of this crucial communication, she gave no outward sign, simply adjusting her machine, typing on her keys, and consulting her screen.

"Coming right up, sir," she said finally, indicating that screen.

The words were the typed transmission of text that had accompanied the original radio call. They slowly took shape, and Jackson's hands clenched into fists as he read them.

"USSS *Troy* . . . tack . . . calling USSS *Pegasus* . . . emergency . . . Arcton . . ."

"That's all we could get, sir," the sailor noted. "There's probably a source of interference near the *Troy.* Either that, or she could still be mostly over the horizon of that planet. It *is* huge, sir."

"Thank you, Roberts," Carstairs said. He looked at Lieutenant Commander Seghers and then at Jackson. "It seems our sister ship is in trouble."

"I agree, sir," the XO replied, and Jackson nodded.

"Helm," the captain barked. "I want all engines full. XO, take the crew to general quarters. We're going in with everything we have." He glanced up as if suddenly remembering that the SEALS officer was present. "You'd better join your Team and stand by, Tom. I don't know what's at stake here, but we have to expect some action."

"Right, sir. I'll await your orders below. Request permission to keep an eye on things."

"Granted," Carstairs said. "But only after you get four hours of sleep. We're at least six or seven hours out, so you'll still have time to enjoy the show."

"Very good, sir. And thank you."

The captain nodded. "And when you get up, L Deck is a good place to watch from. I have two men there crewing that particle beam cannon. When we swing around, you all will get a firsthand look at wherever we're going."

Four hours later the SEALS still were strapped into their bunks, following their officers' orders to get some rest. Jackson decided to let the men sleep for the time being. They were still several hours away from the target, and even if the Team went into action, they wouldn't do anything until the frigate reached the scene. He knew they would respond immediately when it was time to go, so he'd give them an hour or so of warning. The LT himself, however, was refreshed and ready as he made his way to the ship's stern.

There wasn't much to see on L Deck because the ship was still accelerating toward Arcton II and thus her nose was pointed at the destination. The two sailors crewing the particle beam weapon sat in their seats and, after a polite greeting to the SEALS officer, continued to monitor their instruments.

The weapon itself had been salvaged from an Assarn ship at the end of the Batuun mission. In effect, it had been a gift to the SEALS and the navy from Captain Olin Parvik, a piratical Assarn pilot who had shared a great deal of harrowing adventure and a nail-bitingly narrow escape with the Team as they had fled the planet of the Eluoi slaver Tezlac Catal. Parvik's own ship, the *Starguard*, had been destroyed while orbiting Batuun. In gratitude for the SEALS' help, he had offered to help them salvage the undamaged weapon from his ship.

Now the particle beam cannon was mounted externally on the stern of the *Pegasus*. To Jackson it looked like something out of a Buck Rogers story: a wicked slender barrel surrounded by coils that glowed an eerie blue when the weapon was activated. Unlike a laser, the blast of the cannon could cut through gas and vapor barriers, striking a target like a superheated cutting torch. A concentrated blast could knock out a ship's electronics, and a sweeping barrage could cut a hull in half.

The two men who operated the particle beam weapon were seated inside the hull. One aimed the device, and the other controlled the power output. While the weapon drew on the frigate's own engines for its energy, careful control was needed because it was fully capable of draining the entire production of all three fusion engines. Now Jackson was glad that the device was a part of the U.S. Navy's arsenal.

An hour later he heard the chirping beep signaling imminent weightlessness, and the lieutenant secured himself by grasping one of the nearby handrails, holding on for several minutes as the ship wheeled, turning her stern toward the planet.

Arcton II came into view during that graceful spin, and he couldn't help feeling a twinge of awe. The sphere was much huger than Earth, half-illuminated by the blazing radiance of the star called Arcton. He could see a couple of the moons, similarly half-lit, and guessed that the other two must be behind the massive planet. The *Pegasus* approached at an angle that would put her into a polar orbit, and Jackson watched in growing awe as the great body loomed to fill almost the entire forward view.

His communicator chirped as a disembodied voice from the CIC informed him that they were an hour out. Unwilling to leave his front row seat, he contacted Sanders and ordered the junior lieutenant to get the Team up and outfitted for potential action. Until they moved, there would be nothing for him to do in SEALS country, and he didn't want to miss the chance to see what was on the other side of the planet.

Finally the *Pegasus* started to move past the pole of the great rust-colored body. The "surface" below him, Jackson knew, was in reality a churning mass of gases, though it looked remarkably solid from space. The nearest of the moons sparkled with many twinkling lights on the dark side, proof of a large, industrious population. And then that body was past, and the frigate curved into an orbital path, still decelerating as it swept past the roiling mass of the gas giant.

"We've got bogeys on screen!" one of the two gunners called.

Jackson could see flashes against the dark backdrop of

space like sparks in a shadowy room or fireflies dancing in the summer night.

"There's the *Troy*!" the other sailor called out. The ship was too far away to see with the naked eye, but he consulted a vidscreen that showed the other frigate in amazing detail. "She's been hit!"

Jackson leaned over the man's shoulder, sickened at the sight of the damaged frigate. One engine smoldered, and flames spewed and then faded along the punctured hull. "She's under attack by a whole fleet!" he said, observing other ships in the picture. Some of them were large and were shooting at the U.S. Navy frigate. Others were smaller and swooped in and out of the melee, firing small cannons.

Then something smashed hard into the Plexiglas dome of the *Pegasus*. Jackson reeled, stunned.

But even through his confusion he heard the terrifying sound of air escaping from a ruptured hull.

Nine: Broadsides

The impact of the explosion threw Jackson to the unforgiving surface of the deck. When the ship was in deceleration, the surface of L Deck was the Plexiglas sheet separating the interior of the ship from the cold vacuum of space. His face was pressed against that transparent barrier. His nose throbbed, and he wondered if it was broken; the pain brought tears to his eyes and blurred the nearly infinite vista on the other side of the glass.

But he could feel and he could hear in spite of his ears popping from the changing air pressure. The scream of gushing air increased in volume and depth, suggesting that whatever hole had been breached in the hull was growing wider. His right arm and right leg were icy cold as the air blast rushed over his limbs, so he knew that the breach was to that side. Frantically, he flailed with his left hand, his fingers closing around one of the many rails mounted on the deck. Holding on for everything he was worth, he pulled himself against the force of that pummeling wash of air, hooking his leg over the rail to hold himself in place.

His vision cleared, and he looked around. One of the sailors of the gun crew was slumped in his seat, blood spraying from a gash in his forehead. The spray formed a misty cloud in the rush of escaping air, and Jackson followed the stream down to the deck.

There was a hole in the Plexiglas!

The *Pegasus* had taken a hit, and something had punched right through the reinforced crystal barrier that was L Deck. The damage must have jammed the armor cover that normally would have slid down over the plastic after such a strike. The breach was a circle barely twenty centimeters in diameter, but already he could see a plume of vaporous debris spewing into space beyond that opening. Ice formed around the rim of the breach, but before it could block the passage, each chunk of frozen water was torn away by the force of the escaping air.

With growing fear the SEALS officer saw that the second gunner's station was gone, with only the twisted base of his chair remaining in place. Neither the man nor the rest of his seat was anywhere within the confines of L Deck. Another glance at that six-inch hole gave horrifying proof of the pressure of the escaping air and the fate of any person or thing tumbling around in this compartment. Wherever the missing gunner was, the sailor was beyond the effects of any pain.

"Damage control, all decks report!"

The loudspeaker crackled, barely audible above the rush of escaping air. Jackson didn't dare release his grip to seize his communicator; survival had to come first. He saw that the wounded sailor was coming to, looking around wildly. As if by instinct, the man grasped for the buckle of his safety strap.

"No!" Jackson shouted, his head throbbing from the force of his own voice. The sailor looked at him and stopped fumbling with his belt.

The lieutenant pulled himself along the handrail, buffeted by the wind, until he could get one hand on the wheel of the air lock hatch at the base of the axial transport shaft. Another fear occurred to him: How much time did they have?

As in a submarine, a hull breach in a spaceship was a serious, potentially fatal problem. Instead of water pouring in, of course, the hole allowed air to escape from the pressurized ship into the vacuum of space. To protect against catastrophic failure, the individual compartments in both types of ships could be sealed so that the breach to the outside doomed only one compartment, not the entire vessel.

The problem was that if you were inside the breached compartment when it was sealed off, you were screwed.

Gritting his teeth, Jackson spun the wheel of the air lock, relieved when it moved. His ears were popping, and his breathing grew frantic and raspy as the air pressure rapidly declined on L Deck. But he wasn't doomed yet.

The sailor, still strapped into his seat, looked at Jackson and then turned his head to stare in horror at the hole in the deck. The blood, no doubt dried by the force of the wind, had crusted around the gash on his skull, leaving his forehead and cheeks caked with red, his eyes white-rimmed and staring in the middle of the garish mask.

"I'm going to reach for you!" Jackson shouted. "I want you to take my hand. Do you understand?"

The sailor nodded mutely and once again put his hand to the quick release buckle of his scat strap. He extended the other hand toward the SEALS lieutenant.

Jackson was clinging to the hatch with both white-knuckled fists, and it took all his courage to release the grip of his left hand. Immediately the wind pulled him toward the hole, and his right shoulder nearly was wrenched out of its socket as the grip of that one hand held him in place.

But he could feel already that the force of the wind was easing, no doubt because the air pressure on L Deck was falling rapidly toward vacuum levels. His left hand touched the sailor's extended finger and then moved past the palm until the SEALS could wrap his hand around the sailor's wrist. He felt the corresponding pressure as the man held on to him while still keeping one hand on the release latch of his belt. The sailor stared into the lieutenant's eyes, alert and waiting for the next command.

Jackson's head was hurting from more than just the blow to his nose; he could almost feel his eyeballs expanding. But he waited another few seconds until he could feel that the sailor wouldn't immediately be pulled out of his grasp.

"Release it!" he barked finally.

Immediately the man snapped out of his belt. Jackson pulled him toward the air lock, the force of the wind little more than a breeze now in the thin air. The other man's eyeballs were bulging, the officer saw, as he pulled him into the small confine of the transport compartment.

Jerking the hatch shut behind him, Jackson spun the wheel to secure the air lock, then pressed the repressurize button. He was woozy, almost unconscious from imminent suffocation, but before he passed out, he breathed a large, lifesaving lungful of air.

"Seal the air locks!" Carstairs barked. "All engines full speed. Mark a course for two four zero, with forty-five degrees inclination." He drew a breath. "Damage control parties, make your reports."

Lieutenant (j.g.) Dennis Sanders could only try to stay out of the way as the officers and crew of the *Pegasus* fought to save their ship. The jolt of the impact had been a pounding explosion, and it seemed amazing that the frigate hadn't simply disintegrated from the force of the blast. He wondered about the Team, hoping that none of the explosion had ripped through SEALS country on H Deck.

Immediately the pulse of the engines thrummed through the decks. The ship maneuvered wildly, although the IDS kept the crew from being wrenched around too violently. Sanders merely held on to the handrail at the wall as he watched the images on the CIC computer display.

"Engines operating at full capacity, sir," came the first report. "No sign of external or internal damage on A, B, or C Deck. We seemed to take the hit in the stern."

"We have a breach in the glass on L Deck," crackled another report from one of the ship's female petty officers. "We've lost the integrity of the dome, but the air lock is secure between L and K. One dead, lost to the vacuum. Two more wounded, now secure in the transport compartment."

"Damn," Carstairs cursed, and Sanders knew the personal pain that the captain felt upon hearing news of the death. With a chill, he remembered that his own CO had gone to L Deck to observe the approach to the planet. Was the LT the dead man or one of the wounded in the transport compartment?

"Who the hell is shooting at us?" Carstairs demanded. Despite the IDS, the interior of the ship seemed to lurch violently from side to side as the frigate maneuvered frantically.

"Looks like a real brouhaha out there, sir," reported one of the sailors who was studying his screen in the CIC. "We've got a couple of big ships shooting at something like a dozen smaller vessels. It was one of the big boys that snapped off the shot at us. Seemed to be some kind of projectile, sir, apparently nonexplosive but capable of punching right through the hull."

"Permission to check on the wounded, sir?" Sanders asked, already heading for the hatch as Carstairs waved him on.

The small car of the transport compartment slid smoothly to a halt in the passageway just outside the CIC. Sanders was relieved to see Jackson there, sitting up and cursing, although the junior officer was shocked by the blood smeared across his CO's face. The other wounded man, a sailor, was even bloodier than the LT. He seemed to be unconscious.

Sanders reached for the intercom button. "Corpsman! We need medical attention at the transport hatch on C Deck!"

Almost immediately two sailors were there. Jackson

shrugged off their attentions, though he consented to take an insta-ice compress to hold against his nose. The LT rose shakily to his feet and gestured to the bloody sailor.

"This man needs your help. I need to see the captain," he barked in a tone that would allow no argument.

Sanders stepped so close that Jackson had no choice but to lean on his shoulder; together the two SEALS officers passed through the hatch into the CIC.

"Tom!" Carstairs declared, shocked by the lieutenant's appearance.

"Just a scratch, sir. I came to report on the damage to L Deck." Quickly and tersely he described the puncture of the Plexiglas, the jammed shield, the missing sailor, and the damage to the gun crew position.

"The particle cannon itself—did it get hit?" the captain asked.

"I don't think so, sir. It might be operable if you can get men into the L Deck compartment."

"I already have gunners suiting up. They can work in a vacuum if they have to. But we took that hit from ten thousand klicks away. Our rail guns and missile launchers won't be any use unless we can close the range. That particle gun is the only thing we have with enough range." He turned back to the CIC screens. "What's the status of the fight out there?"

"*Troy* is not making way, sir. She's still firing. Looks like she's given one of those alien destroyers what for."

Indeed, the screens displayed a remarkably high resolution image of ships that were a continent's breadth away from them. The *Troy* and two other large ships appeared to be stationary, and smaller ships were weaving between them. Periodically the flashes of weaponry would light up the screen.

"Mark a course for that fight," Carstairs declared, making up his mind. "And get a crew down to that particle gun."

"Already there, sir," came the voice of the female petty officer who first had reported the lower deck damage. "We need to do some rewiring, but I think we can be up and running in a few minutes."

"Good work, Amy," the captain said, grimacing silently before turning back to his helmsman. "Give us some juking but no more deceleration; I want to mix it up with those bastards!"

"Aye, aye, sir."

"Captain, we're getting a hail over the ship-to-ship!" the radioman announced.

"Put it on the speaker!"

An accented voice, its tone muted by the effects of a translator program, came over the system a few seconds later. "Ahoy there, humans! Is that the *Pegasus*?"

Carstairs glared at the speaker as if it had offended him. "Who the hell—?"

"Sir! That's Olin Parvik!" Jackson declared, wincing as his voice again brought throbbing pain to his nose.

"Damn, you're right!" the captain declared. "Parvik! What's the sitrep? That's our sister frigate down there!"

"I thought so," the Assarn warrior replied. Even through the translator, his tone was grim. "She came to our rescue, she did, when these Eluoi buggers were trying to blast us out of space. And she's paid for it in spades."

"We're on the way," declared Carstairs. "See if you can draw them off."

"Righto, Captain."

Jackson could picture the swashbuckling pilot as he heard his voice. Courageous and loyal to a fault, the Assarn would do whatever he could.

"Captain. We have the particle gun ready," Chief Petty Officer McClennan reported.

"Fire at will. Target those two destroyer-class types on either side of the *Troy*."

"Aye, aye, sir."

Now the viewscreen was illuminated by a new brightness,

a greenish tint that swept outward from the *Pegasus* in a pulsing pattern, bolting toward the space battle as the frigate continued to race closer to the combatants.

A flare billowed around the nearer of the two destroyers, flickering and surging on the screen. Again and again the particle cannon fired, each blast pulsing through the hull of the frigate. Jackson felt the stutter in the engines as the energy-hungry weapon sucked power away from the ship's drives. But the volleys were having a telling effect: Already one destroyer was peeling away from the stricken *Troy* while the other turned its batteries on the rapidly approaching *Pegasus*. Bursts of light flickered on the screen, and the frigate jumped and twisted, vibrating hard, shaking from powerful forces. Jackson couldn't tell if she was being hit by enemy fire or simply maneuvering hard to try to avoid the barrage.

Suddenly there were more ships visible on the screen as the smaller Assarn vessels reversed course with the firing of their powerful rockets, swooping back toward the fight. A half dozen or more were visible, little specks emitting big flashes of light that were indicative of the powerful armaments the Assarn had installed in their ships. Their fire was concentrated on the destroyer that was shooting at the *Pegasus,* and McClennan continued her own relentless bombardment with the particle gun. The firing built to a frenzy, flashes and clouds of debris obscuring the image on the screen for moments at a time.

"Decelerate! Full power!" Carstairs barked. The order carried immediately to the engine room. The fusion reactors surged, though the inertial dampening system prevented the crew from feeling the effects of the powerful thrust.

"Missile battery one, have you acquired a target?" the CO demanded next.

"Aye, aye, sir," came the voice from the gunner's control turret. "Locked and loaded."

"Fire one!" the captain ordered.

Jackson saw the bright flare of the missile as the speedy rocket roared away from the frigate. The brilliance faded not because the propulsion was waning but because it was vanishing rapidly into the distance. The LT clenched his fists, hoping to see that deadly missile strike home. He cursed, along with several of the sailors, when the flicker of a beam weapon flashed from the Eluoi destroyer and incinerated the rocket while it was still dozens of klicks away from the target.

The firing ship turned its batteries back to the *Troy*, catching the frigate in a lethal cross fire as the other destroyer continued its pounding of the U.S. Navy ship. "Fire two!" Carstairs barked, and once again a rocket flared away from the *Pegasus*.

Abruptly the screen went completely, terrifyingly white: A wash of energy erupted from one of the ships to spread across the entire image. For long seconds the obscuration lasted, and when the image finally returned, the men in the CIC groaned audibly in the display. The space before them was much emptier than it had been moments earlier.

"The *Troy* blew up," said the viewing officer, his voice breaking.

Jackson could barely believe it. He would have denied the fact if not for the evidence before his eyes. It seemed unthinkable that a ship the same size as the *Pegasus*, crewed by more than a hundred brave men and women of planet Earth, could be so utterly destroyed.

But it was simply gone.

Another burst of particles streamed out from the *Pegasus*, targeting the blazing destroyer that was now caught in a cross fire between the Assarn scouts and the approaching frigate. Puffs of explosive force, gases and flames and debris, burst from the Eluoi ship's hull. One engine went dark, and the other three flared wildly, sending the ship careering away from the fight as her fusion reactors began to burn out of control.

Again the screen went white, washed out by the emissions of a violent explosion. Jackson winced but couldn't take his eyes off the screen. When the picture returned, this time it was the Eluoi ship that was gone.

The remaining destroyer's four engines flared as it raced away, curling around the horizon of the massive planet. The Assarn ships, some dozen of them now visible, regrouped among the wreckage, declining pursuit for the time being. Where the *Troy* had been, a cloud of debris drifted in space. Some pieces of the ship were large enough to hold out some hope, and Carstairs ordered a course—now slowing dramatically—toward the wreckage.

"Let's see if we can find any survivors," he said, his voice as grim and cold as the lonely dead drifting eternally through space.

Ten: Seeking Survivors

The *Pegasus* moved slowly through the detritus of the space battle. The crew, watching the screens in the CIC or looking out through the portholes and domes of the A and L Decks, spotted bits of flaming engine debris, shattered sections of hull, even bodies. The core of one reactor seethed and churned, burning like a miniature sun as its energy slowly dispersed into the cold vacuum.

One of the *Troy*'s shuttles, twisted like a child's toy after a major tantrum, drifted lifelessly past. Half of a deck compartment, with chairs and benches from the mess hall incongruously attached, spun dizzyingly, slowly dropping toward the nearby planet.

"Captain! I'm getting some electronic signature!" called one of the sailors who sat at a computer console. "Twenty klicks away, bearing about two o'clock off our course."

"Keep your eyes and ears on it," Carstairs ordered before instructing his helmsman to make the necessary course adjustment. The frigate moved under very low power in a weightless condition.

"There it is!" reported one of the lookouts in the bow a few minutes later. "Looks like the CIC. I see lights on the outer surface; it might still be secure."

The combat information center of the *Troy* was an armored compartment just as it was on the *Pegasus*. The nerve center of the ship was designed for maximum survivability in the event of an explosion, and a visual inspection seemed to indicate that the CIC of the *Troy* was intact, floating within the steadily expanding cloud of debris that was all that remained of the frigate. Still, even if it held survivors, the compartment lacked any means of propulsion and of necessity could possess only a limited amount of life support supplies, primarily air. Still, the discovery gave the crew of the sister ship at least some hope that they might recover survivors.

The helmsman aboard the *Pegasus* set the ship into a steady course, drifting under minimal power a hundred meters away from the large, circular metal disk. Several sailors in pressure suits ventured out and, by virtue of the time-honored technique of pounding on the metal and hearing a returning series of blows, confirmed that at least one person was alive within the sealed chamber.

At the same time, some of the Assarn scouts, smaller and more maneuverable than the frigate, swarmed around them in a protective barrier, ready to ward off any hostile approach. The supply crew of the *Pegasus* was able to snare the compartment with her robot arm, but the module was too large to be pulled into either of the frigate's docking bays even if a drop boat was expelled temporarily to make room. They could see that the CIC had an air lock, currently sealed, but it was an interior hatch, not a match for any of the external entry points on the *Pegasus*. There seemed to be no way to get the crew members out without exposing them to hard vacuum.

It was the chief of the boat, Swanson, who came up with the lifesaving idea. He affixed a flexible metal tube, a duct that was more than a meter in diameter, to the brackets on the frigate's air lock. Working with several sailors, all of them in pressure suits, they first glued and then welded the outer end of the tube around the sealed air lock of the *Troy*'s CIC. All the while they kept up an encouraging series of taps, resorting to Morse code to determine that there were eighteen crew members in the drifting compartment. None of them was seriously wounded, but their air supply was running low.

Working quickly and efficiently, the chief and his seamen secured the two ends of the tube. The air lock to the *Pegasus* was opened, immediately pressurizing the duct. Chief Swanson tapped several times on the drifting compartment, now leashed to the frigate, and was rewarded with a feeble but audible response.

Two medical corpsmen in pressure suits went into the duct and all the way to the air lock on the disembodied command center. The hatch opened and the pressure held, maintained within the flexible tube, albeit with a few small leaks spitting air into space. The corpsmen pulled the survivors out of the CIC and propelled them toward the open air lock on the *Pegasus*. One by one the *Troy*'s survivors—four officers, including Captain Kilkenny, and fourteen enlisted men—were pulled to safety in the other frigate. Faces gray from oxygen depletion, they were moved quickly to the infirmary or to bunks in the frigate's crew compartment and immediately began to recover.

Even so, it was a hollow victory. One-half of the spacefaring ships of the United States Navy had been destroyed in a surprise engagement. Of further concern to Captain Carstairs was the fact that there was still no sign of the *Pangaea* or any indication of where she and her complement of crew and VIP passengers might have gone. As soon as Carstairs learned that Captain Kilkenny had recovered enough to talk, he went to visit his fellow skipper in the crowded infirmary.

"Damn, Pete, they lured me into a trap. My crew! My ship . . ."

Kilkenny had regained the ruddy color of his skin, but his eyes were hollow, his voice stricken. "Were there any other survivors—besides those of us in the CIC?"

Carstairs could only shake his head. "We did a thorough

search. We had help from some of those little scout ships piloted by the Assarn. But there was nothing to find. It was
only the armor around your compartment that allowed the
CIC to survive."

"Dammit, Pete, it should have been me! Ninety brave
sailors, dead on my watch . . ."

"I know how you must feel," Carstairs said, realizing that
the statement was at best an exaggeration. He could barely
begin to imagine the sickening sense of loss that must infuse
the spirit of a captain who lost his ship and much of his crew
but personally survived.

But there was no point dwelling on that.

"Listen, Skip. This mission is not completed. We don't
have any word about the *Pangaea*. Were you in contact with
her after you made the jump to Arcton?"

The question seemed to restore some of the grieving captain's spirits. "Yes," he replied firmly. "We got separated on
the jump itself, but we had a message from her within a few
minutes of arrival. She was going to mark a course for the
free port and use Arcton II as a sling point. We were supposed to come after her at flank speed."

Carstairs understood: A sling point was a body in space
exerting a powerful gravitational field. When a ship needed
to change course dramatically, it could do so with much improved efficiency if it could use the gravity of such a body to
sling its course around. With the right coordinates, a sling
point could alter the course of a rapidly traveling vessel by as
much as 180 degrees without burning off a great amount of
speed.

"We made good time coming after her, but it was right
around here that we got the last signal. The *Pangaea* reported
some ship traffic in her vicinity, but there wasn't any indication of alarm. Then, by the time we got here, she was gone,
and the damned Eluoi were waiting to jump us. They would

have taken us out right at once if it wasn't for those little scouts. You said they were Assarn?"

"Yes. One of their pilots, the leader, I think, is a captain I encountered on our first jump."

"Ah, yeah. To the Batuu system, wasn't it? To collect those SEALS that got hauled off from Mars."

"That was the one."

"Then where do you suppose the *Pangaea* is hiding?" asked the skipper of the *Troy*. "You don't think she was wrecked—blown away or something?"

Carstairs shook his head, partly because he didn't believe it and partly because he couldn't imagine the scale of the disaster if the ship carrying the diplomatic party was lost with heavy casualties.

"Captain to the CIC," came the summons from Lieutenant Commander Seghers.

"Listen, Skip. You need some rest. Soak up the oxygen, let the IV do its work. I'm going to need your help on this, but not yet."

"Yeah, okay, Pete. And . . . thanks."

Carstairs shook Kilkenny's hand, clasping it hard for several seconds, before turning to leave the infirmary. In thirty seconds he had traveled up to C Deck and pulled himself into the crowded combat information center, where he was met by a visibly excited XO.

"We've got some information from this Assarn pilot, Captain Parvik. He's been talking to Lieutenant Jackson." The exec indicated the SEALS officer, who was listening attentively to a headset that he was wearing at the communication station.

Jackson nodded. "No sign of the *Pangaea* anywhere around here. But that Eluoi destroyer was dinged pretty bad in the fight. She's gone into orbit around the ice moon. The Assarn say there's signs of a lot of shuttle traffic between the ship and the Eluoi base down on the ground."

"And what is that supposed to mean?" To Carstairs, any pursuit of the Eluoi ship seemed to be a wild-goose chase when what they really needed to do was find the civilian ship.

The SEALS officer met the captain's frank stare. "Sir, that crippled ship is our only link to the *Pangaea*. Doesn't it seem likely that she encountered those Eluoi bastards when she was coming around the planet to her sling point? After all, the *Troy* came up on them as she was trying to catch up to the *Pangaea*."

"What do you suggest we do?" Carstairs asked, intrigued in spite of himself. He was forced to admit that Jackson was right: They had no other known link to the fate of the civilian vessel.

"I might suggest, sir, that you bring your frigate in on the far side of the ice moon, screened from the Eluoi ship and the base on the ground. Get in as close as you can and send my Team down in the boats to see what the hell is going on over there."

"What the hell is an ice moon?" Mirowski demanded irritably. "Can't say I much like the sound of it."

"What do you care?" Robinson asked him genially. "You'll be bundled up all nice and warm in your pressure suit. Shit, it can't be any worse than cold space, can it?"

All the men knew that Smokey's bluff heartiness masked a grim, angry determination. Keast, Robinson's partner for the last year, would be staying behind on this mission. Although X-rays had proved that his leg was not broken, he had suffered a messy wound, with a contusion of bone and flesh complicated by lots of swelling and significant loss of blood. The medical officer, Lieutenant Alderson, had restricted him to bed for another few days, and Jackson, despite the protest of his men, had refused to override the doctor.

Smokey Robinson was ready to go after some revenge.

"I'm not worried about getting frostbite," Mirowski said. "I just don't like the sound of it is all."

"All right, you old ladies!" Ruiz barked, standing up and speaking in a voice that easily carried through the large, crowded compartment that was SEALS country aboard the *Pegasus*. "Now, we've got a job to do, and I'm going to see that each and every one of you does it! If you're thinking about a career change, this isn't the time or the place. But put your name on the waiting list and I'll see that you're next in line for guard duty at the old sailors' widows' home!"

"I'm just wondering is all," Mirowski said under his breath. Robinson ignored him, as indeed did the rest of the Team. Each man had checked and rechecked his weapons, collected his ammunition, and triple-checked his own and his partner's survival packs, all while keeping one ear on the litany of details Lieutenant (j.g.) Sanders was providing in his very illuminating briefing.

"Let's see, gusting winds that can exceed a hundred kph. Temperatures hovering around seventy-five below, Celsius. Mostly mountains, with the only sea consisting primarily of methane. That's where we'll be taking our leave, of course, after the mission is wrapped up," Sanders noted cheerfully. "And good news: By all reports, the beaches aren't crowded at all even though this is the height of the season."

"I wonder what kind of alien tail we'll see on *those* beaches," Mirowski wondered, brightening.

They went over the details again while waiting for the go command. The Team would go in both drop boats, as usual. The two craft would rely on visual and very local radio transmissions to keep in contact. The intent was to come in low and slow, using the horizon of the moon to let them get as close to the Eluoi base as possible. Once they found the base, they'd try to infiltrate and gain any possible intel about the Eluoi plans, including, they hoped, the current position of the *Pangaea*.

Encouraging signs included the dense clouds on the moon that were characterized by a pattern of raging electrical storms. Those clouds, it was hoped, would keep the enemy detection devices from noticing the SEALS. Discouraging signs included the same dense clouds on the moon that were characterized by a pattern of raging electrical storms. They, it was feared, would make it a little dicey for the insertion crews to keep in contact with each other and pick out a proper LZ.

All those questions were running through the minds of the men and their officers alike, though none displayed any outward signs of misgivings. Instead, they showed an almost comical bravado as they waited, and worried, and listened.

Finally the loudspeaker crackled into life, and it was time to go.

The two drop boats skimmed above the atmosphere of the ice moon, buffeted by stray tendrils of wind that seemed to reach right into space to try to swat them down. To Jackson, the ice moon looked like nothing so much as the teeming coils of a tropical cyclone—but a hurricane that was so large that it engulfed an entire planet, with no sign of a pastoral eye.

"We're coming up on the last minute," Grafton reported to the lieutenant. "We're going to have to descend now or we'll run the risk of exposure to the destroyer in orbit. I don't have to tell you we won't be hard to pick out against this mess down below."

"No, you're right, Grafty," the officer replied. He swallowed his misgivings, as always hating the part of the ride where he had no control. "Better take her down."

"Aye aye, sir," Grafton flashed an external light that was visible to the men on *Tommy* barely five hundred meters to port, indicating his intention to enter the atmosphere. He was rewarded immediately with a corresponding reply: Message received and understood.

The pilot used his stern thrusters to drop the boat's nose, and almost immediately they were swallowed in the gusts of a maelstrom. The craft rocked and heeled, and if the men hadn't been strapped down, they would have tumbled all through the cockpit. As it was, they hung on for dear life, and many an ice-blooded SEALS felt the blood drain from his face and the acid churn in his belly as they entered the grip of the stormy atmosphere.

"Where the hell is *Tommy*?" someone asked, and the truth sank in: They couldn't see more than a few dozen meters in this murk, and they already had lost visual contact with the other drop boat.

"Damn, Lieutenant. My gauges are going all to hell. We're getting a ton of interference; it's masking radar, radio, even the magnetometer."

"No signal from the other boat?"

"Negative, sir. Nothing but static."

"Hold her steady, Grafty," Jackson said, hoping he sounded calmer than he felt. He toyed briefly with an unpleasant question: Should they abort the mission? But there was no way to communicate that intent to the other boat even if he was willing to give the order.

And the truth was that he couldn't do it. They were in, come hell or high water.

Although, it looked like they were more likely to end up in a snowdrift than either some semblance of Hades or anything even remotely liquid. White gusts swirled past the canopy; snow was blowing so hard—and was matched to their considerable speed—that it was merely a blur of whiteness. The green lights illuminating the control panel reflected eerily in the frigid murk. Jackson's small computer screen had gone to its own realm of white, a chaos of static that completely obscured even images that he called up from his own hard drive. It was as if they were in the middle of some kind of powerful electromagnetic pulse.

"Keep trying to raise *Tommy*," Grafton barked to his gunner, who doubled as the radioman. "You never know when we'll get a break in the static."

Jackson glimpsed the bright strobe of the other boat just once through the swirl of cloud, and he had to be impressed by how well the two pilots were holding formation. They were descending steadily, and he remembered the scouting reports: This ice moon was a very mountainous place. Now he couldn't help imagining jagged daggers of frosty rock jutting from the moon's surface to slice the drop boats out of the sky.

"Keep the nose up—shit. I'm losing her," Coxswain Grafton snapped. His hands were steady on the drop boat's helm, but *Mikey* was pitching and hawing violently as the little craft descended through the cloudy, raging atmosphere. "Not much air pressure, sir," he reported to Jackson. "But what there is seems to be howling past us at about two hundred kph. And damned if it doesn't switch from a headwind to a tailwind in the blink of an eye."

It seemed that the gusts did just that as the drop boat suddenly careered forward recklessly, a stomach-churning jolt that had all the SEALS lurching against their safety straps. For a heart-stopping moment it seemed as if they were smashing into a physical object, and then the speedy descent resumed, each man pressed tightly into his seat as the boat took a steep, plummeting dive.

"How far to the ground?" Jackson asked, trying to speak calmly through his clenched teeth.

"Can't say for sure, sir. The electronics have crapped out on every level. Best thing is to try to get a visual."

The odds of anything visual did not look good, not when each viewport and canopy was utterly masked by the howling fury of the storm. But there was nothing else for it.

Lights blazed in all directions, powerful landing lamps designed to brighten even the darkest environments. Here they showed little or nothing except the raging storm.

In the end, it was the proximity sensors—the one piece of electronics that seemed capable of penetrating the dense curtain of that churning atmosphere—that saved them. A howling alarm clanged, and Grafton immediately pulled back on the stick, bringing up the bow as the engines pushed, working hard to halt the craft's plummeting descent.

Then they crashed. The impact was bone-jarring, and Jackson painfully bit his tongue as the boat came to a sudden halt. There was still that blinding whiteness outside, but it was clear that they no longer were moving.

"*Tommy,* come in. This is *Mikey.* Do you read? *Tommy,* come in!" the radioman repeated, clutching his mike as if it were the last remaining link to civilization, even to humankind in general.

But there was only that churning storm.

Eleven: Ambush in Ice

"Everybody check in," Jackson ordered. "Any broken bones?"

A series of "Negative" replies crackled through his communicator. The cabin lights were on, and he could see all of his men moving out of their seats. The two pilots were working with instruments at the front of the drop boat while the gunner climbed into view, emerging from his low front turret. The SEALS, meanwhile, unstrapped themselves from their seats and picked up their gear, checking each piece for damage. Jackson heard a certain amount of muted cursing and grousing, but he was pleased to see that despite their dire straits, there was no sign of panic among the members of his Team.

"Grafty? I take it we're not driving anywhere from here?" the LT asked Coxswain Grafton.

"Sorry to say, sir, I don't think so. We took some structural damage on the gear and knocked the crap out of our port thrusters. I've got some battery power, but I wouldn't trust the rockets even if I could get 'em to fire. I'm pretty sure there are some fuel leaks out there, and we don't want to blow ourselves up."

"No, I guess we don't," the lieutenant replied. "Do you think you can get the canopy open?"

"Looks like we'll be able to, LT. I figured I'd wait till the last minute, since it doesn't look too nice out there," the coxswain replied.

"We'll be moving out on foot. You and your crew better come with us. We'll get you outfitted with some firepower."

"Aye, aye, sir," Grafton replied. All three navy crewmen wore pressure suits, unarmored versions of the heavier SEALS Mark IV suits, so they would be able to survive in that environment. Though they lacked the rigorous training and physical fitness regimen of the Teammates, they wouldn't be carrying anywhere near as much gear, so Jackson hoped they'd be able to keep up.

Anyway, there wasn't another alternative. Chief Harris took care of arming the boat's crew, giving each of the two pilots one of the spare VP90 pistols, high-powered handguns firing 10-mm rounds, their accuracy enhanced by a laser spotter attached just above the barrel. The weapon could be set to semi- or full-automatic firing, but Harris encouraged the swabbies not to use the latter setting unless they wanted to use up all their ammunition in the first ten seconds of firing. Next, the chief was able to dig up a spare G15 for the gunner.

Jackson already was turning to the next order of business. "Any idea where *Tommy* came down?" he asked the coxswain.

"Well, off to the port side somewhere, sir," Grafton replied. "But it could be a hundred yards or ten klicks for all we can see through this shit. Excuse me, this crap."

"'Shit' will do," the lieutenant agreed, looking at the storm howling beyond the clear Plexiglas of the drop boat's upper canopy. He saw swirling snow, icy needles pounding against the hull, occasionally easing enough for him to see drifts some ten or twenty meters away. Once the variable gale shifted direction, and he caught sight of an outcrop of rock about fifty meters to starboard; he grimaced at the thought that the boat could have come down right on top of that spire.

But there was no point sitting there and taking in the scenery. "I guess it's time to take a walk in this winter wonderland," Jackson decided. "Can you pop the top?"

Grafton pulled a manual release lever, and the explosive bolts securing the canopy blasted away, throwing the shield upward, where it immediately was snatched by the wind and carried away. The eight SEALS and the three sailors emerged into a snowfield that was nearly thigh-deep.

"We move out single file," the officer ordered. "Rotate point and take turns breaking trail." He consulted his navscanner, which was a combination of miniature pocket radar and electronic compass. The radar was a mess of crackling static, but the compass provided a semblance of a bearing, even if it wobbled unsteadily. Remembering Grafton's speculation about the location of *Tommy,* the LT chose a course of east by southeast.

"I got the point, sir," Robinson volunteered.

Jackson nodded, and the squad started out.

Immediately the storm surrounded them. Jackson looked back after half a minute, and the wreck of the drop boat already had vanished in the white gale. Although it was not strictly night, neither could it be called daylight. Instead, this side of the ice moon was shrouded in a kind of gray twilight, dominated in all directions by snow in the air and snow on the ground.

The terrain was rough, scoured by ravines and outcrops of rock, though, fortunately, it was not exactly mountainous. Robinson followed along the edge of a deep ravine until he found a place to descend and then waded through chest-deep snow within the depression before climbing out on the other side. Jackson was going to suggest that a second man take the point, but the lanky Minnesotan pressed ahead before the LT had a chance to give the order. Remembering the man's grim determination and the fact that his shooting partner, Keast, remained in the infirmary aboard the *Pegasus,* Jackson decided to let him continue in the lead for the time being. The lieutenant wouldn't let the man exhaust himself, but right now the exertion might be just what he needed.

The SEALS tried to raise the other drop boat on their comlinks and used magnetometers and infrared detection viewers to seek their comrades, but in the end it was good old eyesight that led them to their target. They found *Tommy* less than a kilometer away, amid a halo of illumination caused by the bright landing lights shining through the blizzard.

The second boat had come down much more roughly than the first. It lay on its side, and the force of the impact had shattered the main canopy. If the SEALS inside hadn't been protected by their pressure suits, they would have frozen to death in the seventy-five minutes that it took the men from *Mikey* to find them. As it was, the men of the second squad still were assembling around their disabled boat. None of them were badly hurt, and Sanders, like Jackson, had arranged to outfit the three navy crewmen with weapons, knowing that the only way any of them would get out of there would be by walking.

"I can't even get a goddamn compass to work," groused Sanders. "Every damn piece of equipment I own got the crap knocked out of it in the crash."

"I'm having a little better luck with my navscanner now that we're on the ground. We're just going to have to hold to our bearing," Jackson countered. "But we have to move, and move as fast as we can."

He was truly worried about the Team and their navy comrades. Despite their pressure suits, the deep chill of the ice moon's atmosphere was pervasive. They had no clear idea how far it was to the target, and though no one had been in-

jured seriously, the rough landings had left his men bruised
and battered, with several of them limping noticeably.

"Keep the man in front of you in sight," Jackson ordered,
standing to the side as the file of SEALS—strangely anony-
mous in their bulky pressure suits, trudged past him. They
were traversing a steep ridge, sticking to the snowbank just
to the lee of the summit. Barely a dozen meters overhead the
lieutenant could see a film of ice crystals scoured by the furious wind blowing off into the distance. Faintly illuminated
by the light of distant Arcton, the plume of frost looked like
a sheet of smooth blue silk.

He had learned that it could cut like a knife when he had
dared to stick his head over the top of the ridge. The wind-
blown crystals had struck his faceplate like sand from a
power blaster, and he had ducked hastily down again, fearing
that even his rugged suit could not stand up to that kind of
pressure for long.

Still, on the plus side, the storm was not quite as intense
on the planetary surface as it had been in the midlevel atmosphere. Now visibility was at least ten meters, and sometimes a gap in the gusts would allow him to see five or ten
times that far. It was enough to confirm that the file of
SEALS was advancing down a deep, troughlike valley surrounded by icy sheer heights on both sides. Marannis was
now in the lead, forging a trough in the snow that made walking much easier for the men behind him. His ghillie cloak
caused him to vanish against the white background, disappearing so completely that it looked as though his tracks in
the snow were being left by a ghost. The sailors brought up
the rear of the column, except for Chief Harris, who followed a couple of hundred meters behind, keeping a keen
eye out for unwelcome visitors.

It was such perfect ambush country that it made his skin
crawl.

To counter the danger, he had the men employ any and all

components of their detection arrays that could be made to work. Several men activated the IR filters on their face-masks. It was that visual enhancement into the thermal spectrum that saved the Team from disaster.

Marannis, still at the point, knelt in the deep snow and raised his hand to halt the file while he waited for Jackson to catch up to him.

"LT," the scout reported in a matter-of-fact tone. He indicated his fellow scout, Sanchez, right behind him in the line. "Willie called my attention to something. I switched on the IR scanner and got a line of hot spots up on each slope of the valley. Couple dozen—at least—on both sides. They're actually more warm than hot; I had to double-check to see if there's really anything there. They don't have much of a heat signature, but they're hunkered down on those heights. If we keep moving, we walk right down the middle of Ambush Alley."

Jackson nodded, considering. Surprisingly, he felt a vague sense of relief at the prospect of action. It certainly beat walking through the blizzard for days until their life support ran out. Furthermore, if they encountered sentient creatures out there in the blizzard, those strangers must have come from somewhere presumably a little more sheltered than the surface of the ice moon. If they could defeat the ambush and find out where the hostiles were based, they might actually find somewhere they could get shelter and perhaps even find a way to call for help.

"Any idea if they've spotted us yet?" he asked his scout.

Marannis shook his head. "Not by any reaction they've made, sir. And our own IR signature is pretty washed out right now; the outside of our suits is damn near as cold as the rest of this place."

Jackson whistled into his helmet as he made a sudden deduction. "But these guys are making some kind of heat signal. That means they might not even be in suits, doesn't it?"

"Now that you mention it, that makes sense, sir. Though how they can live in this stuff is beyond me. But they're up there on the heights for sure, to the left and right of us. Do you think they might be native?"

Jackson was very curious about that point as well and knew they weren't going to get any answers sitting around in the snowdrift at the bottom of the valley. He waved his junior officer over and explained the situation to Sanders. Both of them scanned the heights through the IR filters on their face-plates and were able to—barely—pick out a few warm spots in the snowdrifts. The potential ambushers were about halfway up the steeply sloping walls of the U-shaped valley.

If ambush was, in fact, their intention. The officer was not yet willing to take that for granted and wasn't willing to make an unprovoked attack on what, for all he knew, might turn out to be a bunch of miners taking their lunch break in the middle of a blizzard. He needed more data, and he had an idea how to get it.

"Sandy, I want you to take your squad straight up the hill from here, to the left. Get to an elevation where you're higher than those bogeys and start moving along the slope until you're above their position. How long do you think that'll take?"

The lieutenant (j.g.) studied the terrain for a moment. "Give me forty minutes, sir. And then what?"

"And then," Jackson said, hoping the idea wasn't as stupid as it sounded, "the rest of us will start walking down the valley of death. We'll find out soon enough what their intentions are."

Sanders was breathing hard, the sound of his respiration rasping harshly through his earpiece. He was on point for the last leg of the climb, and his men had made good time in moving up a very steep slope of snow-covered rock. They had followed a shallow gully, which meant that the snow was

extra deep, but had remained out of view of the unknown
aliens arrayed along the ridge's heights. He checked his
watch and saw that twenty-seven minutes had elapsed since
he had taken his squad off at right angles from the Team's
line of march. It was thirteen minutes before Jackson and the
first squad moved down the valley.

Finally he climbed to the lip of the gully and saw that they
indeed had climbed some fifty meters higher on the slope
than their targets, which looked like vaguely outlined red
splotches on the snow. Already he could see twelve or more
of them, and they didn't seem to be moving.

Waving his men forward, he led the SEALS of the second
squad onto the barren slope above the mysterious strangers.
It was steep, but that grade actually worked to their advantage, since the snow was only a few inches deep. The rock
beneath it was hard and gritty, so their footing remained
fairly solid as they began to move out along the side hill.

Through the IR screen he got a better view of the targets,
eventually counting two dozen of them in his initial inspection. They were humanlike shapes, with heads, torsos, and
limbs, and they appeared to be lying prone in the snow. Their
attention seemed to be directed downward, suggesting that
they did indeed intend an ambush. He was further startled by
the size of each imprint: The heat image seemed to be somewhat larger than that of a man. He wondered if they might be
wearing oversized suits as protection against the extreme environment, but they were still too far away to get an actual
look at them.

His men moved deliberately, taking care not to knock free
any snow or rocks that might tumble down to alert the aliens
to their presence. Advancing in a single file, with some ten
meters between them, the squad had moved into position
above the right flank of the ambushers when another glance
at his watch confirmed for Sanders that the LT was going to
start moving out. Another glance at the images showed that

none of them seemed to have noticed anything amiss to the rear of their position; they all lay still, attention directed toward the valley floor. The SEALS started to inch downward in line abreast, carefully approaching the unknown creatures.

"Lieutenant Sanders!" It was the other scout, Willie Sanchez, his voice hissing with astonishment. "I got a look at one of these things—it's like a goddamn polar bear, sir. But it's packing—looks like a damn big rifle of some kind."

Polar bear? Sanders didn't know what to make of that, but he didn't like the fact that it had a gun. "All right. Keep an eye on them. We're gonna let them make the first move, but if they're hostile, we give 'em a real kick up the ass."

He was barely done speaking when he saw movement. The nearest of the creatures rose to a kneeling position—it did look like a goddamn polar bear!—and raised a gun, sighting down the slope toward the valley floor, where Jackson and the rest of the Team should just be coming into view.

That was enough intent for Sanders. He released a controlled burst—three 6.8-mm rounds—from his G15, shooting the creature in the back before it could squeeze off its own shot. Each bullet struck home, impacting right between what should have been its shoulder blades. The burst would have been lethal to a man, but this target seemed to find the attack merely annoying. It rose with a roar, spun around, and cracked off a very loud shot from the long rifle.

The round went wide, and Sanders opened up on full automatic, sending a stream of thirty slugs into the creature in the space of a few seconds. It tumbled onto its back, the rifle falling from its hands, a wide crimson stain spreading across the white fur of its belly.

It was, Sanders realized with shock, like a goddamn polar bear with opposable thumbs. At least, it towered some ten feet tall and was covered all over in shaggy white fur. The face was more apelike than bearlike, and its limbs, too, suggested a simian suppleness. But it was huge and powerful, and now its companions were fully up in arms. They rose from their firing pits, shooting those big guns at the SEALS above and below them, and the SEALS returned fire with the full complement of their arsenal.

Each of the alien guns seemed to release a single shot, but it was like the burst of a small cannon, accompanied by a gout of yellow flame and a billow of smoke. Sanders felt the impact when one round hammered into the rock nearby, splintering the stone and sending a cloud of snow flying. The officer returned fire and watched more of the aliens fall backward, shredded by dozens of G15 rounds.

One of the white, shaggy creatures lunged up the slope, dropping to all fours and springing with catlike agility toward Marannis just as the scout was snapping a new magazine into his G15. In the blink of an eye the SEALS dropped his gun, letting it dangle from the sling, and raised the breaching tool he kept strapped to his hip. He brought the breacher, an axlike tool with a superhardened blade on one side and a puncturing spike on the other, down in a slash across the alien's face, cutting into the cheek and drawing an outraged howl. The creature slapped at the scout and sent him tumbling with a powerful blow.

As soon as Marannis fell, two more SEALS opened up with their G15s, cutting the charging beast down. More rounds boomed from the big guns, and Schroeder, Baxter, and Mirowski replied with grenades fired from the assault guns' underbarrel launchers. The rocket-propelled missiles sputtered through the stormy blizzard, booming and flashing as they impacted the shaggy aliens. Each blast cut one of the big fellows down, leaving a bloody crater in the middle of the shaggy coat.

The nearest of the alien ambushers had all been cut down, but the rest of the group, those that had been farther along the ridge than the SEALS when the battle began, roared and howled for vengeance. More of the aliens charged, some carrying their guns and lumbering on two legs, others dropping the firearms, which dangled from slings below their bellies, as they galloped on all four limbs. The caseless rounds from the Team's G15s tore through the attackers, but the aliens seemed unaffected by the initial hits; it took the force of a full burst to cut one down.

More grenades spit outward, adding to the chaos on the steep slope. Sanders dropped to one knee in the deep snow, aiming carefully and emptying his weapon into the nearest beast. The alien continued to lunge closer, looming over him before it collapsed with a groan and started rolling down the hill, leaving blood imprints every time its belly contacted the snowy ground.

Rocky Rodale released his G15 and hoisted the M76 Wasp with a four-round clip of rockets loaded in place. He fired them in quick succession, his steady hand and keen eye guiding each missile unerringly into a big, shaggy target. Those rounds, each of which packed the punch of a whole volley of grenades, literally blew the aliens to pieces, scattering blood and bits of skin, bone, and fur across a wide area.

By the time the fourth rocket struck home, the ambushers seemed to lose their stomach for the fight. Sanders didn't know how many were left, but he saw at least four or five of them spin away, running on all fours as they pounced and leaped down the slope of the ridge to be swallowed quickly by the swirling murk of the stormy world. The officer momentarily considered ordering a pursuit, but a look at the flashes, tracers, and explosions in the valley showed that a furious firefight still raged down there.

"All right, SEALS!" the junior lieutenant snapped. "Lets boogie down this hill and see if the LT needs a hand!"

Smokey Robinson was in the lead again, at his own request, but Jackson followed his point man, staying about ten meters behind. All of his senses tingled, as he knew that his column of SEALS was coming into view of the unseen aliens hunkered down on the snowy heights to either side. He resisted the urge to study the heights, limiting himself to the occasional glances upward that might be normal for any reasonably alert soldier to make. He wanted to reach around to scratch the itch in the middle of his back where he imagined some hostile shooter drawing a bead, but there was no way to reach the spot.

As a result, it was almost a relief when the shit hit the fan up on the ridge where Sanders's squad had taken position. The streams of tracers clearly showed that the SEALS' G15s were finding targets, and the booming explosive blasts of the single-shot rifles proved that the enemy was armed and dangerous. Knowing that the eight SEALS up there would give the enemy on the left a lot to think about, Jackson ordered his men to focus on the ambushers up to the right.

Almost immediately, a series of flashes erupted from the snowfield where the second rank of attackers waited in concealment. Snow puffed nearby from the impact of the heavy slugs, and the SEALS of the first squad, together with the six armed drop boat crewmen, returned a withering barrage into the heights. Some of the men launched grenades, the missiles exploding in billowing cascades of snow, while others raked the slope with streams of 6.8-mm rounds from the G15s.

A new weapon chimed in suddenly from the enemy position, marked by the stuttering chatter that was unmistakably a heavy machine gun. Flames spewed from an unseen barrel that was at a right angle to their position. Jackson saw the line of impacts, clearly marked by flying snow, approaching him from the left and threw himself flat, his helmet and faceplate pressed into the snow, as the stream of bullets went past. He popped to his knees and fired a sustained burst at the place where he had seen the blazing barrel, though by then it had fallen silent and he could only guess its exact location. More spurts of flame indicated the long guns of the enemy infantry. They seemed to be single-shot weapons, but they fired faster than muzzle loaders.

"Harris!" the LT barked into his comlink.

"Right here at the back of the line," the chief replied.

"Take your fire team straight up the hill. See if you can catch that machine gun nest in the flank. We'll try to keep 'em looking at us down here!"

"We're on our way, LT. Teal, LaRue, Falco, you heard the boss—move out!"

The four men of the first squad—the second fire team—moved away from the line of march while Jackson, Dobson, Robinson, and the six sailors continued popping away. The snow didn't offer protection from the enemy's big slugs, but it did provide concealment, and the men burrowed in as much as possible. The bullets continued to thunk into the rocky ground around them, each impact causing a shudder in the bedrock itself. Fortunately, the shooting was not terribly accurate.

Then the heavy machine gun opened up again, spitting slugs across the valley floor, shattering rock and pulverizing snow. Jackson once again pressed his face to the ground as the stream passed. When he raised his head, he saw the shots pounding the snow nearby and heard Coxswain Grafton curse.

They were in a hell of a pickle, the LT knew. They couldn't advance and couldn't retreat without exposing themselves to that lethal barrage.

He could only hope that Chief Harris and his team would get up the hill and take out that gun, right about *now*.

Twelve: Shelter
from the Storm

Harris led his fire team in a sprint up the steep slope of the valley's side wall. He thought longingly of the .1 gravity of the asteroid, realizing that this moon's mass rendered their weight close enough to Earth's that it didn't make any difference. Between his suit and his gear, he was carrying some two hundred pounds up the hill, and he was beginning to feel every one of them.

Still, the four SEALS already had climbed several hundred meters, and they continued to make good time. They were nearly as high as the heavy machine gun emplacement, which continued to be revealed by the flashing muzzle blasts every time the gunners directed another barrage into the men pinned down on the valley floor. Harris glanced to the side as the gun fired again, considering a path of approach that might bring them around to the high side.

As a result of his focus, he almost stumbled into the massive white-furred alien that abruptly reared up in front of him. The chief found himself staring into the barrel of a gun so large that it looked like a piece of field artillery, and he did the only thing his instincts allowed: He threw himself backward, landing flat on his back as the alien's weapon discharged. He felt the concussion of the blast against his helmet but had his G15 up even as he fell; with a single squeeze of the trigger he pumped a controlled burst of three rounds into the alien's chest.

Unfortunately, that only seemed to make it mad. The creature pumped the loader on the underbarrel of his gun, which appeared to be very similar to a typical shotgun—albeit with a very large barrel—and uttered a bellowing roar, displaying a muzzle full of sharp white teeth.

"Fuck it," Harris muttered, flipping the G15 to fully automatic. Before the beast could pump its round into the chamber, the chief fired a whizzing stream of rounds into its belly, sweeping the barrel upward to the wide throat. The magazine emptied quickly as the alien dropped its gun from nerveless fingers and started to topple forward. Harris rolled out of the way just before the corpse, which probably weighed six or eight hundred pounds, could land on top of him.

"Christ, Chief. What the hell *is* that thing?" Falco demanded, kneeling next to the bloody shape.

Harris saw the apelike muzzle, the deep-set eyes sheltered under a craggy brow, and the long fingers, each the size of a bratwurst. The teeth were sharp but not as long as a big dog's fangs, and the body was lankier than he had first thought; it merely looked like a bear because of the thick coat of hair.

"It's a goddamn yeti is what it is," Teal said, coming up with the G-Man.

"Huh?" LaRue demanded.

"You know, the Abominable Snowman," the corpsman explained impatiently.

"Yeti, sure," Harris agreed, turning to eye the machine gun nest again. "Let's make some more dead yetis."

Another burst of flame emerged from the big muzzle as the automatic weapon spewed a series of rounds into the valley. The machine gun was still active, and Harris knew that the big slugs could wreak havoc among his Teammates if the aliens got the range down.

"Falco, do you think you can take out the gunners from here?" he asked the sniper.

"I dunno, Chief," the sniper replied. "In this visibility, it would take a bit of luck. I can't even see who's shooting the damned thing."

"Yeah, I know," Harris grunted, wondering if they should simply charge the emplacement.

"Uh, Chief. What about Baby?" LaRue asked. "We can't see the gunners, maybe, but I can sure as hell see the gun." He hoisted the rail gun; Harris saw that he already had clicked on the power source in his battery pack.

"Sure, G-Man. Give it your best shot," the chief agreed.

The other three SEALS moved to the sides, each of them watching for signs of any nearby alien as they avoided the imminent backblast. Apparently the yeti who had surprised them had been a lone flanker; he didn't seem to have any pals in the immediate vicinity.

LaRue brushed aside the few inches of snow that had accumulated on the high slope and knelt on the stony ground. He raised the rail gun to his shoulder, sighting carefully through the aiming system. The battery pack pulsed, shooting a supercharged burst of energy from its series of high-density capacitors. The electric charge shot down the barrel, slinging the heavy copper-jacketed slugs down the rails and on a high-velocity flight toward the target. The counter-recoil blast from the rear of the weapon raised a cloud of snow but otherwise went unnoticed as the rail gun's projectile hit the target.

The impact was almost instantaneous. It seemed as though the slug, with its core of depleted uranium, must have hit the machine gun right in the breech as a blossom of fire erupted from the emplacement and shards of superheated metal shot through the murk like the tracers of a major display of fireworks.

Beyond the gun, a number of the shaggy aliens popped into view, rising to their feet in reaction to the loud, violent explosion. The three SEALS sprayed them with their G15s, and the rest of the Team, pinned down in the valley, added their own fusillade of grenades and bullets to the mix. The yetis apparently had had enough. As the barrage increased in fury, the remaining aliens, guns swinging from slings, dropped to their hands and feet and galloped away, quickly vanishing into the eternal murk of the swirling snow.

"They went thataway, Sheriff," Marannis drawled, using the muzzle of his G15 to indicate a notch between two looming pillars of rock. "Seems they can't help but leave some tracks in the snow when they're running for their lives."

"Good," Jackson said before adding, "And Pete, nice work on spotting that ambush. Those shaggy SOBs could have put a real hurt on us if we'd kept on going."

"Thank you, sir." Marannis seemed almost embarrassed by the compliment. He nodded toward Sanchez, who was reloading his assault rifle. "It was Willie who first sensed something. He waved me over to have a look."

Jackson nodded, unsurprised. "I'm glad the Team has you two for eyes and ears."

He spotted Coxswain Grafton, approaching with a stricken expression on his face, and immediately the LT suspected the worst.

"It's Zimmer," the petty officer said grimly, speaking of his copilot. "He took two rounds from that machine gun in his back. He was dead before I even got to him."

"Damn," said Jackson, keenly feeling the loss of a man under his command. "I'm sorry, Grafty."

The coxswain nodded slowly. "I . . . I don't want to just leave him here. I mean, there's nothing we can do for him; we can't even dig a decent grave."

"No, of course not," the LT replied. "Have your men rig a sledge, maybe using Zimmer's suit with some of the cables. We'll take him along and get him off this rock with the rest of us."

"Sure, LT. And, well, thanks, sir."

"We'd do the same for any one of our own," Jackson replied, meaning it. "Let's make ready to move out as soon as we can."

Grafton immediately gathered the other four sailors, and they set to work rigging a means to carry the dead man. The rest of the SEALS were assembling, reloading, and checking their suits for leaks or other damage. Harris and Teal approached, tromping down the slope in long, lunging strides after their inspection of the enemy dead.

"They're big, shaggy assholes, LT," the chief reported. "Teal called them yetis. Lots of 'em showed flesh wounds. They didn't seem to react much to hits in the extremities. Got a layer of blubber like a damn polar bear or something."

"Not surprising," Jackson replied. "How'd *you* like to try living on this ice cube?"

"I've already booked my cruise out of here, sir," Harris replied with a grin. "I'm thinking Aruba or Barbados."

The levity overlooked the fact, still at the forefront of Jackson's mind, that they had two disabled drop boats and no way to get a signal through the electronic clutter to let the crew of the *Pegasus* know that they were alive, much less what their position or situation was. He saw that the men were ready, standing around at ease. The officer knew that even in their climate-controlled pressure suits, they would need to find some sort of shelter before long, preferably an installation that would give them a chance to send a message out of there. There was no point wasting time.

"All right, Team. Move out, standard file. Everybody keep your eyes open. We want to find wherever it is these . . ." He searched his mind, seeking the right word, and finally settled on Teal's suggestion. "Yetis call home."

"A yeti," Sanders repeated with an appreciative whistle. "Aye, aye, sir. We finally discovered the Abominable Snowman, and he's armed and dangerous."

Once again the two scouts went first, Marannis preceding

Sanchez for a time. The rest of the men fell into single file, taking advantage of the trough in the snow created by the passage of the leader.

All the men stayed alert, weapon safeties off, fingers on or near the triggers. The five sailors alternated pulling Zimmer's body along like a makeshift sled, two at a time bearing the load. Harris, as usual, acted as rear guard. Leaving the immediate foreground to the point men, the trailing SEALS scoured the heights to either side, continually looking for any anomalous marring of the snow or other indication of unfriendly observers.

Not that the environment wasn't unfriendly enough. Jackson studied the pillars of rock, the two prominences that flanked their forward path. They were so steep that snow couldn't collect on the precipitous faces. Instead, he saw surfaces of rock so dark that they were almost black. The pale light from the distant star illuminated enough that he could make out numerous shelves of vaguely luminous ice draped like beards from ledges and cracks in the irregular surface. Some of the gaps were chimneys extending hundreds of feet up the cliff; others were dark and menacing, suggesting anything from shallow niches to caves extending deep into the icebound rock.

Mindful of the need to conserve his battery power, he nevertheless flipped on the IR detector for a few minutes. The environment immediately darkened, but he carefully scanned first the right and then the left cliff, seeking any sign of warmth, anything that didn't belong in the frigid icescape. He was only moderately relieved when he couldn't pick up any sign—he remembered how thoroughly the yetis had concealed themselves before springing the ambush.

Switching off the IR screen, he saw the gray-filtered landscape as it really was, watching as the Team moved through the gap without incident. Beyond, the slope dropped steeply away into the deepest valley they had encountered on this

ice-encrusted moon. The far side was a virtual wall of cliff
formed by the same black rock as the two pillars they had
just traversed. Even in the dim light he could see several
klicks to the right and left, and in neither direction did he see
any sign of possible egress if they continued straight ahead.

Not that that was the most important thing. Looking down
the slope before him, he saw that Marannis already was curling to the left, still on the tracks of the fleeing yetis. The
SEALS was glissading on his sturdy boots, using them almost like skis to move through the deep powder, kicking up
a plume that swiftly was swept away by the scouring wind.
Sanchez remained a hundred meters behind the point man,
his G15 held at the ready, keen eyes searching the surroundings for any sign of danger.

A few seconds later Marannis dropped into the snow to
take up the watch position. His ghillie cloak blended with the
snow so perfectly that if Jackson had not seen where he had
stopped, he would have lost him against the icy backdrop.
Sanchez repeated his Teammate's glissade, and one by one
the rest of the men came after. Jackson was the fifth man
down and dropped prone next to the two point men as he
neared the bottom of the steep-sided valley.

"The yetis took a right here, LT," Sanchez reported. "The
tracks are filling in—mainly from the blowing, I think—but
I'll be able to follow for a while yet."

"Might as well keep moving, then," the officer replied.
"Unless you want to stay here and soak up some rays for a
while."

"Nah. I've never been much for the beach life," the veteran scout replied drolly. "Thanks anyway, sir."

He was up and moving again, and the rest of the Team
continued to follow. The valley was a winding course, a deep
trench in the rock with steep cliffs on both sides. Not surprisingly, the track of the retreating ambushers led right along
the bottom. In many places now it was drifted over, but

enough stretches remained apparent for the keen-eyed scouts to be certain they were still on the trail.

The SEALS pressed forward for several hours. Jackson alternated Ruiz and Teal, then Dobson and Robinson, through the point duties. Since the first man in line had to push through snowdrifts that were often waist-deep and occasionally higher than even the G-Man's head, it was fatiguing duty. By changing the position every twenty minutes, the lieutenant did the best he could to keep his Team fresh.

At the same time, Jackson kept a watchful eye on the sky. The pale disk of Arcton—the star that passed for a sun in that bleak environment—was hard to place against the raging, stormy backdrop, but he became aware after a few hours that it was getting darker. Abruptly, over the course of just a few minutes, it seemed that the moon rotated away from the starlight, and night fell with dramatic suddenness.

Each suit was equipped with a headlamp capable of both high- and low-intensity beams as well as an IR "night-vision" beam, but Jackson was reluctant to have the men light up. He knew that it was easier to spot the source of a light from the darkness than to find any potential threat with a sweeping, inexact searchlight. So the men continued through the almost impenetrable darkness, using their IR scanners periodically, mostly just pressing ahead by pure force of will.

They no longer could see the proof of the yetis' trail before them, but the steep walls of the valley—it was virtually a canyon—seemed to promise that they only could have continued forward. At the very least, the SEALS suspected, if they had sought shelter somewhere along the trail, their hideout would have to have some kind of heat signature that would show up on the frequent IR scans each man was making.

Barely conscious of his own weariness, Jackson knew that fatigue was as dangerous to his Team as were the hostile conditions. Finally, he used the lowest setting on his comlink to order a halt. He posted four of his fire teams as pickets, each twenty meters out from the makeshift bivouac, while the other seven SEALS, including the CO, and five sailors used their hands and their long-bladed knives to excavate a deep snow cave along the base of the valley wall.

Consulting his wrist computer, into which he had downloaded all the data about this moon that the sensors aboard the *Pegasus* had been able to amass, Jackson estimated that the dark period would last some fourteen hours, of which two already had passed. He decided that eight hours would not be excessive for a rest halt and set up a rotation—four men on watch while the others slept—that allowed each SEALS to get six hours of much-needed recuperative sleep. The sailors, exhausted and demoralized by the extreme conditions, for which they had not been trained, and the loss of one of their own, were encouraged to get as much sleep as possible.

Because the moon's atmosphere contained a significant amount of oxygen, the men did not need to breathe bottled air. They had energy bars to stave off starvation and water within the life support systems of their suits. Nevertheless, they needed to continue to drain their batteries to prevent hypothermia. The snow cave at least sheltered them from the wind, and Jackson was pleased, albeit unsurprised, as the men broke camp rested, refreshed, and ready to get on with the mission.

It was still dark, and the wind and snow whipped past with undiluted fury. Baxter and Falco both attempted to raise the *Pegasus*—or anything else—over their portable radios, but the electrical interference, like the storm, seemed to be an eternal fixture in this place. Unwilling to waste any more time on what was likely to be a futile attempt, Jackson gave the order to move out.

Of course, the tracks of the fleeing yetis were long gone. The lieutenant wondered if it *ever* stopped snowing in this damned place. Nevertheless, the Team resumed its trek down the narrow, steep-sided canyon with a fair degree of certainty that they must be on the right track. Once again the point position rotated every twenty minutes, Marannis breaking trail first and then yielding to Sanchez. Jackson was pleased to note that they were making better time than at the end of the previous day. Master Chief Ruiz took the lead after Sanchez's shift, and by the time the rangy Puerto Rican was ready to turn the job over to Harry Teal, the black fury of the blizzard was brightening to the muted gray that seemed to be the best daylight the ice moon could muster.

Falco took the lead next, his squirrel gun slung over his back while he carried his G15 cradled in his arms as he waded through the snow, sometimes almost swimming through the deep drifts. The grade of the valley floor began to climb, making the work even harder, but the Team pressed forward relentlessly. A low crest materialized before them, emerging into view through the murk of the storm when it was barely two hundred meters away.

Jackson took heart from the line of horizon before them. It might be just a low ridgeline, some kind of glacial moraine crossing the base of the canyon, but it was a feature that broke the monotony of the trenchlike channel that they had followed for so long. The rest of the Team seemed to share his anticipation as, without orders or conversation, all the men picked up the pace. Falco, in the lead, lunged like a snowplow up the shallow grade, leaving a deep trough in the snow that each following SEALS tramped down further, so that the men in the back of the file had an almost solid track underfoot.

Approaching the crest, Falco lowered into a crouch to avoid suddenly silhouetting himself for any potential observer on the far side. He crawled the last five meters on his belly and lay prone at the top, waiting for the rest of the team to catch up. The other SEALS spread out, moving through the deep snow to the right and the left. Jackson was the fifth in line, and he made his way to Falco's side, worming forward until he was right beside the sniper.

His first indication of something interesting before them was the grim smile on Falco's face. "Well, LT," he said. "It ain't exactly the Little House on the Prairie, but I think we might have found ourselves a destination."

At first glance the officer didn't see anything anomalous before them. The far side of the shallow crest gently descended into a bowl-shaped depression, probably a couple of klicks in diameter and surrounded to the right and left by sheer cliffs. Vaguely visible across the valley was another notch in the cliffs, similar to the gap currently occupied by the SEALS, that seemed to promise a continuation of their canyon. It was not exactly the kind of destination he was looking for.

"Look for hot spots, sir," Falco suggested.

Jackson flipped on the IR filter and immediately saw what the man was talking about. In the exact center of the bowl was a shimmering area of warmth, smoother and more reflective than anything they had encountered on this icy world. It took him a moment to realize what he was seeing.

"Is that water?" he wondered aloud and incredulously. "*Open* water?"

"Well, it's something liquid, sir," Falco replied. "And it seems to be a helluva lot warmer than the snow. But look over there, about three o'clock."

The lieutenant followed the sniper's pointing finger and picked out another spot of warmth: a disk of pale red against the dark blue backdrop of the frosty landscape. Shutting off the IR screen, he studied the place, using the magnifying aspect to zoom in on it. "Looks like some kind of hatch, doesn't it?" he mused.

"That's what I was thinking, LT," Falco replied.

"Well," Jackson decided, thinking aloud. "Maybe we should go and see if anybody is home."

Two hours later, the lieutenant was waiting for his recon teams to report back to the makeshift command post he had established at the crest of the ridge. Marannis and Sanchez, concealed by their ghillie cloaks, had moved as close to the hatch as they dared. Dobson, Robinson, Schroeder, and Mirowski had inspected the pool of liquid in the center of the bowl-shaped depression. It was the last two men who returned first.

"It's water, sir," Mirowski reported, shaking his head in amazement. "Good old H two O! About five degrees above freezing temperature."

"Any sign of what's warming it up?" the LT asked.

"Not yet, sir. We came back to give you the initial report. We could see a steady stream of bubbles rising to the surface on the far side. A quick scan indicated they were just air, so there must be a pressure source under the water, releasing air. Seems likely, if it's warm air, that it could be enough to keep the water liquid."

"Makes sense," Jackson concurred. "Might be some kind of vent."

Mirowski nodded. "Robinson told us about something they called the Polar Bear Club back in Minnesota; said he was going to qualify for the first interstellar membership as he jumped in. We've been busting the ice off him for a while now."

Jackson nodded, worried but not entirely surprised. The Mark IV pressure suit was effective in many environments, water being one of them, and he reasoned that the best way to investigate the mysterious pool would be direct examination. Even so, there were so many things that could go wrong.

"Okay, good work," he said. "Team, remember to keep your heads in the game. Be ready to move out."

He raised his head slightly and looked at the pond. The surface was as smooth as before, rippled by the effects of the wind. From there, a kilometer away, he couldn't see the bubbles Mirowski had described, nor could he see any sign of the other shooter pair. Robinson, he presumed, was still underwater. Dobson had concealed himself very effectively near the edge of the pond; there was no visual suggestion that he was there.

The two scouts were the next to report back, gliding over the crest of the low ridge, their cloaks matching perfectly the gritty white color of the snow.

"It's certainly a metal hatch, skipper," Sanchez reported. "The white color is a paint job. About as big as the door to a two-car garage. We saw a few peepers and periscopes around it, probably sensory stuff, although they could be weapons emplacements. Anyway, that's got to be the front door to the place."

"Good work. But I hate going in the front door," Jackson groused. He didn't bother to ask if the two men had been observed. If there were any humans who could effectively become invisible, it was the veteran pair of SEALS scouts. Furthermore, the pressure suits were very effective at masking an IR signature, and the ghillie cloaks made detection by vision almost impossible.

But if not through the front door, how in hell was his Team going to get inside this installation, thus far the only outpost of civilization they had discovered on the whole ice-covered rock?

It was the final team of scouts who brought the answer as Dobson and Robinson returned over the crest. Robinson's suit still carried bits of ice on it in spite of the enthusiastic assistance of his Teammates. Still, his underwater foray had yielded promising results.

"It's an exhaust vent for the installation," he reported. "The warm air melts the snow, and that's created the pond down there."

"How come the water doesn't drain down the vent?" the officer wanted to know.

Robinson made a gesture like an inverted fishhook. "It's got a downward-facing bell. The air comes up from below, then emerges through a grid to bubble right into the water."

"What kind of grid?" Jackson asked, a little worried.

"Simple steel, sir," Robinson replied with a grin. "Nothing that Baxter won't be able to cut with his soldering iron."

"All right," Jackson said. "I think I've got the beginnings of a plan."

Thirteen: A Knock
on the Door

Like any sensible commander, Jackson hated to divide his forces before an engagement. But when he considered the risky, almost desperate, nature of the task before them, he decided that there was no decent alternative. The trick for the CO was to determine the right balance of men for the two tasks he had in mind. In the end, that balance weighed heavily in favor of the infiltrators, with only one fire team held out to create the all-important diversion.

The elements favored the operation, he told himself. Whether it was because this steep-walled valley protected them from the wind or the storm itself was waning, he couldn't be sure. But the force of the gale and even the intensity of the snowfall had eased considerably. From their position at the rim, they could see more than two kilometers now, all the way to the far side of the depression. The valley was a circular space there, like a wide spot in the canyon, with sheer cliffs to the right and left. The only obvious points of access were the gentle pass where the Team was positioned and a similar gap that led to the continuation of the canyon on the far side of the bowl.

After some consideration, he had decided to have the five sailors, the crewmen from the drop boats, accompany the larger group of SEALS, the men who would seek to penetrate the enemy installation. After he explained his plan to Coxswain Grafton, the sailors laid Zimmer's body near the side of the ridge, with a small cairn of rocks to mark the spot. If the Team was successful, they would return to get the remains. If they were not successful, Grafton readily understood that there would be a lot more bodies to worry about.

"G-Man, Falco," he explained tersely. "I need you to hold position on this ridge. When you see the last man get into the water, start a twenty-minute countdown. On zero, I want you to make these hostiles think that an all-out attack is coming in the front door."

"Gotcha, LT," replied the big SEALS, the tallest and strongest operator in the Team. He patted the long barrel of his rail gun. "I presume you want me to use Baby to ring the bell."

"Right. Give 'em a wake-up call and wait for a reaction. If nobody shows after sixty seconds, send in a second shot." He turned to the sniper. "I don't need to tell you to be ready if they sortie."

"I'll be ready, skipper." Falco cradled his Mark 30 rifle. The long gun, tended carefully by the sniper, was dry and clean, the lenses of the scope covered for now to protect them from the elements. The 10.2-mm round fired by the sniper rifle had a lot more stopping power than the 6.8-mm rounds of the G15, and Falco seemed to think he could drop a yeti with a single shot, if necessary. "At this range and with that snow, they won't have much chance of getting over to us unless they send a tank."

"I *hope* they send a tank," LaRue noted with a chuckle that was totally devoid of humor. "Baby likes big game."

"I remember," Jackson said drolly, thinking of the dinosaur-like reptile the big man had blown apart on their last combat mission. "Good luck."

"Thank you, sir. You, too," the big man replied meaningfully.

The rest of the Team was ready to move out. Robinson, the

man who first had investigated the pond that was their destination, took the point, with Dobson close behind. Jackson
came third, with the rest of the Team filing after him. Though
only the two scouts wore the ghillie cloaks, the adaptable
camouflage of the pressure suits rendered all thirteen of
the SEALS pale ghosts, moving soundlessly and carefully
through the snow. The five sailors were less effectively camouflaged in their pressure suits, which had been designed for
flight operations, but they would keep low, following the
trench plowed by the SEALS, and by doing so avoid discovery.

Jackson confirmed again that the wind was falling a little
bit, because the trough in the deep drifts marking the path of
the fire team's initial reconnaissance was still visible, though
it was half-filled by blowing snow. Aided by the gradual descent, they made good time, reaching the edge of the incongruous pond less than ten minutes after moving out from the
crest of the low ridge. The lieutenant looked back at that
horizon and was not surprised that he could make out no sign
of LaRue and Falco. Nevertheless, he knew they were there,
and he was acutely conscious of the clock that would start
ticking as soon as the last man entered the water.

The plan had been outlined before the Team had moved
out, and so they wasted no time there, exposed on the pond's
shore. The bank was a steep slope of snow plummeting one
or two meters almost straight down into the dark liquid. Despite the wind, the pool was sheltered by those banks, and so
the surface was only moderately rippled. Jackson easily
could make out the bubbles rising to the top on the far side,
roiling the water and quickly evaporating into the frigid air.

In contrast to the dry powdery snow that seemed to cover
this whole moon, the banks of the pond proved to be wet, almost slushy. It was possible to kick steps solid enough to
support a man, and Robinson and Dobson wasted no time
moving right down to the surface. They entered the water

feet first, quickly vanishing beneath the surface. Jackson stayed at the edge, tapping the SEALS on the shoulders as, one by one, they passed him and entered the frigid liquid. Their headlamps were visible in the darkness, and the lieutenant could see them moving away from the bank, the lights dimming as they dropped deeper and deeper.

Ruiz and Teal moved past, sliding down the chute that had formed in the snowbank to plunge into the pond. Next came Grafton and the four other sailors. Jackson was impressed that despite the harrowing and unique nature of the task, none of them had displayed any hesitation about the mission when the LT had outlined the plan. Three of the men, including the coxswains, were armed with pistols, and two carried the spare G15s and had demonstrated already that they knew how to use the weapons. The extra men had the potential to improve the Team's firepower significantly if it came to that.

Finally Jackson was alone out of the water. He took one last look at the crest, again feeling that tug of reluctance to divide his force. But there was nothing else to do. He didn't even risk a farewell wave to the fire team concealed on the ridge top. For now, G-Man and Falco were on their own. Instead, the lieutenant checked his watch and slid down the slushy snow to plunge into the water of the alien pond.

The suit's heating unit was adequate to protect him from the cold, but he was immediately conscious of the resistance caused by the cold water. Because of the heavy loads of ammunition carried by each man, the SEALS had negative buoyancy, which was an advantage for this part of the mission because they wanted to remain underwater and, presumably, out of sight. Sinking gradually, Jackson finally stood on a bare stone bottom, his head perhaps four or five meters under the surface.

The headlamps bobbed through the surprisingly clear liquid, and Jackson quickly counted all seventeen men of the infiltration party. They were moving forward, led by the intrepid Robinson. When the LT caught up to his point man, the lanky Minnesotan was pointing upward, tilting his head so that his light illuminated the objective. They were underneath an overhanging ledge of rock, and the SEALS could make out clearly the gaping mouth of the air vent, pointed straight down. The aperture was more than a meter across, blocked by a metallic grid that looked to the naked eye to be something similar to stainless steel. A steady stream of bubbles churned there, proof that this was an active exhaust vent.

Jackson's breathing was the only sound in his ears, a raspy but reassuring in and out of air hissing slowly in his earphones. As per the plan he had outlined on the ridge crest, the men had their communicators turned off to avoid broadcasting any kind of signal. Still, they knew the drill: Baxter already was moving toward the front, his battery-powered plasma cutter in his hand.

The wiry SEALS was lifted by Dobson and Robinson, each man holding one of his legs so that he easily could reach the metal grid blocking access to the air vent. The cutter sizzled brightly, turning the water it contacted into steam, masking the actual touch of the tool to the metal. But it worked like a charm. Baxter pressed the cutter against one bar of the grate, and in the middle of a cloud of bubbles Jackson saw a red glow. The illumination started as a pale hint, but within five seconds it was bright, intense enough that the heat was not dissipated immediately by the cold water. Ten seconds after he started, the first of the grid's bars had been sliced off right where it was anchored into the frame of the air vent.

Still, there were nearly a hundred individual contact points, and as the SEALS continued his cutting, Jackson was keenly aware of time ticking away. Already they had been in the water for ten minutes. In another ten, the diversion attack would begin, and his intent had been for the Team to be ready to infiltrate at the same time LaRue fired his initial round at the hatch.

Perhaps Baxter sensed his urgency, or maybe the warming water—the LT's external thermometer indicated it had warmed nearly forty degrees Celsius in their immediate vicinity since the cutting had begun—made the task easier. In any event, the tool-wielding Teammate began to cut faster, and the timer showed seventeen minutes elapsed when he sliced through the last bar. The heavy grid fell away, sinking past the watching SEALS to come to rest on the bottom.

Again according to the prearranged plan, the two scouts went first, Marannis and Sanchez pulling themselves up out of the water. They slid single file into the exhaust vent as one by one the SEALS and sailors of the attack party moved into the unknown installation.

Jackson came fourth, and just as he pulled himself up and out of the water, the digital timer on his wrist clicked to eighteen minutes.

"It's time," Falco whispered to himself. Like the infiltrators making their way into the enemy installation, the two men on the ridge had their comlinks switched off, but each had been keeping an eye on the clock. Both SEALS lay prone in the snow, and the wind had dusted them over so much that they were virtually invisible to anyone more than a few meters away.

Of course, that was all about to change. Falco glanced at the big man next to him and saw that LaRue already was resting Baby's barrel on the fold-down bipod, taking aim at the metal hatch. The sniper cradled his squirrel gun and removed the protective covers from the scope. He scanned the rest of the valley, leaving his partner to concentrate on the initial target.

The battery pack powering the rail gun was hot, and the weapon was ready. LaRue had braced the rail gun along the trough he had cleared through the snow, and he drew a bead on the steel door in the rock outcrop near the center of the circular valley. He pulled the trigger, and the counterblast erupted from the back of the weapon in a fiery burst even as the copper-jacketed slug shot unerringly through the air to impact against the steel hatch.

To the two men, the only visible effect was the bright red glow of the puncture hole that appeared almost directly in the middle of the hatch. They knew that bits of superheated metal had sprayed immediately, almost like a splash of liquid, through whatever occupied the space on the other side of the door. The copper coating would have sheathed off the depleted-uranium core as it penetrated the metal door, and the whole of the round's kinetic energy might have liquefied it into a lethal spurt, a spray of deadly heat spreading in a searing shower through whatever was on the other side of the door. Those molten projectiles would slice flesh and bone without even slowing down and would inflict a lot of damage on metal or stone objects as well.

For long, dragging seconds they waited. LaRue kept his eyes on the hatch while Falco scanned the crater, even checking over his shoulder to see if anything was moving in reaction to the violent assault. Conscious of the LT's order to fire a second round after a minute, G-Man prepped the next slug simply by cocking the trigger and steadied his aim for the next shot.

It was Falco who spotted the movement. "Heads up, G-Man," he snapped. "Ten o'clock."

Some five hundred meters away, an object was rising from the snow, a pillar of dark metal that had been concealed in the ground. Narrow slits were visible in the sides, and one of those slits sparked and flamed as a barrage of high-velocity rounds spit toward the crest where the two SEALS were concealed. Both men ducked instinctively, watching as the burst chewed through the snow along the stony ridge. "Whattya know?" G-Man said. "It's a fucking robot gun."

"I think that one's got your name on it," Falco said laconically as the burst continued to sweep back and forth. The bullets came at them in a dense stream, the gun firing faster than a G15 on full automatic. It seemed to be concentrating on the ridge at their exact position, though occasionally the bursts swept to the right and left. High-speed rounds whizzed past, cutting through the air and the snow like a crazed buzz saw.

LaRue rolled over and over until he was about eight meters to the side of his original firing position. Falco, meanwhile, pushed his gun barrel through the snow, stirring up the powdery stuff, sending up a plume that could be seen by an observer on the other side. Immediately the barrage focused on the diversion, giving G-Man the chance he needed to swing Baby over the crest, take aim at the turret, and fire another round. The slug tore through the metal of what seemed to be an automated turret, and immediately the gun fell silent.

Falco popped up again just in time to see the hatch explode outward, toppling heavily into the snow. "Did you do that?" he asked his partner in surprise.

"Negative. Take a look."

The two SEALS saw a tanklike vehicle riding on a pair of wide tracks burst from the now opened hatchway and churn through the snow toward their position. Apparently the enemy had released an explosive charge to move the punctured barrier quickly out of the way. A machine gun chattered from a turret on the armored vehicle, but the first rounds sailed high as the firing platform pitched and lurched through the soft powder. Immediately beyond the tank came what looked like a full platoon of infantry, soldiers dressed in parkas and large webbed footgear. Even a cursory glance was enough to confirm that the hostiles were manlike, very different from the large lumbering yeti.

LaRue was lining up another shot for the rail gun. Falco concentrated on the soldiers, who were virtually sitting ducks in the scope of his sniper rifle at that range. He squeezed off one round and watched the leading man fall backward; a second shot produced the same result. By the time he dropped the third infantryman, the enemy troops had perceived their peril and dropped prone into the snow. They snapped off a barrage of rounds from their guns, which fired like assault rifles. Rounds impacted at and below the crest or whistled over the heads of the two SEALS.

Falco ducked for cover as LaRue, unrattled, fired his third round. He gaped in disbelief for a moment, then ducked down and called to his partner. "I hit the goddamned tank in the windshield, but the round went right through! It's still coming!"

"Aim for the engine block," Falco suggested, popping up to snap off another couple of rounds from his Hammer. With the enemy troops prone in the snow, he couldn't tell if he was hitting them, but he wanted to make sure they kept their heads down.

G-Man pushed forward and took aim again. This time the round flew true, right through the front grille of the churning snow machine. Fire and smoke spurted through the hatches, and the back end was rocked by a series of secondary explosions as ammunition and fuel cooked off. The vehicle stopped where it was hit; from what the two SEALS could see, none of the crew made it out.

More soldiers charged from the open hatchway, and Falco picked off two of them before they, too, joined their companions in the snow. "How damned big is that place, anyway?" he wondered, guessing that something like forty men had emerged already.

He rose slightly, looking for a target, when something

smacked him hard in the faceplate. He fell backward, wrenching his neck, tasting blood, and feeling cold, dry air chill the skin of his face.

"I'm hit!" he croaked, shaking his head, which only provoked more stinging pain in his neck. Where had the shot come from? He hadn't even exposed himself to the men who were emerging from the hatch.

"Shit!" LaRue cursed, the sound of his voice tinny and rattling in Falco's ears. "Big trouble!"

Releasing his rail gun, G-Man left the weapon lying in the snow as he snatched up the G15 slung across his chest. Raising the gun to his shoulder, he sighted along the barrel and snapped off one controlled burst after another. Most confusing to Falco, he was shooting to the left, not toward any of the soldiers they had seen emerging from the hatch.

Rolling back to his stomach, Falco pushed himself up to his hands and knees. His cheeks were numb, and his eyes teared from the cold air that surged through his shattered faceplate. Blood ran down from his forehead, and he impatiently wiped it away. Then he saw what LaRue had seen.

A concealed hatch in the side of the cliff had popped open directly to their left, less than a hundred meters away. More soldiers emerged from it, charging toward the two SEALS. As G-Man shot several of them, the others spread out, returning fire from their lethal short-barreled assault rifles. Some knelt, covering the advance with short, well-aimed bursts, while the others came on at a run. They were closing fast.

"We gotta get out of here," LaRue said, his voice surprisingly calm under the circumstances. Falco nodded, adrenaline driving his pain into the background. He shook off his partner's hand when the big man tried to hoist him up.

"I'm okay," he snapped. "Let's move!"

He snatched up his squirrel gun while G-Man hoisted Baby over his shoulder. Staying low, the two SEALS backed

down from their ridgetop position for a dozen steps. When
they were low enough for temporary cover, they turned and
sprinted through the snow, heading up the canyon, away
from the base and the rest of the Team. Counting their steps,
they ran for about fifty paces until they guessed that the attackers would be nearing the crest they had just vacated.

At the same instant, the two SEALS dropped prone in the
snow and aimed their carbines toward the crest. A few seconds later, three or four of the parka-clad soldiers appeared
there, crouching low, advancing at a lumbering run. With a
few precise bursts, the shooter pair cut them all down. For
another few heartbeats they watched until it was clear that
there were no other pursuers eager to cross that deadly horizon. Springing to their feet, they ran, covering fifty or sixty
meters through the deep, exhausting snow.

Once again they paused, turning back to wait but only for
a second. The pursuing company came over the ridge in a
wave, dozens of men charging into view, diving over the
crest, tumbling into the deep snow where Falco and LaRue
had set up their firing position. The SEALS snapped off
more short bursts, but there were too many targets, and even
as they shot down some of the enemy soldiers, more of them
poured over the ridge, guns blazing.

Rounds zinged through the snow on all sides of them, and
Falco felt another impact, this time on his left shoulder. It
was more of a punch than a penetration, however, so he
hoped that the suit's armor had deflected the blow. There was
nothing he could do about it in any event.

Again the two SEALS took off running, staying low, carrying their long weapons strapped across their backs while
they cradled their G15s in their arms. LaRue made for a
large outcropping of rock near the right-hand wall of the
canyon, and Falco fell into step behind his partner, grateful
for the trough the big man was excavating through the deep
drifts. The sniper spun and cracked off a few more bursts,

trying to hold the pursuers at bay. His magazine empty, he tossed it away and chased after G-Man, who had tumbled behind the snow-capped clump of boulders.

Each breath was a blast of frost shooting straight into Falco's lungs. He knew he'd suffer frostbite on his face in a few minutes if he didn't protect his skin, but that was the least of his problems. He crawled to a vantage point between a couple of square-topped rocks and snapped another full magazine, his second to last, into his G15. The pursuers were fanning out as they moved down the crest, and at the last second he lowered his carbine and picked up the Mark 30 Hammer rifle.

At less than 200 meters' range there was no way he could miss, and in rapid succession he squeezed off six rounds, killing or wounding an equal number of the enemy. LaRue snapped off controlled bursts, the 6.8-mm slugs churning the snow around the pursuing soldiers, dropping several of them onto their faces. The SEALS could see several places where the pristine white snow was being stained a shocking bright red.

They heard it before they saw it: a grinding engine, treads crunching the snow. It loomed suddenly on the crest of the ridge like some arctic-equipped Abrams tank, rumbling up the crest and immediately toppling over to descend the near slope. Snow flew from the churning treads as the second snow tank came into view, veering and juking wildly to present a difficult target. The barrel in a low, flat turret was aimed toward the SEALS' position, and it immediately spit a gout of flame. A high-explosive round smashed into the rocks before them, sending both men tumbling backward.

"Looks like you got your wish," Falco said bitterly, climbing to his feet, "You *had* to hope they had tanks, didn't you?"

LaRue didn't reply as he was busily prepping Baby for more action. Certain he was ready, the big man stood up, lifting his huge, powerful weapon to his shoulder and aiming over the rocks toward the roaring snow machine. Stifling a curse, Falco rolled farther away from the backblast zone, still cradling his long rifle. Rising to a kneeling position, he aimed and shot, aimed and shot, successfully driving the accompanying infantry onto the ground again.

The tank and the rail gun fired, apparently at the same time. LaRue's aim was true as he matched his other successful shot, the round penetrating the front air intake of the snow tank and incinerating the guts of the engine and fuel line. The tank's round, meanwhile, crackled overhead with a sonic boom that knocked both SEALS flat. The shell itself, fortunately, passed a hundred meters beyond them to explode against the wall of the canyon.

They didn't need to look to know that the infantry still was coming on: Rounds spattered all around them, chipping away at the rocks, speeding past in whining ricochets. Once more they crouched low and started to run, keeping the clump of rocks between themselves and their pursuers as much as possible. Here, in the very shadow of the canyon wall, they found that the ground was surprisingly clear of drifted snow, and they were able to make good time, sprinting away from their pursuers. The canyon favored them with a gradual bend to the right, and within a few dozen steps they had advanced around the curve to the point where they no longer could be seen by the shooters arrayed on the ridge and around the burning snow tank.

But both men were gasping for breath now, staggering with exhaustion and shock. Falco's lungs were raw, and the water vapor from his breath had formed a layer of frost around his nose and mouth. He blinked and had to work to snap his eyelids shut as they were becoming frozen in place. Stumbling, he felt himself going over, and only with the greatest desperation was he able to keep his footing. He staggered up to the canyon wall and braced himself with one hand.

"Keep going," he urged LaRue. "I'll hold 'em up for a bit, let you get a firing position. Then I'll join up."

"Fuck that," the big SEALS snarled. "And let you get all the glory?"

Instead, G-Man hoisted Falco's arm over his shoulders, between the barrel of the rail gun and his neck, atop the heavy battery pack. Somehow he found the strength to continue running while Falco did the best he could to help out, which basically meant striding with one of his feet whenever he was able to reach the ground.

The deep canyon straightened, eliminating their advantage of cover, and more rounds zinged past them, sparking off the cliff. They reached a small side niche where flowing water at some point might have scoured a small creek bed. In any event, it served as a makeshift trench, and the two SEALS tumbled in, their landing cushioned by the deep layer of snow.

Falco strained to see, wiping his gloved hands over his face and feeling the minimal warmth of his heated gloves as a searing but welcome pain against his face. LaRue had his G15 up and snapped his final full magazine into place across the top of the weapon. Rising up to peer over the rim of the trench, he fired off a few careful bursts.

With a ragged gasp, Falco lifted his carbine and joined his partner at the rim. They both understood that there could be no more retreating: They were trapped there. For some odd reason, the sniper recalled a line from a movie he'd seen as a lad, one of the classics of twentieth-century cinema. He fired another round and turned to his partner.

"Hey, Sundance," he said. "Who *are* those guys?"

Fourteen: A Lot of Hot Air

The exhaust vent was a long shaft that ascended gradually, wide enough for only one man at a time. Unable to see much beyond Chief Harris's feet, Jackson found himself wishing that he was in the lead. Immediately he suppressed that selfish urge; he trusted Marannis as much as any man and knew that the CO of the outfit had no place crawling point in a dangerous infiltration. Gritting his teeth, his G15 protected against his chest, he crawled along on his elbows and knees, listening and watching.

The readout on his wrist indicated that the air in the shaft was very breathable, but he kept his helmet on and knew that his men would do the same thing in the absence of orders to the contrary. If they were discovered, it would be too easy for the enemy to disable or kill them with a simple infusion of gas, and so each SEALS would rely on his own self-contained universe of warmth and oxygen. Most important, they had to get out of the ducts, and *fast.* Jackson acutely sensed the Team's vulnerability while it wormed through those confining passages and chafed against the inability to take any offensive action.

The distant explosion reached him with a thump that was more felt than heard, and he knew LaRue had commenced the diversionary attack against the installation's outer hatch. Immediately afterward, he heard the caterwaul of some kind of siren as the enemy's alarms went off. Still crawling, Jackson moved into an intersection of ducts where three branching passages led to the right, forward, and to the left. By prearranged plan, the three men in the lead had split up, one going down each duct to seek some egress that would allow them into the compartments of the base.

Grimacing against the necessity of violating radio silence, the LT switched on his comlink and waited for a report. The siren continued to wail, and it was less than forty-five seconds before Sanchez's voice came over the radio: "Take a left, Team," he said tersely.

Jackson, waiting at the intersecting ducts, immediately moved out. He crawled forward until he saw the scout's boots before him. There was a glow of external illumination ahead of Sanchez, apparently coming up through a grid from a compartment down below. As soon as the officer touched the other man's foot, Sanchez initiated a small incendiary charge, the sudden white-hot flash searing through the duct. A second later the man dropped through the burned-out grate, tumbling headfirst out of the duct.

The LT squirmed forward to see Sanchez rolling on a catwalk about ten feet below. The scout bounced to his feet with his G15, noise suppressor attached, in his hands as he scanned the chamber, which was large, clean, and filled with machinery. As Jackson dropped behind him, Sanchez extended a hand, allowing the officer to land on his feet. The SEALS had landed on a catwalk that circled the entire compartment; they were some four meters above the main floor, but because of pipes and more ductwork they could see only a small portion of the room. The lieutenant waved his scout forward and waited to assist the next man, Dobson, who came tumbling out of the duct.

Sanchez ran a dozen meters along the catwalk and then fired a burst, slugs spattering blood out the back of a humanlike guard who had recovered from the initial shock to come charging forward. The G15 was whisper-quiet but deadly, and two more armed men were cut down before they could raise their weapons. The trio had been standing near a large door.

Jackson moved along the catwalk in the direction away from Sanchez as Dobson helped the next SEALS out of the duct. There were other men on the floor of the compartment, but they didn't seem to be armed; instead, they scrambled for cover behind the large domed device that dominated the chamber. Jackson couldn't be certain, but he guessed it was a nuclear reactor, probably the power source for the whole installation.

As the Team streamed into the large room, the CO took stock of their surroundings. He'd counted nearly a dozen men diving for cover and took them to be technicians.

"Take out any potential shooters," he barked into his communicator. "Capture the rest of 'em."

By then Sanchez, Dobson, and two more SEALS had skidded down gridwork stairways to the floor of the room. They wasted no time rounding up the workers, corralling them in a section of office cubicles and covering them with the suppressed muzzles of their lethal G15s.

"LT," the scout reported, sounding more than a little surprised. "These are some green-eyed operators down here. I think we've dropped in on an Eluoi base."

"You don't say?" Jackson replied, unsurprised. After multiple violent skirmishes with the Eluoi on Batuun, he had no regrets about fighting more of them, and it seemed logical that this ice moon was peopled by more than the fur-covered brutes the SEALS had christened yetis. Still, that fact supported his and Carstairs's observations about the destroyer orbiting this world, which clearly had been an Eluoi ship. He filed the data away for future reflection as his men secured the rest of the reactor room.

"Eleven prisoners, sir," Ruiz reported. "Three guards, all dead."

The officer looked over at the terrified workers. They were huddled together, wide-eyed and in many cases trembling. They wore matching green coveralls; none of them seemed to be armed. He couldn't bring himself to order them killed, but neither did he want to split up his unit by detaching even a single fire team to watch over POWs.

"All right. Any place we can secure these guys?"

"Got a storage locker over here, skipper," Schroeder reported, emerging from a small chamber off the main room. He indicated the metal lever that operated the door latch. "We can secure it from the outside."

"Did you look around inside?" Jackson asked Schroeder. "Any weapons or anything useful in there?"

"Some crates of supplies. They seemed to be small items, paint, and the like. Oh, and there was an intercom on the wall, but I smashed that."

The LT nodded, feeling the need to move out in a hurry.

"You!" Jackson barked, striding up to the prisoners, waving the menacing barrel of his assault rifle at them and then indicating the door. "Get in there!"

He didn't know if they had the typical translating devices implanted, but even if they didn't, his gestures made his meaning clear. The Eluoi technicians practically fell over one another in their haste to retreat to the storage locker. The SEALS slammed the door and secured the latch with a length of light chain that Schroeder had scrounged from the locker. A minute later they stepped past the bodies of the guard and opened the door connecting the reactor room to the rest of the installation.

Immediately the noise of the siren hit them—it had been muffled by the walls of the reactor facility—but there was no one in sight. The corridor outside was well lighted, and they saw a metal-grid stairway rising to the next level a short distance away.

"Let's clear this floor first," Jackson declared, waving two fire teams to the right and two to the left.

"Hey, Lieutenant," called Baxter, who was peering through the small window in a door.

Jackson went over to the electrician's mate and looked, whistling in surprise as he saw a large, dimly lit chamber with some fifteen or twenty large, shaggy figures sitting list-lessly on metal bunks. One or two turned their big muzzled faces toward the door, but the rest simply slumped where they were. "They're those yetis," he remarked in amazement.

"Maybe the ones that got away from the battle. We did track them here, after all, sir," Baxter suggested.

Jackson noted the sturdy steel door with the lock and latch clearly visible on the outside. "It looks like they're being treated more like prisoners than loyal allies."

"That's what I was thinking, too, sir. You want me to do anything about it?"

The lieutenant shook his head. "Might as well leave them here for now. We can work out the details later." Even so, it was an interesting development, and Jackson began to think about how he might turn it to the Team's advantage.

Three minutes later the reconnoitering SEALS returned. "More storage down this way, sir. Looks like food, clothing, that kind of stuff," Ruiz reported. "No people, though. I think we're in their basement."

"There's a weapons locker over here, LT," Dobson said, coming from the other direction. "The door's still open, and lots of racks are empty; I think them sumbitches grabbed their gear already and headed upstairs. I did find another one of these here stairways."

"All right." He turned to the navy coxswain, who had led his men out of the ductwork behind the SEALS. "Grafty, I want you and your men to stay here for the time being. You're going to be our reserve, but be ready to move after Sandy or me if we need help."

"Aye, aye, sir," the petty officer said.

"Well, let's take the next level, then," Jackson declared. He turned to his second in command. "Mister Sanders, take your squad with you up this ladder. The rest of you, come with me. Dobson, lead the way to the other stairs."

The men moved out at a jog. Ruiz and his detachment swarmed up the near ladder, which was a spiraling grid of bare metal rising into a cylindrical shaft overhead. The second stairwell, thirty meters away and around a corner, was a similar structure, and Sanchez led the way up that one, with Marannis and then Jackson following close behind.

As they emerged onto the upper floor, they saw flashing lights, heard the shrieking wail of the siren, and surprised a dozen Eluoi troops who were rushing away from them, presumably moving toward the outer hatch. The first three SEALS up the ladder opened fire while the rest of the men scrambled up, and the Eluoi went down without getting off a return shot.

But the attackers had been discovered. Jackson heard the bark of a loud automatic weapon and hurled himself prone as slugs zinged off the walls and floor. Realizing that the shooting had come from beyond the dead soldiers, he squeezed off a burst against the unseen enemy. Marannis and Sanchez did the same thing while, behind him, one of his men launched a high-explosive grenade.

"Duck and cover!" came the warning—it sounded like Mirowski's voice—and the helmeted SEALS pressed their faceplates to the floor. The blast was a sudden, jarring blow, filling the corridor with smoke.

"Charge!" Jackson barked, immediately springing to his feet and sprinting toward the target.

Something slammed into his chest, and he was lying on his back, straining to fill his lungs. The rasping of the breathing apparatus suddenly seemed terribly loud; there was no other sound. A film of red crept across his eyes, and he wondered with a sense of vague detachment if he was dying.

Finally, with a great effort, he drew a ragged gulp of air, expelled it, and inhaled again. His ribs throbbed, and his gloved hand went to his chest, feeling the semirigid plates of his body armor. There was a notable gouge in that armor, right over his sternum, but he probed further and determined that the slug hadn't penetrated. Ignoring the pain, he rolled onto his side and then pushed himself up to one knee.

His heart sank at the sight of two more of his men down, one lying still and the other struggling feebly to roll just as Jackson himself had. Beyond, four SEALS were visible, hunkered into alcoves to either side of the passageway, shooting carefully aimed bursts from their silenced G15s. Return fire chattered loudly, and Jackson could see the sparks of impact as the slugs skipped along the floor or bounced from the walls and ceiling.

It was a hell of a pickle. The far end of the corridor was concealed by smoke, masking any potential targets. Sitting on the floor, with his back against the wall, he racked an incendiary grenade under the barrel of his gun, sighted, and launched. The mild recoil jarred his bruised chest, but he watched the round as it vanished into the smoke. Almost instantly a blossom of orange fire erupted, seething through the murk, fading into a billowing cloud of thick black smoke.

The Team didn't need orders. Every one of the five mobile SEALS instantly sprinted toward the target, the two leaders snapping off several bursts of suppressing fire. Jackson pushed himself to his feet and saw that one of the fallen men, Rocky Rodale, had done the same thing and was checking his beloved rocket launcher. Spotting the LT, he gave a cheerful thumbs-up and turned to walk, a little unsteadily, toward the melee.

The other downed man was Schroeder. His helmet had

been shattered, and his scalp was bleeding from a long gash. Jackson cursed silently as he wiped the blood away and was elated to see the man's eyelids flicker.

"Stay here, son," he said, clapping the burly SEALS on the shoulder. "We'll be back for you."

Rising to his feet, he jogged after the rest of his Team. He found them clearing a circular chamber at the terminus of the corridor. Three adjoining passages led away from there, and a spiral stairway climbed through the ceiling in the center. The far passage was wide enough for a small truck to pass; those to the right and left were the size of an average hotel corridor. The blast and incendiary grenades had done some damage, but the place looked to be a meeting room; the remnants of chairs and tables were scattered among more than a dozen dead Eluoi.

"Chamber secure, LT," Chief Harris reported. "This wide passage seems to lead toward the outside hatch."

Jackson pressed the speak button on his comlink. "Sanders, give me a sitrep."

"We're up against a tough nut, sir," came the crackling response. "There's a dozen or more hostiles holed up in a series of compartments. They have cross fire down the approaches, and we can't get line of sight to hit them with a grenade. Orders?"

The lieutenant looked at the stairs climbing up through the domed ceiling and made a snap judgment. "I want you to leave those guys alone for now. Fall back down the stairs and follow the route we took. Tell Grafton to set up a defensive position down there, right outside the reactor room where we came in. Make sure he understands that he has to watch our backs. Someone will guide you when you get back up to this level."

He sent Chief Harris and Teal, asking the corpsman to check on Schroeder while the chief brought Sanders's detachment in. Meanwhile, Sanchez and Marannis checked out one side corridor while Dobson and Robinson investigated the other. The wide passage, they could see, ended in a sturdy steel door some twenty meters away from the room. Rocky Rodale had his rocket launcher trained on that barrier, ready to react to any surprise.

The two scouts returned on the run, followed by a bang and a cloud of smoke.

"They have automatic guns sighted down that way, LT," Sanchez reported. "Including grenade launchers."

"Okay, defend at this end, then," the lieutenant ordered.

Jackson was relieved when Harris returned a minute later, bringing not only Sanders's squad but Teal and a limping, cursing Schroeder out of the battered corridor.

"Grafton has a good position," the junior officer reported. "One of his gunners found another of those laser-type weapons like Ruiz was testing. He's got it operational, and if the hostiles try to come at us that way, those swabbies will give them a hot reception."

"Good." Jackson took stock of the situation, thinking fast. His Team was almost complete, with the notable exception of LaRue and Falco. He described the situation to his second in command, and Sanders nodded when he heard about the defenses the scouts had discovered.

"Probably part of the same complex, sir," he noted. "It's the same direction, anyway. Must be where the garrison is holed up."

The CO concurred. "No sense in a frontal attack," he announced. His attention turned to the gridwork of the spiral steps rising from the middle of the large room. "I'm guessing we'll find the CP up those steps," he said, reasoning that the installation's command post would be on the highest level. "I want to make it ours."

"I'll take the point, sir," Mirowski declared, eyes gleaming at the challenge. Schroeder's squad mate clearly was looking for a little payback. "I checked it out already; there looks to be a landing and a sealed hatch about six or seven meters above us. Want me to plant a little C-6 door knocker?"

"Explosive breach," Jackson agreed. "Do it."

Mirowski took a small packet of explosive from his pack and climbed the steps, disappearing onto the cylindrical landing above.

The CO explained his plan to the rest of the Team. Ruiz and Baxter would go next, with the LT and Dobson following. Sanders would send up reinforcements as necessary while making sure they held the large central compartment against any potential counterattack. By that time Mirowski had slipped back down the steps, a remote detonator held in his hand.

Jackson nodded, and the SEALS pressed the button. A *whump* of explosive pressure blasted down the stairwell, accompanied by a cloud of smoke and a skittering rain of metal shards.

Immediately the big Pole started up the steps at a run, the rest of the attack party racing behind. Mirowski tumbled through the open hatch at the top, snapping off bursts from his suppressed G15 as Ruiz and Baxter rushed behind him. Jackson followed the charge, finding that they had burst directly into some kind of control room. Consoles and screens lined the walls, with a large bank of controls in the center of the room.

More significantly, a number of Eluoi troops had dived for cover after the explosion, but now they had recovered from the shock to squeeze off shots at the SEALS. Baxter slammed against one wall and dropped, and Jackson felt a tug at his shoulder. He spotted the shooter kneeling behind a chair and dropped him with a burst to the throat that nearly tore his head off. Rodale came up from behind, shooting a pair of Eluoi with an extended burst, a few stray slugs shattering one of the vidscreens right behind them.

Ruiz and Mirowski charged farther into the control room,

shooting to the left and right. Jackson spotted a hostile diving behind a bank of computers. He didn't want to launch a grenade—the equipment could prove useful if they captured it in working condition—so he rushed after the fellow, shooting him in the head as he tried to scramble to his feet.

Something whizzed past the lieutenant's head, knocking him sideways as it detonated against the wall behind him. He saw a burly Eluoi, his face swarthy and his green eyes narrowed, dark with fury. The fellow held a small but lethal-looking rocket launcher and smoothly racked another round onto the short rail of the barrel. He leveled the weapon at Jackson and fired.

But Mirowski was in the way! Somehow the SEALS had stopped and spun, charging toward the rocket-launching Eluoi in a fury. The blast caught the Pole in the chest, but not before his G15 had chattered off a long ripping burst. The slugs tore into the Eluoi, and the weapon dropped from the fellow's nerveless fingers as the force of the rocket, full in the chest, blasted Mirowski against the wall.

"All clear, sir," Ruiz was reporting, checking the rest of the fallen hostiles.

Jackson barely heard him. He stumbled over to Mirowski and saw the gaping hole in the armor of his suit and the torn flesh underneath.

Even before he knelt beside him, he knew the big SEALS was dead.

Fifteen: Cold Vengeance

A few more suppressed shots coughed through the control room as the grim SEALS stalked around the large compartment. With Mirowski's body still lying against the far console, they gave no quarter: When they came upon an Eluoi hiding behind a piece of equipment, the alien died quickly. Jackson, his jaw clenched, watched the search with cold detachment for a second, then returned to the slain SEALS. He knelt and found himself compelled to look at the ghastly wound, a crater of flesh, bone, and blood in the man's chest.

"Teal!" he barked as the corpsman entered the command center. "Get over here! See what you can do!"

Harry Teal ran to the LT's side and knelt beside the body, taking in the horrific wound that had torn away the man's body armor and gouged deeply into his chest. He was about to say something to Jackson when something in the officer's eyes caused him to change his mind.

Instead, he consulted the dials on the life support module of Mirowski's backpack, which were visible from the side so that he did not have to move the body. "I'm sorry, sir," he said. "But there's nothing to do for him. I think he was gone as soon as the round hit him."

"Dammit, I know that," Jackson said, slumping into a sitting position with his back against the console. He wiped a gloved hand across his faceplate. "He saved my life."

"He was a good man," the corpsman agreed, reaching out

to unlatch Mirowski's helmet gently. Removing the head-gear, he took a hand and solemnly closed the big Pole's—"Polish-American's," Jackson reminded himself—eyes.

The LT shook his head, fighting off weariness, realizing that they still had a lot of work to do. He activated his communicator and set it to full power. "Falco? G-Man?" he called. "Do you copy?"

The only answer was static.

Suddenly the lieutenant felt terribly discouraged and weary. The enemy installation had proved to be far more extensive than he could have imagined, and he knew there were still two pockets of enemy holdouts, maybe more, within the maze of tunnels, caverns, and compartments. Two of his men were outside, and God only knew how they were faring.

He looked around the command center and saw that Baxter was studying the main computer center in the middle of the room. Other monitors and drives had been shattered in the brief but violent firefight, but the central bank of equipment seemed to have escaped damage. Schroeder, the other electrician's mate, went over to the machines and also started to study the keyboards and screens.

Jackson shook his head, banishing his weariness and discouragement with an effort of will. They were still in a dire situation, and his men needed him. He activated his communicator and spoke into the microphone built into his helmet.

"Sandy?" he called to his second in command. "What's your situation over on the flank?"

"The bastards are still forted up down here, sir," the lieutenant (j.g.) reported. "They can't get to us, but we can't get to them, either."

"Very well. Steady as she goes, for now. Grafty, do you copy?" he continued.

"Right here, Lieutenant," the coxswain came back.

"Had any visitors down there?" Jackson asked.

"Actually, we had a hot little dance going on for a few

minutes. Some of the bastards came down the stairs, just like you warned me, and tried to get at you through the basement. Gunner's Mate Roberts microwaved a few of them with that captured laser, and the rest of 'em turned back."

"Good work," the lieutenant replied, impressed. "Keep your finger on the trigger. This thing isn't over yet."

"Aye, aye, sir," came Grafton's reply.

Feeling a little more energized, Jackson pushed himself to his feet and started over to the two electrician's mates who were studying the alien control consoles. He paused, though, to watch Teal and Ruiz carefully wrap Mirowski's body in a cloth they had found below, but he snapped his attention back to the job when Baxter called to him.

"What can we do from here?" the officer asked.

"I can make out these controls, LT," Baxter reported after studying the command console for a few minutes. He was the first of the SEALS to complete one of the new alien language courses at Quantico, specializing in the Eluoi alphabet, and what were bizarre hieroglyphics to Jackson apparently made at least a little sense to the electrician's mate. "This is the climate control system, and over here you've got the defensive systems. They had an external gun turret, remotely controlled, but it looks like it's been taken out."

"Good," Jackson said approvingly, suspecting that LaRue might have had something to do with that.

The electrician's mate twisted a dial, and a screen illuminated, displaying an image of geometric shapes, including several grids marked by lines and bars. Jackson couldn't read the symbols, but it looked like a series of charts or tables. "These are their inventories, I think. Supplies of food and fuel and ammunition." He indicated a circular display that resembled a pie chart. "That place we came in is the reactor, and this graph seems to display the power situation for the whole installation."

"What about the remaining hostiles? Anything you can

learn about the tactical situation?" The LT tried to keep the impatience out of his voice. In truth, he was amazed at the man's ability to decipher the alien technology.

"I'm working on that right now, sir. I think I might be on to something." Baxter punched a few keys, and a three-dimensional schematic appeared on the large central wall screen. One bullet hole in the lower left corner marred the image, but the rest of the screen functioned perfectly. Another few keystrokes brought an array of green dots into sight, perhaps fifty of them scattered about the diagram. Thirty or so were off to the right, mainly on the second level, and more than a dozen were clustered around a central circle and in the compartment just above that circle. Five more were down on the bottom level, right near the entrance to the reactor room.

"This is the floor plan of the installation," Baxter explained. "The green spots are living beings, including us and the hostiles." He pointed to the quintet on the lowest level. "These five are Coxswain Grafton and his sailors." He next indicated a nearby compartment on the lower level, and the LT discerned another group of green spots that were so faint that he hadn't noticed them previously. The electrician's mate continued. "These pale spots down here are probably the yetis we saw in that cell. They don't cast much of a heat signature, and this image is obviously based on IR detection."

"I understand," Jackson said grimly. One section of the screen indicated a large compartment adjacent to the outer hatch, but the image was dark. "What do you make of this?" he asked.

Baxter could only shrug. "That looks like, for lack of a better word, the garage, sir. At least, it's some kind of access to the outside, probably the interior of that big hatch we spotted from the ridge. The sensors in there aren't working. They probably took some damage when LaRue started tossing slugs their way."

"Makes sense." Jackson's attention was focused on the area of the installation occupied by the hostiles. "These sections to the right are held by the Eluoi, correct?"

"Yes, sir. We hold the high ground in here— this command center—and about half the middle and lower levels. The Eluoi have a pretty good garrison here, to the left, in the middle level. They tried to move through the basement, but Grafty's men seem to have stopped them short."

"Okay." The officer continued to study the schematic, thinking aloud. "So there are only two points of contact between the remaining Eluoi and our Team. Here, where they tried to get down to the lower level, and here, where Sanchez and Marannis are blocking the door."

"And probably here, too, LT," Baxter pointed out, indicated the area where the sensors had been blacked out. "If this is the garage, or motor pool, or whatever, it's open to the elements outside, but we can gain access through a door on our side, and the Eluoi can enter it through this other door over here."

"What about air locks? Is there any kind of locking mechanism you might be able to use from here to secure the hatches? Seal the bastards up?"

"Let me have a look, sir," Baxter said.

Jackson paced impatiently around the control room while the technically gifted SEALS manipulated the computer and security controls. The officer barely could contain his fury. He wanted to get after the enemy with every weapon, every man, at his disposal. But he knew that a frontal assault against the Eluoi troops would be costly, potentially disastrous. In room-to-room fighting, the defender always had a significant advantage, at least once the possibility of surprise had been removed.

Five minutes later Baxter looked up. "It might be possible to secure the hatches, sir. I'd like to give it a test."

"Sure." Jackson wanted to seize the possibility. "What do you want to do?"

The electrician's mate pointed at a compartment just below the control center. "This is a storeroom. We cleared it on our way up here." He moved a cursor until it stopped over the image of that room's entry door. The cursor switched to a hollow square and began to flash. "I suggest we have someone down below keep an eye on this hatch and report what happens in the next few seconds."

"Chief Harris," Jackson called, and received an immediate reply. "Are you in the anteroom down at the bottom of the stairs?"

"Affirmative, sir."

"Is the door to that storeroom open? Keep an eye on it. Baxter's going to try some remote-control wizardry."

"Aye, aye, skipper."

The LT nodded to the SEALS at the computer console, and Baxter flipped a switch. Immediately the hollow flashing square on the schematic screen became a solid red block. At the same time, Harris's voice came over the communicator.

"Holy shit, sir! I'm glad I didn't have my fingers on the frame. The hatch slammed shut like my girlfriend Rosie's legs on prom night!"

"Can you open it, Chief?"

"Negative, sir. It's locked tighter than a drum."

"Okay, good." Jackson studied the screen, looking over his man's shoulder as Baxter manipulated the cursor once again. "Nice work, Fritz. Can you do the same with the hatch leading down into the lower level and the one where Sanchez and Marannis are guarding the door?"

Within a minute the SEALS mate had secured both passages. "It looks like there's three of the bastards on the downside of the basement hatch, sir," he pointed out. "But we've cut them off from the rest of their men."

"Okay." Next Jackson contacted the coxswain on the lower level. "Grafty? You've got three hostiles at the far end of your corridor. They can't get away. Just hold on where you are and we'll send you some backup to clean 'em out of there."

"Aye, aye, sir, I copy," the coxswain replied.

"LT?" Baxter asked, pointing to a third junction that appeared on the screen next to the blacked-out compartment leading to the outside. "I think I can secure the door on the far side of the motor pool. That will keep them from getting out of the installation or coming after us through the garage."

"Make it so," Jackson replied, forming a plan while he watched the SEALS slam the last hatch shut. With the exception of the three Eluoi on the lower level and an unknown number in the garage, all of the surviving hostiles were secured behind sealed air locks.

"What about the air supply?" he asked when Baxter had sealed the final access point.

"I think I can figure out how to manipulate the oxygen controls, sir. In whatever manner you want."

"Shut off the air," Jackson ordered without hesitation. "Kill the sons of bitches."

Baxter immediately set to work, punching keys and bringing up control screens, while Jackson paced around the control room. Mirowski's body was carried reverently down the stairs toward the central room, and the officer had to forcefully repress the urge to punch something. If one of the apparently slain Eluoi on the floor had stirred, the lieutenant willingly would have strangled him with his bare hands. As it was, there was no one to attack, no reasonable way to strike out.

Chief Harris climbed the stairs to the command room.

"We got more hostiles behind that big door, skipper, in the motor pool. Robinson got it open a crack, and we spotted a big tractor in there, like a tank equipped for snow. It's colder than hell in there, like it's open to the outside. They got a couple guys working on the tank, and at least a dozen more are waiting around for a ride. Probably going out after LaRue and Falco, eh?"

"Or else they're trying to make a getaway," Jackson noted, and seized the chance for action. "Let's blow the door and see if we can't get our hands on the AFV," he declared. He wasn't sure what they would use an armored fighting vehicle for, but it seemed a wise precaution to keep it from the enemy's hands. Also, it was a chance for a little more revenge against the Eluoi, whom he was starting to hate with a deep and abiding passion.

This time it was Harry Teal who set the charges: two packets of C-6, one at each side of the garage-door-size hatch. The attack would be made by eight SEALS as Sanchez and Marannis stayed back to watch the hatch leading into the large compartment and Baxter continued to work on the Eluoi installation controls. Grafton and his swabbies remained in their holding position below, blocking the trio of trapped hostiles in the lower level. Jackson hadn't forgotten about them but decided they would keep for the time being.

Taking up positions just around the corner from the breaching charges, the men waited for the charges to blow. Teal watched for the lieutenant to give him the go sign. When Jackson pointed, the corpsman pressed the button on his clicker, and a *crump* of sound and pressure shot down the corridor, filling the compartment with smoke.

The SEALS moved out immediately to find that once again the reliable C-6 had worked perfectly. With Dobson and Rodale leading the way, the attacking Team charged into the large garage area as the hatch still was bouncing on the floor. A couple of hapless Eluoi were trapped under the ton or two of metal, and several others had been thrown to the floor by the force of the blast.

Still, there were others there, armed and ready for battle, and they recovered quickly. Some dived for cover behind the big snow tank, and others shot bursts at the SEALS as they charged into the large compartment. Rounds zinged from the deck, and Dobson went down hard, punched by a shot in the chest that was absorbed by the armor of his pressure suit. Jackson, coming from behind, killed the shooter, who was standing behind the turret, with a well-placed shot right through the middle of his face.

The Eluoi were wearing heavy parkas and winter gear but did not have pressure suits. The SEALS exploited that advantage, charging full tilt across the floor, trusting the armor of their Mark IV suits to protect them from the few haphazard shots that found targets. Dobson and Rodale scrambled up onto the tank's deck, shooting down the Eluoi who had sought shelter behind the turret and then using that armored dome as they sprayed rounds into the far side of the hangar.

Ruiz and Teal took out the two Eluoi on the far right and moved through what looked to be an empty bay, possibly a parking space for another of the big tractors like the one that loomed before them. Jackson saw that the whole space was open to the frigid outdoors via a large doorway that no longer was protected with a hatch. The interior showed plenty of damage, including numerous spots where it looked like the walls, lockers, and equipment had been sprayed by superheated drops of metal. The very visible aftermath of the rail gun rounds provided tangible proof of the effects of LaRue's diversionary attack.

More sniping came from the left, and two shooter pairs leapfrogged into an assault, one man firing while his partner advanced. A series of long freestanding shelves like the stacks of a library provided cover, and they quickly closed in on the shooters. Robinson snapped off a couple of rounds, spattering some cans of liquid—paint or sealant, apparently—and driving a hostile from cover. Ruiz cut him down with a short burst just before the Eluoi reached shelter behind the snow tank.

The blast of heavy machine-gun fire took everyone by surprise, slugs sparking off the floor between Chief Harris and Dobson. The two SEALS dived for cover as the gun chattered again, firing high, sending a stream of big rounds spattering through the motor pool.

"Where the hell did that come from?" the master chief demanded.

Jackson finally noticed the movement of the low, flat turret atop the big snow tank. The barrel of the gun was recessed into the swiveling dome so that it was almost invisible except for the flames that issued when it fired. Like a half dozen other SEALS, he shot at the gun with his G15 but stopped after two bursts. Clearly, the slugs were simply bouncing off the armored plate. When the turret swiveled toward him, he dived unceremoniously behind a workbench, keeping his head down as the rounds chewed through tools and supplies, sending a shower of metal splinters raining down on him.

The turret swiveled farther, with the gun firing like a buzz saw, gnawing through the shelves where four SEALS clutched the floor, trying to melt into the ground. The heavy storage unit gave them some protection, but when the gun aimed another burst, one of the shelves was torn in half, and a cascade of cans and crates tumbled down onto the men trying to avoid the machine gun.

The LT wanted to capture the tank, but not at the expense of any of his men. "Rocky!" he barked, signaling Rodale.

The gunner's mate (missile) merely nodded and raised his rocket launcher to his shoulder. He flicked the setting for direct fire and pulled the trigger.

A flash of fire and smoke blasted from the back of the launcher as the sleek, arrowlike projectile streaked toward the target faster than the human eye could follow. Playing it safe, Rocky hadn't aimed for the steeply sloping armor of the turret dome. Instead, he had fired right at the narrow glass windshield. The rocket impacted and exploded, spewing fire out several side windows, blowing out a hatch on the top of the snow tank. The turret immediately stopped moving, and the SEALS could only duck and watch as secondary explosions rocked the doomed vehicle.

In another two minutes, the garage area was secured. There were bays for three of the big snow tanks, and two of those bays were empty. The hatch to the outdoors had been impacted by at least one of Baby's copper-coated uranium core slugs; the impact had started a fire inside the garage that appeared to have been extinguished quickly. A number of lockers lined one wall of the big area, and although most of them were empty, a few contained insulated parkas, trousers, and snowshoes. Nearby was a rack of small arms, also mostly emptied, so Jackson was forced to conclude that a fairly muscular sortie force had charged out of there after his diversionary fire team.

The lieutenant and his men tried to raise G-Man and Falco on their comlinks, but even when they stood in the open doorway, they could pick up nothing but static. Jackson stared into that storm-swept landscape, noting that it was still daylight, and the wind and snow appeared to swirl unabated. The wreckage of a snow tank, still smoking, dominated the view from the open hatch. He barely could make out the ridge where his two men had been posted. A number of bodies littered the snowy bowl, many of them right outside the hatch, with others—now half-covered in white powder—scattered through the valley.

Did it *ever* stop snowing in this godforsaken place?

He was heading back to the interior of the installation when his earpiece crackled and he recognized Baxter's deep, gravelly voice asking for him.

"Jackson here," he replied, walking more quickly toward the interior hatch.

"I've got a signal from Falco, sir," the electrician's mate reported. "It's faint, but I'm picking it up on the installation's radio set. It's a lot more powerful than our portable units."

"What's he saying?" asked the LT.

"No verbal message, sir. Just a standard Mayday broadcast. Been going for at least ten minutes, it sounds like."

Jackson felt a stab of dismay. His men were in trouble, and he wasn't with them. "Location?" he asked tersely.

"About two klicks from here, back up that canyon we came down, sir. Shit! The signal just cut out."

"Keep trying to raise him!" the SEALS CO barked. He turned around, looked at the looming gap of the blasted hatch and knew there was really only one option, whether or not Falco or his partner came back on the air.

"Now hear this, SEALS," he declared over his comlink. "Our Teammates are out in that storm. We're going to go bring them in from the cold."

Sixteen: Assault from the Rear

The preparations for the rescue op took only a few minutes. Jackson would leave Sanders in charge of a small detachment holding the installation, including Baxter, who was to continue to mine whatever data he could from the Eluoi control room. Robinson and the still bruised and shaken Schroeder also would stay behind. All in all, the LT would take a party of eight men into the cold canyon of the ice moon.

The expedition was heading for the gaping hatch to the outside when Jackson was halted by another call from Baxter. "Sir, if you can come up here for a second, I can show you something that might speed you up some."

Biting back a curse of frustration, the LT sprang up the steps to the command post, taking the stairs two or three at a time. He was glad that he had done so as soon as he saw the new schematic Baxter had raised on the screen.

"This is an access tunnel, about eight hundred meters long, sir," the electrician's mate reported. Jackson could see the passageway extending straight as an arrow toward the ridge where Falco and LaRue had been situated. "You should find it a lot faster going than if you have to wade through two meters of snow."

"Right, good work," Jackson said. "We reach it on the bottom level, it looks like." He didn't voice the other thought that immediately had popped into his head: The Eluoi could

have used the tunnel to send a party that would have come
out practically under the fire team's noses. He took heart
from the fact that Falco had broadcast an SOS: At least they
hadn't been taken out by the first counterattack. But there
was no time to waste.

A minute later the lieutenant and the seven additional
SEALS of the rescue party found the access hatch to the tunnel, which was not far from the reactor room where they first
had burst into the installation. The corridor was wide and
smooth, excavated directly from the bedrock of the ice
moon, and they jogged along it in their pressure suits. In
mere minutes they reached the end, where a ladder led up to
an escape vent. The hatch there was still open, as proved by
the drift of snow that had collected at the terminus of the
tunnel. Wasting no time, the Team, with the two scouts in the
lead, scrambled up the ladder and out into the frigid landscape of Arcton V's ice moon.

Marannis immediately started for the ridge where the
shooter pair had set up for their diversion. The scout was virtually invisible as his ghillie cloak matched the color of the
snow to perfection, even swirling and shifting in its degree of
whiteness as the flurries waxed and waned behind him. He
made good time because a considerable trough remained in
the snow from a previous sortie, confirming Jackson's fear
that the Eluoi had come up through this remote hatch to surprise his two men.

Sanchez, equally invisible, came right behind his partner,
followed by Jackson, Dobson, Master Chief Ruiz, Rocky
Rodale, and Harry Teal, with Chief Harris bringing up the
rear. Approaching the crest of the low ridge, the lead scout
crouched low and sprinted over the high ground, rolling into
the snow on the far side. In another moment he popped to his
feet and waved the rest of the SEALS forward with an all-
clear sign.

Following at a run, Jackson immediately noticed the hulk

of a second snow tank some hundred meters past the crest of
the ridge. It confirmed that LaRue and Falco had been making a fighting withdrawal, and the officer felt a surge of pride
at the proof of their impressive fighting capabilities. He
vowed again to do everything in his power to bring them
back alive.

Here, too, they found a number of Eluoi bodies scattered
in the snow, most felled by a single gunshot wound, proof
that Falco, as well as LaRue, had been active when the pair
fell back from the ridge. Their initial firing position was visible, a pair of flat spots where they had lain in the snow. The
route up the canyon was littered with Eluoi corpses, but there
was no sign of a living hostile or of their Teammates.

"Damn, sir," Ruiz said with a low whistle. "Talk about a
diversion. Looks like they pulled a whole company after
them."

"Right, Master Chief. Let's follow up—on the double!"

Sanchez moved smoothly into the point, jogging as much
as possible, taking advantage of the packed trails through the
snow that had been created by the Eluoi pursuit of the two
SEALS. They came around the tank to see that it had been
punctured in the front, obviously by a round from Baby, and
had been wracked by secondary explosions. One Eluoi, his
body charred, had made it halfway out of the side hatch, but
there was no sign of the rest of the crew.

In a few minutes they reached a cluster of rocks, a shelter
that seemed to offer good cover and indeed had been chipped
and chiseled by an intense fusillade of gunfire. They came
around the obstacle to see more depressions in the snow but,
thankfully, no sign of blood or, worse, a body. Without missing a step, they continued on.

The canyon curved gradually to the right from there, and
the SEALS followed along in single file, still moving at a
loping jog. When Sanchez began to breathe heavily, Dobson
passed him to take the point, traversing the deep snow in

easy strides, his long legs carrying him smoothly forward. They stayed near the right-hand wall of the canyon, where the snow was not very deep, and continued to make good time.

Jackson wished they could move at a full sprint. The fear that they would be too late gnawed at him, causing him to clench his G15 with white-knuckled intensity. He second-guessed his decision to bring the Team down to this icebound hellhole, feeling the loss not only of Mirowski but of the sailor Zimmer, who also had been brought into this situation on the SEALS commander's initiative. He was not much of a praying man, but he put his most fervent thoughts into the hope that Falco and LaRue could be brought out of there alive.

For several long minutes he was alone with those thoughts and insecurities and the harsh rasp of his breathing within the earphone of his comlink. None of the SEALS spoke, for there was nothing to be said. With the good going and light snow cover on hard rock, Dobson didn't tire of breaking the trail, and the LT let the file move on as quickly as it could without bothering with another change in the point man.

Then, suddenly, Dobson halted and raised his hand. The rest of the Teammates stopped as well, with Jackson quickly advancing to the side of the lanky Alabaman. Dobson gestured to his ears, and Jackson listened, clearly picking up the sounds through the external auditory device every one of their suits was equipped with: the *pop-pop-pop* of sharp reports echoing through the canyon, many of the noises coming in rapid succession. The truth was obvious.

Somewhere not too far ahead, people were shooting at each other.

LaRue snapped his last magazine into the mechanism of his G15. "Fifty rounds left," he told his partner.

Falco nodded; he had installed his final magazine a few

minutes earlier, and even though he was conserving his ammo, he had only about twenty shots left, plus another ten for the Mark 30 sniper rifle.

"Of course I have a round for Baby," G-Man said conversationally. "If I could get these bastards to stand in a nice, straight line, I could shoot through the whole lot of them."

"Wouldn't that be nice," Falco said—or tried to say. His lips were virtually immobile, chilled through with frostbite. His nose, cheeks, and forehead were numb and coated with frost as the cold air spilled in through the broken faceplate to scour his skin. He had turned the heating module in his pressure suit up to full power, which had drained the battery nearly to the danger level, but at least the warm air flowing up through the collar had kept him from freezing to death.

Truth be told, he expected that he'd be dead well before the suit's power pack was drained completely.

The two SEALS had been forced into a narrow alcove in the canyon wall, the chute that had been the source of the trench where they had started their last stand. The enemy, some two dozen in number, had circled around to block any further retreat up the canyon and now faced the two men in a semicircle of snapping carbines and hooded, faceless antagonists.

A few jagged rocks marked the entrance to the alcove, and the shooter pair had hunkered down behind them. Several meters back the chute became a chimney leading straight up the almost vertical wall. Even if they'd had the endurance to try to climb it, they would have been completely exposed to enemy fire. There was no escape that way.

The only reason they'd survived this long, Falco knew, was that the enemy troops had come out in such a hurry that they'd neglected some basic preparations. If they'd brought a full complement of grenades, for example, the two SEALS would have been blown to bits an hour before. Instead, the Eluoi had lobbed a few of the explosive devices toward them, but none had hit the mark. And after four or five of them had gone off, those attacks had ceased.

Still, the enemy troops were tenacious, disciplined, and skilled. They wormed steadily closer, using the snow for concealment and the occasional rocks studding the ground as cover. Many of the Eluoi laid down covering fire, rounds zinging and chipping off the rocks around the two SEALS, while a few of their number scrambled forward, bringing the semicircular noose ever more tightly around the pair's dead-end position.

Falco dropped his G15 and picked up the Hammer, steadying the squirrel gun between a couple of rocks while he squinted into the snowbound landscape. His eyes burned and watered, almost freezing shut as the wind whipped past, and when he saw a hostile lunge forward from behind a rock, he snapped off a shot that missed by at least a meter. The Eluoi made it to the next position and dropped prone, unharmed and another six meters closer to his quarry.

With a curse, the sniper set aside the powerful gun and again hoisted his carbine. Unlike the members of the infiltration party, he and LaRue had not bothered with the noise suppressors. Their role, after all, had been to create a diversion. In spite of their predicament, he grinned fiercely at the realization that they had done that in spades.

LaRue snapped off a controlled burst, rounds puffing through snow, cracking into a rock no more than fifty meters away. The Eluoi hiding there rose very slightly to squeeze off a return burst, and Falco fired six precious rounds, watching in satisfaction as the parka-clad hostile twisted around to lie on his back, twitching a couple of times before falling still.

"Any more grenades?" G-Man asked.

"I'm fresh out," Falco answered, having launched his last one five minutes earlier. "As soon as I get to a computer, I'll scan the classifieds and see if I can find a good deal on some more."

LaRue laughed, a sharp and bitter bark of sound. He popped off two more controlled bursts, and then the two SEALS pressed their faces to the ground, using every bit of cover as another blistering volley of rounds spattered their well-protected hiding place. Acutely conscious of their vulnerability, the men popped up as soon as they dared, just in time to see three of their attackers diving for cover behind a low, flat rock no more than forty meters from their redoubt. By the time they got their carbines up, the Eluoi had dropped prone, presenting nothing to use as a target.

A rocket zoomed in from the left, trailing fire and smoke, streaking faster than the eye could follow. By the time Falco flinched back, an involuntary reaction that would have been too late in any event, the round impacted with a sharp, fiery explosion. The sniper's first thought was that an enemy shot, with a new and terribly lethal weapon, had gone wide.

The explosion smashed the flat rock where the three attackers had taken shelter, blowing Eluoi, shards of rock, and instantly melted snow into the air. It took only a moment for Falco to realize that the shot had not targeted the two SEALS, after all. Instead, it had come from beyond the battle, and it looked a hell of a lot like one of Rocky Rodale's M76 Wasp missiles.

"Look, there!" crowed LaRue, the big man's voice cracking in excitement. Falco looked and saw: Two shimmering shapes had risen from the snow and fired point-blank bursts from their G15s into the Eluoi shooters at the outer rim of their semicircular formation. He recognized the ghillie cloaks of the two scouts at once.

Immediately the sniper and G-Man added their own noise-makers to the party, popping up from behind their rocky barricade to shoot into the ranks of Eluoi who were reacting in panic to the sudden attack from behind. A glance to the left showed four SEALS in pressure suits approaching along the edge of the cliff. Two raised their guns, covering their partners, while the other two rushed forward to new firing positions where they fired bursts into the flank of the Eluoi formation as their comrades advanced.

The shock of the counterattack was complete and utterly demoralizing. Falco saw the enemy soldiers scrambling to face the new and unexpected threat, but most of them never got turned around before they were gunned down where they lay. A few leaped to their feet and started to run, sprinting up the canyon, away from the installation—and the only hope of long-term survival on this hostile world. The SEALS dropped most of them with bursts from the G15s.

But one of the Eluoi was already out of range and running fast, pushing frantically through the deep snow. Wiping the frost from his eyelids, Falco once again picked up his squirrel gun. He rested it on the flat rock that had been his lifesaving barrier for the last twenty minutes. Blinking away the tears that almost constantly blurred his vision, the SEALS sniper settled in and entered his "bubble." The snow, wind, and discomfort disappeared for a moment; all that existed for Falco was the target he was aiming at and the weapon in his hands. For that instant of time, the man and the weapon were one. He sighted through the scope, refined his point of aim, and gently squeezed the trigger.

The last round of the battle snapped like a firecracker through the canyon, the report echoing from the walls even as the big 10.2-mm round shot straight and true, dropping the last Eluoi as it punctured his body squarely between the shoulder blades.

Falco blinked again and made sure of his kill.

Then he passed out.

Seventeen: Ursine Allies

Lieutenant (j.g.) Sanders paced the control room in agitation. Baxter continued to punch and tap at the various keyboards and control panels, and the young officer felt about as useful as the proverbial tits on a bull. He confirmed that the three dozen or so Eluoi of the garrison remained trapped behind the hatches Baxter had sealed by remote control. The electrician's mate pointed out that the IR signatures meant that the hostile troops were still alive. He couldn't read the exact quality of the air on the alien equipment but thought that at the very least, the Eluoi would be weakened considerably by the decreasing oxygen content of their self-contained atmosphere.

Finally, Sanders dropped down the ladder to the central room, where he saw that Schroeder and Robinson were hunkered down behind makeshift barriers, ready to hold out if the Eluoi somehow broke through their sealed hatches and mounted a counterattack. How *long* they could hold out was a question Sanders didn't want to think about; he could only hope that the LT and the rescue party got back in a hurry.

The odds of an Eluoi sortie were unknown, unfortunately. The seals that Baxter had dropped remotely to secure the enemy behind their locked hatches seemed to be holding, and there was no sign that the enemy troops were having any success in breaking out of the compartments where they had been imprisoned. But if one of the hostiles was able to come

up with a breaching charge or a powerful cutting tool, all
bets were off. Still, there was nothing he could do but keep
an eye on them and wait for developments.

He recalled the three that were holed up in the lower level
and checked with Grafton to make sure that they had made
no overt move. His last check of Baxter's schematic had
shown that the isolated trio had been unable to rejoin their
comrades. Uncontained as they were, they represented a threat
that would have to be dealt with sooner rather than later.

The young officer's mind wandered a bit, and he thought
of the third group of warriors within the installation. The
shaggy brutes the Team had termed yetis were locked in
a single cell on the lowest level. He hadn't counted but
guessed there were about twenty in there. He was inclined to
share the opinion that they were the survivors of the party
that had ambushed the SEALS but that when they had re-
treated here to their Eluoi "allies," they had been welcomed
with arms that were not exactly open. Remembering the
rudimentary language the Team had heard during the battle,
he wondered how hard it would be to communicate with the
hulking, brutish creatures.

Admonishing Schroeder and Robinson to keep alert—an
unnecessary request that only served to make the junior lieutenant feel like he was doing something—he descended to
the lower level, where he found Coxswain Grafton and his
four sailors camped out at one end of the long corridor leading past the yetis' prison cell, toward the stairwell where the
three Eluoi were trapped.

"Any sign of trouble down there, Grafty?" he asked.

"Negative, sir. A half hour ago one of them took a few
potshots our way, but we drove him back with a volley he
won't soon forget."

Sanders noticed that one of the sailors, Gunner's Mate
Roberts, was wearing the battery pack and holding the en-

ergy weapon they had captured from the garrison. "Do you know how to use that thing, sailor?"

"Sir, yes, sir!" Roberts replied. He used the barrel to indicate the far end of the wall. "You see that cut in the steel? That was about a half-second burst at medium power."

Sanders saw the cut, which was more than a meter long and looked to have gouged all the way through a centimeter's thickness of metal plating. He also saw that he wouldn't be able to talk to the yeti prisoners safely unless they cleaned out the three hostile troops at the far end of the hall. He explained the problem to the coxswain. "Are you and your men up for a little offensive action?" he asked.

"Let us at the bastards," Grafton replied grimly.

Sanders nodded. "All right. I'm going to get their attention with a couple of grenades. Then we hustle down there and see that their troublemaking days are over. Got it?"

Of course, if those men had been SEALS, he simply would have ordered the operation, but the situation went above and beyond what the sailors had signed on for. Thus, he felt it appropriate to gauge how the men felt about what was essentially a commando operation. They didn't disappoint him, all of them dead serious as they nodded their support for his plan.

He readied two grenades, loading one into the underbarrel launcher on his G15. He lifted the weapon and sighted for the corner of the corridor. With a click of the trigger, the grenade shot down the passageway, bouncing off the far wall just where it went around the bend. A moment later a blast of fire, smoke, and lethal fragments erupted from the unseen alcove.

Sanders already had his second grenade loaded and sent it after the first before starting down the corridor at a sprint. The sailors charged behind, Roberts matching him stride for stride with the laser rifle held at the ready. They came around the corner to see that two of the Eluoi were down, killed by the blasts, while the third was stunned, struggling to climb to his feet. The officer opened up with his automatic carbine, and Roberts added a sizzling bolt from the electrical weapon.

The stunned Eluoi never made it off the floor.

"Good job, men," Sanders said with sincere gratitude.

He went to one of the slain Eluoi and tore the bloodstained uniform tunic off the man. Then he made his way back down the hallway through the lowest level of the installation and started looking through some of the lockers in the passageway outside the door of the yetis' cell. He was soon rewarded by the discovery of several communications devices, including comlinks, radio sets, and some of the small in-ear translators all the SEALS were wearing. Most intriguing were some larger, headphonelike devices. Holding one up to his helmet, he saw that it was far too wide for any human-size skull.

"Bingo," he muttered, taking several of the devices and going to the locked door to the imprisoned yetis' cell. The latch was a simple mechanical switch. Glancing through the small window, he saw that the prisoners were still sitting around listlessly; one or two looked up at him with an aura of apathy.

Still, he wasn't sure that he wanted to open the door to a room holding twenty prisoners, each of whom weighed at least three or four times as much as he did and was a good meter taller. He looked at the window closely and saw that the plastic plate could be swiveled free, opening a small hole covered by a grid of sturdy steel bars into the prison cell.

He released the latch and casually tossed the three Eluoi headsets they'd found into the cell. The yetis blinked in surprise, and several growled, baring those long, curved fangs. One, however, regarded him with something like curiosity.

"Pick it up," Sanders said, gesturing to the headset. "I'd like to talk to you."

Suspiciously, the shaggy creature reached down to hoist

the device in his powerful claw-tipped fingers. He was clearly familiar with it and slipped it smoothly over his head so that the padded earpieces covered his furry, ursine ears.

"Can you understand me?" the lieutenant asked.

The creature blinked in surprise, then uttered a guttural grunt. Sanders's translator crackled, turning the grunt into a word: "Yes." Obviously, the Eluoi had deciphered their alien language and programmed it into their translators.

"Who are you?"

"We are Kyne-Ursa," the creature growled; again, the translator changed the animalistic sounds into English. "Who are you?"

"We are humans," Sanders replied. "Enemies of the Eluoi." He tossed the bloodied uniform tunic into the cell. "We killed them."

The shred of clothing provoked a host of woofs and growls as the prisoners rose from their benches, moving forward to gather around the bloody rag. The one who had spoken raised it in his nimble paw, sniffed it, then passed it to his comrades as he looked at the young officer with an unreadable expression.

"Eluoi killed us," the yeti said.

"They locked you in here?" the human asked.

"Yes," the Ursa replied. "Angry we did not kill you . . . humans."

"We humans are hard to kill," Sanders noted. "You're not the first to try and fail."

"Now Eluoi will kill us," the creature said glumly .

"Actually, there are not too many of these Eluoi left," the SEALS officer replied. "They are our enemies, and we killed many of them. We destroyed their tanks and took this place away from them."

The big creature looked at him with wide eyes. "You are hard killers," he grunted, and Sanders took the remark to be a compliment.

"How many installations like this are there on your world?" the SEALS officer probed.

"Only this," the Ursa replied. "But they come here and make this place, and we must obey. The Eluoi with the black eyes, with the brain that speaks loud noise, makes it so."

"An Eluoi with a brain that speaks loud noise?" Sanders repeated. "Why did you allow him to give you orders?"

"Had no choice. His brain-speak destroyed our will, made us his . . . slaves." He barked the last word angrily.

At that moment Sanders's comlink crackled as Baxter started reporting that the rescue party was returning through the tunnel to the installation.

"I will be back," he said. "I need to speak to my leader."

Without waiting for a reply, he turned and headed for the stairs, knowing that Jackson would be very interested to learn that an Eluoi savant had been on this remote ice world.

Jackson led the rescue expedition back to the captured installation after they had rigged a blanket to cover Falco's shattered helmet visor. The man's face looked terrible, but he bore his frostbite with the kind of uncomplaining stoicism characteristic of the SEALS. Two men helped him walk, and the others stopped to collect Zimmer's body from the cairn where he had been laid before the attack. Then the whole party returned to the base through the access tunnel they had used when they had started out on the rescue mission.

Leaving the rest of the Team to attend to the exhausted but cheerful G-Man while Harry Teal did what he could to treat Falco's frozen and blistered face, Jackson quickly climbed the stairs to consult with the junior lieutenant and the electrician's mate. He found Sanders and Baxter waiting for him in the command post.

"Any luck contacting the *Pegasus*?" the CO asked immediately.

Baxter shook his head, grimacing in disappointment. "If

there's a way to send a radio signal through the interference surrounding this ice cube, I haven't found it yet, sir."

"The Eluoi must have had a way to do it!" the officer snapped impatiently.

"Yes, sir. But we did some damage to this place when we took it over. We might have knocked out some of their communicators," the SEALS electrician's mate replied logically.

"Yeah, that makes sense," Jackson, who had become increasingly impressed by the man's abilities, allowed. "But keep trying. And see if you can find anything in there, any reference at all to the *Pangaea*."

"Aye, aye, sir."

"Everything quiet back at the ranch while we were gone?" he asked Sanders.

"Well, there've been a few developments, sir." The young officer proceeded to describe his elimination of the Eluoi trio, his conversation with the Ursa, and his conclusion that a savant must have been the one who had compelled their servitude to the Eluoi cause.

" 'A brain that speaks loud noise'? That's a pretty good description of my experience with Tezlac Catal," Jackson remarked. "He knocked me off my feet just by *thinking*." He all but shuddered at the memory of his encounter with the Eluoi leader, who had possessed uncanny and terrifying mental powers.

"Tezlac Catal?" Baxter said, looking up from the console. "That name is all over these files."

"You don't say," the LT commented. "I wonder why that old son of a bitch is interested in what's going on around Arcton V."

"I can do some digging if you want, sir," the electrician's mate offered. "I have found some intel about a human ship. It made the jump out of this system before that destroyer mixed it up with the *Troy*. It might be a reference to the *Pangaea*."

"Good! See if you can isolate the data. If we ever find a way to contact the frigate, that intel might make this whole excursion seem worthwhile." He thought with a pang of Mirowski's death and wondered if it was even possible that he had spoken the truth. Immediately, he shook off the looming sense of depression and regret.

"Just keep looking," Jackson ordered. He turned to Sanders. "In the meantime, let's go have a talk with these . . . what do they call themselves?"

"Kyne-Ursa, sir. I've just been referring to them as the Ursa. It seems to fit."

The two officers descended into the depths of the installation again, and the shaggy prisoners looked up with interest when they appeared at the window to the cell.

"How did the Eluoi come down to your world?" Lieutenant Jackson asked the spokesman, who had donned his headphones as soon as the two men had returned.

"They fly a fire-tail ship down through sky and snow. They come out of ship."

"And the ship left them here?"

"Many ships come. One stays, in mountain."

"They have a ship here, inside a mountain?" the LT pressed, intrigued but hoping for clarification.

"Very close to here," the Ursa replied.

"Look," Jackson said, making up his mind. "You know that we have killed many Eluoi and locked up the others. They can't reach their weapons, and they have no one here to, to 'brain-speak,' as you called it."

"We saw and smelled the Eluoi blood. You are mighty warriors," the shaggy creature allowed.

"If we release you from this cell, will you accept our friendship, or will you serve the Eluoi and seek to do us harm?"

The Ursa snorted, an inarticulate sound of clear contempt.

"I will help any warrior who defeats the Eluoi. They are harsh masters, and we would be rid of them."

"All right." The officer reached down and released the mechanical latch. He nodded at Sanders, who held his G15 at the ready, and pushed open the door. "We free you as friends of humankind and enemies of the Eluoi."

Slowly, hesitantly, the hulking spokesman, who was apparently some kind of chief to judge from the way the others deferred to him, rose and approached the door. He looked out, sniffed cautiously, and stepped into the corridor, where he loomed above the two humans. "We are free?" he growled.

"Yes. If we can find the ship you talk about, we humans will leave this place, and it will be yours once again. Until then, we are allies, sworn to peace with each other. Do you agree?"

To their surprise, the Ursa dropped to one knee and bowed his massive head. "I agree, on behalf of all of the Kyne-Ursa. Now we shall leave this place."

"Wait," Jackson said. "Before you go, can you show us where this fire-tail ship is? Where is this mountain?"

"I will show you," the huge creature pledged. "But my people must go free."

"All right," Jackson agreed. He thought of an obvious question. "Do you have a name?" he asked.

"I am called Sha," the Ursa said, looking down at the officer with eyes that seemed strangely soft, even intelligent. "And how are you called?"

"Call me LT," the SEALS CO replied without hesitation.

The file of prisoners trooped out past the surprised SEALS in the central hall and the garage. The shaggy creatures didn't even flinch as they stepped through the shattered hatch, marched into the raging blizzard, and disappeared into the growing twilight. Only Sha remained, looking wistfully into the storm with the incongruous earphones on his large, shaggy head.

"You will go with them as soon as we find the ship," Jackson promised.

As soon as they were out of sight, Jackson returned to the control room, accompanied by the Ursa chief. "Sha here has told me about a spaceship or shuttle—some kind of rocket—that is supposedly enclosed in an underground chamber somewhere on this rock," he told Baxter. "What can you find out about it?"

The officer left the mate to his task and checked on the rest of his men. Schroeder and LaRue were much better than they had been an hour before; hot food and rest had worked wonders for each of them. Falco, after a painkilling injection, was sleeping, and the LT spoke to his corpsman.

"How's he doing?"

"Well, he might lose some skin, maybe even the tip of his nose," Teal replied. "But he'll be okay. Once we get home, a cosmetic surgeon might be needed to make him all pretty again."

Jackson nodded, somewhat relieved. There remained only Zimmer's and Mirowski's bodies as reminders that this mission had not come without a terrible cost.

Then, an hour later, Baxter called down on his comlink. Jackson raced up the steps to the control room, and as soon as he looked at the big vidscreen, he saw that the SEALS had struck gold.

"It's another tunnel, LT," the electrician's mate explained. "It was concealed in a coded program, so it took a little searching." He gestured to the diagram. "It leads from the lower level of this installation, about three klicks into—under, actually—the mountains. But the yeti was right: It's an underground hangar, and according to this, it contains one fully fueled and space-ready shuttle."

"All right." Jackson was elated. He looked around the control room, thinking. "Did you turn up any more data on Tezlac Catal? Or the *Pangaea?*"

"Well, yes, sir. As to Catal, he's on record as the CO of this place, but it doesn't seem like he was here within the last six months. Still, it looks like those pirates were working for him; they're not so much pirates as privateers, apparently. If they were able to return here with the 'prize'—and he doesn't say what that is—they were supposed to bring it to him in some place called the Darius system. I gather that he makes a lot of profit from his operations there; they're centered on a station called the Bazaar. He moves a lot of slaves through, if I'm reading this right. With respect, he sounds like a real asshole, sir."

"He *is* a real asshole," Jackson confirmed. "Okay. What about the *Pangaea?*"

"Well, they don't mention her by name, but they make reference to a target, and it seems to be an Earth ship. That almost has to be our big sister, doesn't it, sir?" Jackson nodded, and Baxter continued. "All indications are that the ship jumped in the direction of the Darius system that they were talking about. If Catal doesn't have her already, he might be chasing her."

"Good work. Anything else?"

"Well, just this, sir. Some of these files were created by the savant himself, apparently. They have a different kind of signature, like he didn't use keystrokes but just inputted the material directly onto the memory boards. There's a hatch here on the drive that only he can open, as if he needed to get direct access to the disk without even a thin layer of metal in between. It sounds crazy, I know. Is it even possible? Can he really *do* that, sir?"

Jackson remembered Dr. Sulati's speculation that the savant's powers were in fact some type of electrical signals that he was able to broadcast. He certainly had the ability to interfere with the electrical signals in the brains of his listeners; Jackson had experienced that brutal pain firsthand.

"I'm not sure what he can do, to tell you the truth. But the SOB nearly made me piss my pants when he talked to me, so nothing else would surprise me." Still, it was an interesting piece of data and suggested that somehow the savant's powers were caused by creating some sort of electrical impulse with his mind. The question deserved further investigation, but now was not the time for that.

"What about the Eluoi who are still locked up?" Jackson asked Baxter.

The electrician's mate shrugged. "Hard to say, sir. They're still alive; you can see that by the IR signature on the schematic. But they have to be breathing some pretty skanky air. They're not going to be any too lively."

Jackson realized that the impulse to kill all the sons of bitches was no longer the compelling motivation it had been in the immediate aftermath of Mirowski's death. He shook his head, suddenly ashamed of his merciless impulse: They were a defeated enemy and deserved to be treated as POWs. "Turn the air back on," he said to Baxter. "But leave the hatches sealed. We're getting out of here, and they can have this dump back when we're gone."

But then he went on. "Actually, I think the Kyne-Ursa are going to be in charge of this ice rock, at least most of it. They seem to have evolved to function in these conditions, and as far as I'm concerned, they're welcome to it. And I think they'll be kindly disposed toward the U.S. Navy if we ever get back here again. It will give them a leg up if we don't leave the Eluoi a fully functional station. Let's set a few demolition charges around here so they'll have a little bit of a mess to clean up when they finally break out of their sealed compartments. Take out all the computer equipment, especially."

"You mean *if* they break out, right, sir?" Sanders queried.

"Yes," Jackson replied grimly. Once again, his thoughts turned to Mirowski, the SEALS who had sacrificed his life to save the CO. "*If* they break out."

Three hours later, the SEALS were all strapped into the seats of a large shuttle. They had found the ship easily by following a subterranean passageway and quickly determined that it was fully fueled and ready for launch and had more than enough room for the Teammates and their navy companions. The roof that enclosed the place had been a slab of steel, covered by ice and snow on the outside so that it had been indistinguishable from the terrain all over the ice moon. Fortunately, the controls were right there in the hangar, and they had opened it with no difficulty.

Harry Teal, who had augmented his earlier pilot skills with actual training in spaceflight during the past year, sat in the captain's chair. Jackson rode shotgun, though he would leave the flying up to the corpsman. Baxter was behind the pilots' chairs, ready to try the radio as soon as they broke free from the ice moon's powerful shield of electrical interference. The rest of the men were below them in the long hull, reclining in seats that were oriented toward the bow of the shuttle so that for now they essentially were lying on their backs.

They had brought a number of computer files that Baxter had downloaded from the command center consoles before they had demolished that equipment and made their way down the long, cold tunnel to the remote launching hangar. Sanders sincerely hoped that those files would provide some useful intel on the Eluoi mission in this system and their thwarted capture of the shield drive.

"The sixty-four-million-credit question," Sanders muttered through his communicator, "is whether we'll find the *Pegasus* waiting for us in orbit."

That was indeed a matter of life and death, Jackson and all

the Teammates understood. If the frigate, which had had no contact with the landing party since the drop boats had penetrated the moon's atmosphere, had moved to a new location, they would simply orbit above the ice world until their supplies gave out.

But Stonewall Jackson knew Captain Carstairs very well, and he was willing to bet the lives of himself and all of his Teammates that the captain would have his navy ship somewhere nearby when they finally burst through the clouds.

"Everybody hold on," Teal said by way of warning. He started to flip switches, and very soon they felt the rumble of powerful rocket engines firing. The shuttle held in place, trembling, for another few seconds and then blasted upward with enough acceleration to plaster the SEALS hard into their cushioned seats. Jackson barely had the strength to turn his head sideways. By the time he did, the snow-encased landscape had vanished below them, swallowed by the constant murk.

The G-force of the ascending rocket was extreme but not fatal. The men simply allowed the pressure to hold them against their seats. Here and there a SEALS crossed his fingers or whispered a nearly silent prayer; they knew they were basically powerless to influence their fate on this risky launch.

The ship blasted upward through the stormy atmosphere. For half a minute snow and ice created a whiteout against the windows of the pilot's cabin, but the rocket swiftly rose above the planetary weather. Soon it was coursing through the region of electrical disturbance, and Jackson was worried when he realized that his hair, even on the back of his hands, was standing on end from the powerful ionizing effects. Within another minute even that was left behind, and the strangely reassuring blackness of space yawned before them.

Teal eased back on the throttle, the acceleration force

backing down to a couple of Gs as the shuttle continued to rise away from the ice-coated moon. Jackson was amazed by how happy he was to be back in space; the sense that the lifeless, freezing vacuum could possibly be a welcoming environment seemed incongruous, to say the least. But he was undeniably delighted to be off the hostile, entrapping surface of the ice moon.

Finally Teal shut off the engines, and the SEALS were immediately weightless, held in place only by the straps on their seats. The LT looked around, hoping—unrealistically, he knew—to catch sight of the frigate. There was only that eternal blackness, with the shrouded world below and the distant pale fire of Arcton so many millions of kilometers away.

But Baxter went to work with the radio, holding the microphone in his right hand while his left twirled a dial through a variety of frequencies. "This is SEALS Team Jackson calling USSS *Pegasus*. Come in, *Pegasus*. Come in."

He repeated the call over and over, rewarded only by static, and Jackson began to wonder if his faith had been misplaced. Surely the ship was up there somewhere. They must be able to hear them!

And then he was rewarded with the most beautiful phrase he had ever heard:

"This is *Pegasus*. Come in, SEALS. What is your status?"

Eighteen: To the Bazaar

A locker in the commandeered shuttle's launching bay had contained several serviceable pressure suits, although not quite up to the Mark IV's standards of armor, comfort, and technological advancement. Still, the SEALS had been able to find one for Falco, who was the only member of the Team unprepared to face a vacuum environment because of his shattered faceplate. With everyone suited up, the Teammates and their navy comrades were able to transfer to the *Pegasus* without a direct air lock docking between the two ships.

Carstairs merely brought his frigate into a matching orbit with the shuttle after Teal had killed the engines of the little escape ship. Navy crew members aboard the *Pegasus* used the frigate's docking arm to hold the two ships in close proximity—about twenty meters—and Chief Swanson led a small party through space to establish a static line between the two ships. In the meantime, after double-checking everyone's suit for pressure integrity, Teal had depressurized the shuttle slowly until the interior was as perfect a vacuum as the space beyond the hatch.

Once that had been accomplished, the shuttle's hatch was opened. One at a time, the men snapped D-rings to the static line and pulled themselves hand over hand into the open drop boat dock of the frigate. Once there, each man secured himself to one of the many fasteners in that hold. It took somewhat less than half an hour for the fourteen SEALS, the five drop boat crewmen, and the bodies of Zimmer and Mirowski to be transferred to the *Pegasus*. Finally, the hold doors were closed over the drop boat dock, and the large compartment gradually was repressurized. In a little over an hour from the time the docking arm had been attached, the men who had survived the ice moon were able to remove their suits and weightlessly enter the passages of the *Pegasus*.

Master Chief Ruiz and Chief Harris saw to the establishment of the men back in SEALS country on H Deck, and Jackson, accompanied by Sanders and Coxswain Grafton, wasted no time seeking out Captain Carstairs. The CO welcomed them heartily and invited the trio in to the CIC for a debriefing. Consul Char-Kane was already there, her cool visage softening with a hint of relief as the SEALS entered.

Jackson gave them the CliffsNotes version of the operation on the ice moon, recapping in five minutes the terrible conditions, the landing that had wrecked the drop boats, the attempted ambush by the Kyne-Ursa, and finally their infiltration and capture of the Eluoi installation. He acknowledged Falco and LaRue's bravery in creating the effective diversion, made note of Grafton and his mates' important contribution in the battle for the ice station, and grimly reported the loss of two personnel.

"We learned from the computer records that our old friend Tezlac Catal is in charge of the place," he concluded. "But we still haven't figured out what he was getting out of there. Still, my whiz kid, Electrician's Mate Baxter, was able to come up with quite a dossier of material on Catal, his operations, and the savants in general. For now, it seems that Catal is off in the Darius star system, though he'd been on the ice moon within the last half year. There's some indication that the *Pangaea* might have jumped there as well."

Carstairs nodded. "That's damned good news, and it jibes perfectly with what we've picked up. Tezlac Catal is supposed to be one of the Eluoi delegates at the conference. I wouldn't be surprised if he's behind the disappearance of the *Pangaea*. Remember, the destroyer we tracked to the ice moon was the last ship known to be anywhere near her."

"What about that destroyer, sir?"

"Well, when we didn't hear from you after twenty-four hours, I decided to focus on that destroyer. She was on the far side of the moon from us, but we were able to get a good analysis of her position by picking up the reflected emissions as they bounced off the planet. Apparently, she needed some repairs, and when those were completed, she bugged out. I would have followed her except I was hoping you and your Team would still show up. And you didn't disappoint."

Jackson grimaced. "Still no word from the *Pangaea*?" he asked.

"Well, we haven't come up entirely blank. We did a review of our scanners and were able to track her last position in this system. She jumped, but we didn't really know where. However, judging by her bearing and rate of acceleration, it's more than possible she jumped to the Darius system—it's goddamn likely. Somehow her signal was masked from active sensors, so we couldn't see her or pick up her radar beacon while she was here. But now we have a reasonable idea of where she went—or was taken," he concluded grimly.

"That's what Baxter found on the computer of the Eluoi installation," Jackson noted. "The pirates were supposed to bring Tezlac Catal something, but they failed to deliver it."

"The shield driver?" the captain speculated, a guess that was completely in line with Jackson's hypothesis. "I gather they wanted to take it to someplace called the Darius system, to some location called the Bazaar. Catal has a center of operations there. He uses it to run slaves and God only knows what else through the galaxy."

"And the shield driver would be of great value to anyone who could offer it for sale," Char-Kane interjected. "Although it is still not operational, I have been informed that only a few details remain to be resolved. If it can be perfected, the shield will represent a quantum advance in spaceship defense; the empire that possesses it could well master the others."

She said it with no more emotion than if she had been reciting a grocery list, but the military men who were her listeners could not help feeling a sense of real dread at the thought of that technology in Eluoi hands.

"Good thing we have the prototype safe in our hold," Carstairs muttered. "As for this Bazaar, it gives us a focal point once we make the jump to Darius. And Stonewall," Carstairs added, his tone dropping still further, "that was a nice bit of work down there. I'm sorry about your man and my own as well, but if you hadn't learned what you did, we'd be flailing around the whole galaxy right now."

"Thanks for waiting for us, sir," Jackson said sincerely. "I presume we're going after the *Pangaea* now."

"Already under way. For now, get your Team settled in; see that your men get a hot meal and some rest. We've started the acceleration, but it will be about thirty hours until we're in position to make the jump."

"Very good, sir. Captain?" the SEALS officer asked.

"Yes?"

"This mission has already had more twists and turns than the roller coasters at Disney Galactic. I had an idea that might, well, reinforce our capabilities."

"What is it, Tom? I'm interested."

"We have better than a dozen survivors from the *Troy* aboard, I know. Also, five crew from the drop boats, who I'm guessing are out of work for the time being. As I told you, Grafty's men did a helluva job watching our flank while we were taking out that installation. I'd like to ask for volunteers and have my chiefs give them some basic infantry training. We won't make SEALS or even marines out of them in the course of a few days, but we might get them ready to back up a landing party, give a hand with a rescue attempt if we find the *Pangaea.* You never know."

"You're right, Stonewall—we never know. It's a good idea. Go ahead and make it happen."

"Aye, aye, sir. And, well, thanks again."

The *Pegasus* emerged from her jump and immediately began to decelerate as Captain Carstairs marked a course for the ring of populous planets orbiting the star called Darius at a distance equivalent to that between Earth and humankind's sun.

The transit from Arcton had taken more than a hundred hours, and the SEALS and the crew of the frigate had put that time to good use. Master Chief Ruiz and Chief Harris had taken fifteen volunteers—survivors from the *Troy* as well as Grafton and his four drop boat crewmates—and given them intense training in small arms and basic infantry survival techniques. The ad hoc platoon was led by Lieutenant Wesling of the *Troy,* ably supported by Petty Officers Dawson and Grafton, and all the personnel proved to be apt pupils. Every one of them had a score—many, many scores in the case of the *Troy*'s crew—to settle with the Eluoi, and they relished the chance to play a role in the accounting.

Although it was a makeshift platoon, it was a platoon of men—and two women, sailors from the *Troy*—experienced in space operations and determined to make a difference. Most of them were armed with standard G15s that lacked the bells and whistles of the SEALS versions such as the rocket rounds and underbarrel grenade launcher, though four of them did have grenade launchers. Gunner's Mate Roberts retained possession of the alien energy weapon he had recovered on the ice moon and used to such good effect in the skirmish with the Eluoi.

Schroeder's head wounds had been tended to in the infirmary, and the stoic gunner's mate had declared himself 100 percent ready to return to action. Keast, too, was up and about, without even a noticeable limp—"noticeable" meant that he never limped when he knew someone was watching— to show for the punishing shot to his leg that had cracked but not broken the bone. Teal had wrapped it for him with a supporting compact, and he proved to Jackson that he could run and jump at full speed. Falco, too, was ready for action, though his face was a mess. Cosmetic surgery, he announced loudly and frequently, would wait until he had the full attention of three large-breasted nurses to ease him back to his old good-looking self.

After an eight-hour interval of much-needed rest, the Teammates patched suits and armor where they had been damaged, replaced worn parts on communicators and survival gear, cleaned weapons—or, in a couple of cases, discarded damaged arms in favor of new equipment—and, of course, replenished their supplies of munitions from the frigate's well-stocked ammunition magazines. Ruiz asked for and received permission to carry the other battery-powered energy weapon—he called it a ray gun, and the term stuck— and the ship's engineers were able to figure out how to recharge the power pack so that it, like Roberts's, was furnished with a full fuel cell.

The replenishment and training began while the ship accelerated away from Arcton. It was suspended for an interval of sleep, during which time the ship made the jump to the Darius system. When the recruits had rested, the chiefs started the drill again as the *Pegasus* decelerated toward the new star. By the time they were approaching a steady orbit in the inhabited stretch of the system, the SEALS were rested and reinvigorated, and the navy "commandos," after a crash course of six twelve-hour training sessions, were judged ready to go.

Not that they had any choice in the matter.

*   *   *

Though Carstairs enjoyed the view from L Deck—which had been fully repaired after the breaching shot from the Eluoi destroyer—as they decelerated into the Darius system, he had decided to remain in the CIC, where, as usual, he welcomed Jackson's and Consul Char-Kane's company. They watched the screen that displayed the worlds, fixed stations, and other installations in the system on a highly detailed three-dimensional image. Jackson had never seen so many blips on one image of a section of space.

"I gather this star is kind of like a galactic version of Hong Kong, back before the Chinese tamed it," Carstairs noted. "Lots of commerce done here, some diplomacy and piracy, not a lot of regulation."

"It is both famous and infamous in this quarter of the galaxy," Char-Kane noted. "One can supposedly find anything and everything for sale there. Including people," she added.

"Sounds like just the kind of place Tezlac Catal would choose for his vacation home," Jackson noted sourly. At the thought of the savant, he turned to the Shamani, remembering the problem he'd been grappling with since his conversation with Dr. Sulati.

"What is it about his mental power, anyway? How does it work?" he asked bluntly. "Do you understand what his brain, or his voice, actually *does*? How can he inflict pain, even paralysis, just by speaking?"

"We have done surreptitious analysis insofar as possible, though the savants are rare and guard their secrets well. Rarely will they use their powers when there are recording devices present. All we Shamani have been able to determine is that there is a powerful electrical aura, negatively charged, that the savant can project, as if in a wave of ions. His voice carries the power of the charge, but his mind is the source of the electrical field."

"Savants are rare, huh? I guess I'm thankful for small favors, though even one of the sons of bitches is too many for me," the LT declared. Still, the hypothesis made sense: He knew that a field of electrical charge heavily oriented toward one pole—the negative, in this case—could seriously disrupt normal electrical function. And the brain, when one got right down to it, was an organ that functioned because of billions and billions of tiny but significant electrical emissions. Filing the data away, he returned his attention to the mission.

"How many inhabited planets are there in the system?" Jackson asked.

"Three." The CO indicated two bright blips in equidistant orbits around the star called Darius. "These two are the most Earth-like. One is controlled by the Shamani, the other by the Assarn. They revolve around the star more or less opposite each other."

"That planet, Darius I, is the home of some of our greatest artists," Char-Kane noted. "It is reportedly a world of unprecedented beauty. Ninety percent of the surface is water, primarily warm, shallow seas. It is much favored by those who do not have a lot of work to do."

Her tone was faintly disapproving, and Jackson clenched his teeth to hide his smile.

Carstairs next pointed to a larger blip, surrounded by a dense web of smaller images. "This is Darius III, and it's controlled by the Eluoi, as you might have guessed."

"What are all the smaller blips?" the SEALS officer wondered.

"No less than a dozen large stations. A lot of the blips you're seeing are spaceships. Our data indicates that Darius III is one of the most heavily populated planets in the entire galaxy—a population of something near a hundred billion—and that the level of interstellar trade is right up near the top of the list."

Jackson looked at the ship captain. "Are you thinking what I am?"

Carstairs offered a tight smile. "You think we should begin looking for the *Pangaea* in the vicinity of Darius III? I was reaching the same conclusion myself."

They marked a course for the big planet and paid careful attention to the streams of traffic moving to all sides. None of the other ships were close enough to see with the naked eye, but the vidscreen gave proof that they were in a very crowded region of space.

Darius III loomed larger; the planet was clearly visible, and as they neared it, they could make out some of the large stations, like small moons, orbiting it. Carstairs authorized a coded ID signal, identifying his frigate so that if the *Pangaea* was near and was listening, they could contact the missing vessel. Still, no one was prepared for the reply that finally came through:

"Ahoy, USSS *Pegasus*! This is Olin Parvik, commanding the *Starguard II*. Welcome to the Darius system! Want to get together for a cup of tea?"

"Captain Parvik," Carstairs replied. "I would like to invite you aboard to share the hospitality of the United States Navy, spacefaring version."

Four hours later, the *Starguard II* and the *Pegasus* were running parallel courses, both ships decelerating toward the inhabited belt of the Darius system. Parvik made the transfer in a personal shuttle that was the envy of every human who saw it: a speedy and maneuverable little craft that was 80 percent engine and 20 percent cockpit. It was large enough to carry six, but Parvik flew it alone and docked it easily inside the frigate's drop boat bay.

Jackson, who owed his life and those of his Teammates to the jaunty Assarn, was the first to greet Olin Parvik as he came aboard. The pilot, who himself had been saved from slavery or death by the timely intervention of the SEALS, returned the LT's embrace with a firm hug and a clap on the back for Sanders, Carstairs, and the chiefs. He nodded coolly at Consul Char-Kane, who returned the gesture with aloof disdain; Jackson remembered that their two races were very distrustful of each other.

Nevertheless, ten minutes later, Jackson, Sanders, the captain, the XO, Char-Kane, and Parvik were gathered around a table in the officer's wardroom. The top of the table was a flat-panel viewscreen, and it currently displayed a detailed schematic of the entire Darius system.

"The Orion conference has been canceled," Parvik explained bluntly. "The Shamani filed a preliminary protest over the attack on the *Lotus* and blamed it on the Eluoi. The Eluoi, in their inimitable fashion, claimed that the *Lotus* was on a spying mission and they were just defending themselves."

"That is typical of the Eluoi," Char-Kane noted, a surprising edge of bitterness in her usually passionless voice. "They are ever twisting the truth to blame every circumstance on the wrongdoing of some other people."

"True enough," Olin Parvik agreed, looking shrewdly at the Shamani woman.

"Did either side say anything about a shield driver?" Jackson asked.

"Not so far as I know. I've never heard of a shield driver, myself," Parvik said. "What is it?"

"Well, it's some kind of new defensive technology," Carstairs said smoothly when Char-Kane made no attempt to answer. Even though Parvik was an ally, the captain wasn't about to show all his cards. After all, the shield driver recovered from the pirate base was currently secured in the hold of the *Pegasus*. "We're not too sure ourselves but gather that it was at the heart of the *Lotus* affair."

"So they called off the conference because of that?" Jackson asked.

"Well, that got things started. Then, when the delegation from your world failed to arrive, the Eluoi—and Tezlac Catal in particular—declared that to be proof of bad faith. The old wizard even suggested that his poor, helpless people were being led into a trap. So he took his delegation and left, and the Shamani Consul de Star did the same thing; I think she was worried about further Eluoi treachery. We Assarn could have gone ahead with it if we'd only had someone to talk to," Parvik said, shaking his head.

"Who's the Consul de Star?" Carstairs asked.

"She is the leading diplomat for a planetary cluster," Char-Kane explained. "It is a rank several grades higher than my own, as Consul de Campe."

"Were you part of the delegation?" Jackson asked Olin Parvik.

The pilot laughed heartily and for such a long time that the LT began to feel a little foolish. Finally, Parvik wiped his eyes, and shook his head, clapping the SEALS officer on the shoulder. "I'm sorry," he said. "But the day my people let the likes of me attend a diplomatic conference is the day the galaxy starts to spin the other way!"

He quickly grew serious. "I really am sorry. I know you're not well acquainted with my people."

"Except for you," the LT noted pointedly.

"Right, of course. But we're not all a bunch of swash-buckling star jumpers. We Assarn have a pretty strong mer-cantile tradition and have long been used to transporting goods for both the Shamani and the Eluoi. Only lately, we've been pushed to the side—marginalized, if you will—to the extent that a few of us, myself included, have decided that we're going to start pushing back. Our leaders were going to the conference in the sincere hope that they might be able to negotiate some kind of settlement, but I don't believe that's going to happen. Still, I'm surprised that they didn't even sit down at the table."

"Tezlac Catal seemed to be in a hurry to get out of there," Jackson noted. "We found clues suggesting that he came here, to the Darius system, and went to a station called the Bazaar."

Olin Parvik whistled and nodded. "So you heard that Tezlac Catal was going to the Bazaar? That's interesting—and encouraging."

"Why encouraging?" Carstairs asked.

"It gives us a place to look, and it's a place that's about as wide open as any station you'll find anywhere in the galaxy."

"How so?" Jackson asked, intrigued.

Parvik grinned a sly grin. "Why don't you let me show you?" he suggested.

"So you really want us to go ashore in these dirty coveralls?" Master Chief Ruiz asked Jackson. His tone was neutral, but the look of gentle reproach in his eyes was unmistakable.

"I know what you mean, Rafe," the LT replied. "But the idea is for you and me and Baxter and Teal to get a look around without letting the whole galaxy know that the SEALS are here."

"Yes, sir," the master chief replied. He lifted the suit of mechanic's clothing that Olin Parvik had cheerfully provided. Teal and Baxter already had donned theirs, and Jackson pulled his own on over his uniform. Complete with grease stains and an imperfectly sewn patch on the knee, the garment made him look as nondescript as possible.

They rode to the Bazaar in Parvik's shuttle, which, unlike his sleek destroyer, was unarmed and bore no markings designating its origin or the empire to which its pilot belonged. With Parvik in the pilot's seat, the four SEALS occupied most of the remaining five seats. With its large bubble canopy, the little ship allowed them all a good view, and the humans couldn't help gawking as they zoomed toward the station.

At first, it merely glowed in the reflected light of Darius like a small planet, but as they approached, more details became apparent. The most obvious feature, discernible when even some nearby large starships were simply spots in space, was that the Bazaar was, for a manufactured structure, almost unimaginably huge. The external surface was reflective and studded with a massive array of energy collectors like great vanes turned toward the star. It rotated slowly and maintained a high polar orbit over the large planet called Darius III. Because of the orientation of that orbit, Parvik explained, it was never eclipsed by the planet; that is, it remained constantly exposed to the sun.

"The Bazaar is one of the largest stations in all the galaxy," the pilot informed them. As they drew closer, they could see that it was shaped like a cylinder two kilometers in diameter and something more than ten klicks long. It rotated on its long axis like a rolling pin. Jackson knew that the rotation would create, through centrifugal force, an effect like gravity to one who stood on the inside of the outer hull.

At each of the hubs, a large hangar entrance opened into space. The interior was brightly lit and busy with ships, both large and small, coming and going. The hangar itself was exposed to space and thus hard vacuum, but Parvik explained that an example of virtually every type of air lock in the known galaxy could be found inside, so that most ships could enter the hangar bay and securely attach themselves to the hull for easy on- and off-loading of passengers and cargo in a pressurized environment.

"Only the very largest starships can't enter," the Assarn explained. "A ship like your *Pangaea* would have to stand off and send shuttles back and forth into the station. But most cargo haulers and even a vessel like my *Starguard* or your frigate could fly in there and find a docking berth."

During his tours aboard U.S. Navy ships, Jackson had entered some of the great ports of the world, including New York, Singapore, Sydney, Rotterdam, and Hong Kong. The experience of a first-time arrival in one of those legendary places had always been moving, even awe-inspiring, but nothing in his life had prepared him for this. A quick scan showed no fewer than three dozen spaceships in motion around the mouth of the great hangar bay. A steady stream of vessels followed one another in, while another group emerged. The little shuttle joined a queue of smaller ships, approaching slowly, and in a remarkably short time Parvik had guided them into the bright interior of the massive station. The hangar bay itself was nearly a kilometer across.

The radio crackled with instructions. A traffic controller directed the shuttle to Docking Berth 0042, and the Assarn pilot easily located their parking place, nestling his little shuttle between something that looked like a flying passenger bus and a small, speedy-looking craft that reminded Jackson of a Japanese kamikaze aircraft called the Oka of World War II vintage.

Once they were secured at an air lock, Parvik released the hatch, and the four SEALS, disguised in their common workers' garb, debarked. Passing through the connecting tube, they emerged into a concourse that reminded Jackson of nothing so much as a bustling third world airport, albeit one with zero gravity. They pulled themselves through a throng of travelers, then took hold of handles that moved them through space toward the large plazas where transport shafts would carry new arrivals out toward the rim of the station, where the artificial gravity effect would become noticeable. Here, at the hub, of course, the zero-G state was always in effect.

They had their G15s and some other equipment in several large duffels, and Parvik showed them a bank of lockers where they could store their gear while they did their recon. Jackson wasn't happy about moving around unarmed, but he recognized that the presence of weapons or even mysterious burdens almost certainly would be enough to draw significant and highly unwanted attention. In the end, he allowed each man to hold on to a small sidearm and Teal to take along some of his medical gear. They sealed the rest of their equipment in the locker, and Parvik slid a plastic card through the slot.

"That'll buy you the equivalent of about an Earth week's worth of storage." He handed the card to Jackson. "You can use this to buy food, transport, whatever you might need," he said. "Within reason. If you try to book passage on a space-liner, you'll probably cause a few alarms to go off."

"Thanks," the LT said. "I'll save it for emergencies." He was beginning to feel just how keenly out of his element he was.

From the hangar bay, large transport shafts extended "down" toward the outer rim of the station. Because of the rotation of the massive installation, the gravity at the rim was equivalent to about 1.2 of Earth's. The closer one was to the hub, of course, the weaker the pull of the artificial gravity was.

About halfway down, Parvik suggested that they exit the transport lift to perform a little reconnaissance. "I have some good contacts here," the Assarn said. "And besides, I'd like to wet my whistle."

Jackson was eager to get on with his own intel gathering but appreciated their guide's familiarity with the place enough to go along with the plan. When Parvik led them into a crowded tavern, he even allowed his men and himself to share a pitcher of an alien beverage that tasted remarkably like beer. The four SEALS, in their civilian coveralls, stood at a small table, rubbing elbows with many long-haired mustachioed Assarn, and waited while Parvik went into the back to speak to some people he knew. They passed the time eavesdropping on the conversations at nearby tables, most of which involved women, fighting, and the specifications of various spaceships. As usual, their earpiece translators smoothly interpreted anything spoken in one of the dozen different languages they encountered in the bar.

A half hour later, the pilot returned with information.

"Tezlac Catal is here, on the Bazaar. He's got his own headquarters out on the rim of the station, but there's an area in the third midlevel that has recently been sealed off by his order. He made it public: The area's off limits by order of the savant himself. Rumor has it he has some VIP prisoners in there, strangers that he didn't want to send directly into his slaving operation, but too many of them to keep in the holding cells in his HQ."

"That sounds like a promising lead," Jackson allowed. "It could be the people from the *Pangaea*."

"I was thinking the same thing," the pilot said. "I can show you the place—at least the outside of it—and you can take it from there. Okay?"

"Good," the LT replied. He touched his ear, thinking about a question that had occurred to him. "I know these translators are ubiquitous; everyone seems to have one. But I'm wondering. If we go up to some Eluoi flunky and start talking to him, I know he'll understand us, but is he going to notice that we aren't speaking Eluoi, or Assarn?"

Parvik shook his head. "For one thing, there's a lot more than one Eluoi language. They all use the same alphabet, of course, but there's hundreds of different dialects, speech patterns, and word lists. People on these types of stations are so used to listening to the translation that they're not likely at all to pay attention to the sounds actually coming out of the speaker's mouth. And even if they did, I doubt they could tell the difference between English and, say, the language spoken on Arcton V. Remember, since the Shamani first contacted your planet, the major languages of Earth have all been incorporated into the translation databases."

"Good," the officer said, the answer setting aside one of his concerns.

The pilot led them back to the transport, which was a huge, crowded lift carrying some fifty passengers at a time as it *whooshed* "up" and "down," carrying people from the hub of the station to the outer hull and back. This time they stopped at the third midlevel—Jackson made a note of the symbology so that they could find the place again—and Parvik led them out onto a crowded street.

Both sides were lined with shops and stalls where merchants tried to attract the attention of passersby, luring them with shiny baubles, high-tech gadgetry, garments that ranged from silken finery to denim practicality, and a host of other things too strange for the SEALS to identify immediately. Pushing through the crowd, which was thick but orderly, not unlike a Manhattan sidewalk during the lunch hour, the Assarn brought them to a wide plaza where an amazing array of aromas assaulted them.

"This is a food plaza. You'll find anything you want to eat in the galaxy at one of the stalls around here. But over there is what you're really interested in."

Parvik pointed to the wide avenue leading out the other side of the plaza. Jackson spotted the target immediately: A large, closed doorway was guarded by two armed Eluoi soldiers. Even on the crowded street, the pedestrians seemed to give the place a wide berth.

"That's the place Catal supposedly is keeping his prisoners. You fellows have a look at the situation and come up with a plan. I'm going back upstairs to see about getting your Captain Carstairs a shuttle that might look a little less obvious than a United States Navy space frigate. Good luck," Parvik added.

"And to you, too," Jackson replied, watching the Assarn pilot return to the transport shaft. "Well, men," he said to his three Teammates. "Looks like we've got some work to do."

Nineteen: A Measure of Respect

The SEALS set up an observation post (OP) in the middle of the wide food service plaza, an area that was not terribly different from the food court at any of Earth's large shopping malls. Several hundred stalls were located around the periphery, serving meats, breads, vegetables, and a mixture of entrées ranging from sumptuously appetizing to absolutely horrifying. Ruiz took the spending card and made an individual recon, returning with some roll-type objects filled with a spicy but quite tasty mix of meat and beans. Jackson, meanwhile, picked out a table with a good vantage, and the four SEALS took seats.

But the men were not there to eat. Instead, they used the anonymity of the large open area to watch the mouth of the corridor where the Eluoi guards were posted. The two soldiers stood before a sliding door that remained closed for the first hour. One of the guards stood at a small computer, occasionally checking the screen, and the other one kept his eyes on the crowd. Both carried the lethal ray guns attached to the powerful battery packs.

While the SEALS were maintaining their surveillance, they noticed a commotion in the street, with many people scurrying to get out of the way of some kind of important procession. Within seconds the crowded avenue emptied, and they saw a dozen Eluoi commandos approaching. They, too, were armed with beam weapons but wore the elite berets the SEALS had encountered on Batuu. Immediately after the armed men came a pair of Eluoi, one tall and one short, wearing white tunics with much gold braid on the shoulders and sleeves.

Jackson froze, recognizing Tezlac Catal at once. He didn't dare make the announcement to his men, fearing that even a whispered word might attract the preternaturally powered savant's attention. In any event, the other three SEALS were staring at the hostile lord with the same rapt focus as the LT—as was every other person in the street and food plaza, Jackson noted with some relief.

Tezlac Catal was a tall, hawk-faced man who walked with the arrogance of a Roman emperor. Looking neither right nor left, he strode along at a brisk pace so that his escort of commandos had to march double time just to keep up. The shorter official beside the savant, Jackson guessed, would be his mijar, a spokesman who made the savant's will known so that the great leader did not have to inflict the painful effect of his voice on his listeners every time he wanted to communicate.

The crowd, which had been noisy and boisterous moments earlier, remained utterly silent as the savant and his entourage marched past. The two soldiers guarding the closed door snapped to attention and saluted, but their leader didn't even turn to look at them. Even after he had passed and disappeared from sight, the people in the food court seemed reluctant to speak above a whisper, and the pedestrians moved only hesitantly back into the street.

"Well, at least we know he's here," Jackson said quietly. "And we know to look out for him."

It wasn't until the SEALS' third hour at the OP that the guarded door finally opened as several white-coated servers drove up in a battery-powered cart towing a trailer full of what looked like linens.

The two guards at the outer door merely glanced at a com-

puter screen, cursorily checked to see that the attendants
were wearing badges, and pushed a button that allowed the
sliding door to open. The service crew drove in, apparently
making a laundry delivery. When, thirty minutes later, they
emerged with the same cart and trailer, the trailer this time
piled with unkempt sheets, towels, and garments, the SEALS
decided they had guessed right.

"Let's see where they go with that laundry," Jackson suggested, casually rising to his feet. His three men did the same
thing, and they all sauntered after the laundry cart and its two
crewmen. One was driving, and the other, when he thought
no one was looking, surreptitiously slipped a small flask out
of his pocket and took a drink.

Good, Jackson thought. They're obviously not too concerned about discipline, and that fact could only work to the
SEALS' advantage.

The vehicle, which was about the size of a large golf cart,
moved slowly through the crowded passages of the station's
middle ring. Much of the traffic was pedestrian and included
a mix of all three empires, people of the Eluoi and Shamani
and Assarn all bartering, shopping, and socializing together.
A few other carts, matching the green color of the laundry
truck, scooted here and there, and the stalls and shops that
lined both sides of the passageway frequently spilled out into
the middle of the route, increasing the congestion and making it easy for the SEALS to keep the laundry service in
sight. They moved through a gridwork of streets; the pull of
gravity was less than the strength of Earth's but close enough
that walking, lifting, and working felt more or less normal to
the humans.

After perhaps five hundred meters, the driver made a turn
to the left, pulling the laundry shipment into what looked
like a large, open garage door. Other Eluoi were coming and
going there as well, some of them in the white uniforms of

the laundry workers and others in maintenance coveralls that looked very much like the Teammates' garb.

Once again Jackson thanked his lucky stars for the assistance of Olin Parvik, who seemed to have outfitted them in the perfect disguises. The four SEALS wandered through the door after the laundry cart and watched as it entered a side passage, a long corridor to the left that smelled of steam and soap.

Looking around, the LT took stock of the situation. He saw several carts, three like the laundry vehicle and two that were much larger, along a far wall that was lined with benches and tools. Several technicians in workman's coveralls tinkered with the suspension of one vehicle and, with the rear-mounted hood opened, studied the battery pack of another.

Just beyond was a smaller door leading into a back room. While he watched, one of the technicians headed back toward that portal and pushed a button to open it. Before entering, he called back to his fellow mechanic.

"Don't forget, Fillser, we have to get some new heating elements up to the outer level. They've had some frost problems in D Sector."

"Yeah, well they can put on an extra sweater for now," the second worker grunted. "I need to get this truck running or Commandant Spiker's gonna have my ass for breakfast. And if he chews my ass, you can bet I'll be using yours for a topping!"

"Yeah, fine. I was just reminding you," the first tech said grumpily. He lowered his voice, and Jackson turned away, inspecting a tool bench as he strained to listen. "Anyway, I'm on break now. I'm going in the back to see if Lower's got any action going on."

"Don't drop your whole paycheck," the tech grumbled sourly as his companion moved through the door into the back room and closed it behind him.

Jackson made up his mind and started across the work-shop. None of the technicians gave them so much as a sec-ond glance, and when he reached the door, he pressed the same button he'd seen the worker use. It slid smoothly open to reveal a long, narrow compartment that he guessed to be a parts warehouse.

The LT led the way, with his three men following. They passed the technician they had first observed as he was scru-tinizing a shelf of electronic components, apparently seek-ing a specific part. Turning a corner, they moved down a more shadowy passageway with tall shelves looming to ei-ther side. At the far end, they turned another corner, and there they found a lone Eluoi slouched in a chair. He was wearing one of the small plasma guns and looked up suspi-ciously as the four SEALS came into sight.

He was wary and watchful, Jackson saw, but not because that was his job. It was more like he was goofing off and worried about being caught by some supervisor. The LT was pleased but adopted an air of nonchalance as he approached.

"What do you want?" the soldier asked suspiciously. He didn't raise his gun, but his eyes flickered to a nearby door, an opening Jackson hadn't noticed before.

"I think you know what we want," he said with a conspir-atorial wink. He nodded at the door.

"Oh, well, yeah," the guard said, looking past the SEALS as if making sure they hadn't been followed. "You can go in."

Jackson pushed the button, and the door smoothly slid open. They found five men in there, two wearing tech cover-alls, two in the uniform of the laundry attendants, and one wearing a soldier's blouse. They were kneeling, studying some small objects rolling across the floor. It was a scene that would have been familiar to any sailor in any navy in the modern history of Earth.

"What is it?" the soldier asked suspiciously.

"We heard Lower might have some action back here," the LT said conspiratorially.

"I see," the soldier replied, looking up with a sly grin. "You fellows want in?"

"Oh, yeah," Jackson said. "We want in."

Five minutes later the five gamblers, plus their door guard, had been immobilized. One would have a bruise on his head when he woke up, and two others probably had dislocated elbows, but none was badly injured. After the SEALS had overcome them in a quick burst of unarmed combat, Teal had injected each with a sedative guaranteed to keep them all down for twelve hours.

"And even when they come around," Jackson speculated, "I don't think they'll be in any hurry to tell their supervisors what happened." He reached down and plucked the ID badges off all six tunics, giving one to each of his men, pinning one to his own shirt, and dropping the two extras into his pocket.

On the way out they picked up two large empty toolboxes from the warehouse and, again without drawing any untoward attention, left the maintenance shop and took the transport shaft "up" to the hangar deck at the hub of the station. By the time they arrived there, of course, they were virtually weightless. They pulled themselves to the storage lockers and removed the duffel bags containing their weapons and two pressure suits, which they stored in the two large toolboxes.

Finally, Jackson felt they were ready to make their move. They took the transport shaft down to the midlevel. With Teal and Baxter purposefully carrying the toolboxes and each SEALS sporting a stolen ID badge on his tunic, they marched up to the Eluoi guards outside the secured compartment.

"I have orders to replace the heating elements on this level," Jackson declared sternly. The guard at the front entrance looked at his partner for advice, but the other Eluoi trooper simply shrugged.

"No one told me about that," the first sentry said, his tone a mixture of defiance and apology.

"Well, the order came down this morning. There's some icing up going on in there, and we were told in no uncertain terms to fix it."

"Sorry, but I'm supposed to get authorization." The sentry touched his computer screen, scrolling up and down. "I got nothing about that here."

Jackson grimaced. "Look, if I have to miss a cycle of maintenance because of your stubbornness, you can be sure that Commandant Spiker will hear about it!" he snapped, sounding more like a SEALS lieutenant than a maintenance supervisor. Still, the bark of authority seemed to have the desired effect as the man clearly wrestled with an aversion to responsibility.

The guard looked again at the vidscreen, then checked a backup computer on his wrist. "I don't see any maintenance scheduled," he said, his tone definitely apologetic. "I'm really not supposed to let you in."

"Well, Mac," Jackson said, turning to Ruiz. "What's next? Are we scheduled to reprogram the commandant's transporters?"

"Righto, Joe," Ruiz replied, playing the bored technician to the hilt. "But he's not expecting us until after we get these elements replaced. Should we go see him now? I guess we could explain that they lost our authorization down here."

"Shit," Jackson said, shaking his head, noticing the pale expression on the guard's face. "Look, pal," he said. "I know this isn't your fault. But there's a frost problem, and some VIPs are freezing their asses off while I'm wasting time talking to you. Now, I don't want to tell Commandant Spiker that some pissant down in requisitions misplaced a work order, but I will if I have to. I am *not* catching hell for this!"

"Please don't tell the commandant!" the guard pled, digesting the distressing piece of news. "Do your work here. I will let you in and wait for authorization when it comes."

Jackson nodded casually, as if it didn't make much difference to him one way or the other. "Come on," he told his men as the door to the sealed compartment slid open before him.

Baxter and Teal, each holding a heavy tool chest suitable for carrying heating elements, but actually containing the four SEALS' weapons, followed him while Ruiz made a show of consulting his wrist computer, as if seeking the data on the elements to be exchanged. The door *whoosh*ed shut behind them, and they took stock of their surroundings.

They faced a long hallway with a series of doors on either side; two shorter halls led to the right and left immediately inside the door. There was no one in sight along any of the three hallways.

"Let's scout the sides first," Jackson said, indicating that Ruiz and Teal should go right while Baxter followed him to the left. They quickly learned that this corridor ended in a closed door with an electrical control on the outside. Jackson pushed the button, and the panel slid to the side, revealing a dozen people engaged in various forms of exercise. They wore black tunics and pants, similar to martial arts uniforms, that reminded the LT of his time as an Eluoi captive aboard the captured Shamani ship, the *Gladiola*. Some were jogging around a track, others were working out on various weight machines, and a few were playing a game that looked a lot like basketball.

The distinctive physical difference between the races of the three galactic empires, of course, lay in the color of the pupils of the eyes: The Shamani tended toward shades of red, from bright crimson to pale pink; the Eluoi covered the same range in the green spectrum; and Assarn eyes were

cobalt blue. However, hair color was another telltale sign.
The Shamani he had met all had hair as black as the typical
Asian's. The hair of the Eluoi varied between coarse dark
brown and black, and the few Assarn he had encountered—
including Olin Parvik and his crew—were Viking blond or
redheaded.

Though they were too far away for him to get a close look
at their eyes, Jackson saw that the people in the exercise
room covered the gamut from blond to black hair. Their
racial features included Caucasian, Asian, and African. It
was that fact that caused him to conclude that these were
Earthlings, presumably some of the captives taken from the
Pangaea.

At the same time, not one of them seemed to project an
aura of authority or command, and he guessed that these
were probably the support staff of the embassy mission or
the crew—but not the officers—of the *Pangaea.* He filed
away their location but closed the door and returned to their
starting point, where he met Ruiz and Teal returning from
their own recon.

"That is a big mess hall, skipper," the master chief reported. "Looks like it's staffed by about six human prisoners;
they seem to be working up a meal right now, though none of
the customers have come in yet."

Jackson nodded. "I think we're in the right place, but we
need to find someone who's in charge."

They went down the long hallway, past doors that contained the ubiquitous outer locks. A hundred meters along
they encountered a guard station where four Eluoi sat or
stood behind a desk, each wearing a battery pack and a
wicked-looking plasma gun resembling the Nazi machine
pistols of World War II. When Ruiz consulted his monitor
and pointed straight ahead, Jackson led his little party right
past the guards, acting as if he owned the place. They
watched the "maintenance crew" march by but made no ef-

fort to question them. Apparently, once they made it through the outer door, their right to be there would be taken for granted.

Now they entered a different section of the prisoners' quarters, and Jackson felt that they were getting warm. The halls were narrow but carpeted, the walls lined with decorative patterns. They turned a corner, and once they were out of sight of the guard posts, Jackson knocked on the first door they came to and opened it. It was a small room furnished with a pair of comfortable-looking beds, both unmade, as well as a vidscreen on the wall and a small adjoining room that proved to be a lavatory.

"Looks like somebody lives here but they're not at home," he concluded.

They tried several other doors with similar results, but on their fourth try they received a "Who is it?" response when they knocked.

"Friends from home," Jackson replied before pushing the button to open the door.

This room, like the previous compartments, was a two-bed berth. One man, an elderly Asian, was there, sitting up in his bed and watching the vidscreen. He wore the same black pajama garb as the exercise group and blinked in surprise when he saw the four humans.

"Who are you?" he asked in Mandarin. The translator in Jackson's ear smoothly rendered the question into English. "Friends? From *which* home?" he added pointedly.

"We are looking for the diplomats and their companions from Earth," Jackson replied immediately. "Were you with those aboard the *Pangaea*?"

"Yes!" the man declared excitedly, swinging his legs to the floor. "But . . . who are you? How did you find us?" He tried to push himself to his feet but fell back to a sitting position. "Forgive me. I am unwell," he explained. "I am with the Chinese delegation, Deputy Undersecretary of Trade Chin Lu."

"Don't try to get up," Jackson said. "But maybe you can help us. Do you know where the ambassadors are? Or the locations of any of the UN officers?"

"Yes! Continue down this passage. There is a fork at the end. You will find the UN contingent to the left, the Americans to the right. Do you think you can help us get out of here?"

"I intend to do everything in my power to make that happen," Jackson pledged. "Thank you for the information. Now, please tell no one about this. We'll be back."

Closing the door behind him, he had to restrain his urge to jog, and forced himself to maintain a casual pose in case they were being watched by unseen surveillance. When he reached the fork described by Chin, he turned right. There was a large door at the end of the hall, and he went directly to it, knocking several times.

"Come!" sounded the reply in the unmistakable tone of a commanding officer.

Jackson opened the door and stepped inside the spacious chamber, which looked like a conference room. Several men sat around the table in the middle of the room, and at the far end was the man who had barked the command to enter.

It was Ball-Breaker Ballard.

"Admiral Ballard, sir!" snapped Jackson, instinctively coming to attention. As he was utterly out of uniform, he did not salute. "I'm glad to have found you."

The four-star old sea dog blinked almost comically, then rose to his feet. "Jackson?" he asked. "Of the SEALS?"

"At your service, sir. This is Master Chief Ruiz, Electrician's Mate Baxter, and Medical Corpsman Teal." The LT suddenly felt sheepish about his old coveralls. "Please forgive the costumes, sir. We're on a recon and felt it best to use some disguises."

"Of course, of course, man. It's damned good to see you. How in all the universe did you find us?"

"It's a very long story, sir. You should know that the *Pegasus* is near this station. We haven't been able to locate the *Pangaea*, but Captain Carstairs is working on that problem right now. We're hoping to effect a rescue, and this is only the first step—to establish contact with the delegation."

"Yes, of course. Come in, sit down." There were extra chairs at the table, so the SEALS joined the august gathering, which, as Ballard made the introductions, turned out to include the five-star army general in charge of the Joint Chiefs of Staff as well as high brass from the air force and marines.

"How many humans are being held here?" the SEALS officer asked.

"Something like a hundred, I guess. They left most of the crew and passengers aboard the *Pangaea* but took the ones they judged to be the most important, as far as I can tell," Ballard replied. "We were taken by surprise—pirates, we thought, until this savant bastard came aboard. Just one look from the SOB was enough to turn my knees to water, I'm ashamed to admit." The blustering admiral truly did look chagrined. "He opened his mouth, and the most god-awful noise came out—damn near made me pass out! So help me, when he talked, I swear the lights flickered!"

"I understand, sir. I have been a prisoner of an Eluoi savant myself. Their powers go beyond the normal." Jackson noted without comment the admiral's comments about the lights flickering; surely Char-Kane and Sulati were right about the electrical component of the savant's power.

Ballard nodded. "Captain Pickens said that they brought some sort of masking device aboard the ship; that's no doubt why you couldn't find her." The admiral's face flushed. "Do you know?" he said grimly. "These bastards are holding us hostage. This Tezlac Catal intends to blackmail our whole goddamn planet into accepting his 'protection.' Needless to say, Lieutenant, I will die before I allow that to happen!"

"Captain Carstairs is still looking for the *Pangaea*," the SEALS CO offered hopefully. "And we're due to report back to him as soon as possible. But first, we'd like to set up a plan of escape."

"Well, a lot of things would have to go right for that to happen," Ballard declared. "But I'm all ears."

Twenty: The Trail
of the *Pangaea*

"I've got something, Captain," reported the female electrician's mate operating the area scanner in the *Pegasus*'s CIC. "It's blurry, no heat signature, but there seems to be something distorting the magnetic fields in space."

"Mark a course for it," the CO ordered immediately.

The search for the *Pangaea* had occupied all of his attention since Olin Parvik had carried Jackson and the recon party toward the large station orbiting Darius III, the place the Assarn had called the Bazaar. While he waited for communication from Jackson or Parvik, the captain had maintained all his detection systems at full power, though he grew more and more discouraged as the hours passed with no sign of the large starship.

The frigate moved through space under low power, barely generating enough acceleration for a single G of gravity. The crew consulted all the sensory equipment while the gunners stood by the rail gun and missile batteries. They were in a very crowded area of the star system, with cargo and passenger ships accelerating, decelerating, or merely orbiting around them in all directions.

Every cryptographic tool was used to make her signature seem to be merely that of another merchant ship. No recognizable call signs were broadcast, no military radar was employed, and no communications were made with any of the

nearby vessels as the *Pegasus* made her stealthy way into an
orbital pattern above Darius III.

"We're going to get close enough for optical confirmation," Carstairs declared. "Engines to low power. Helm, start
your turn."

Despite the matchless technology at his disposal, he felt
much like a submarine commander must have felt when taking his boat into the Inland Sea of Japan or silently approaching a North Atlantic convoy 110 years earlier.

The powerful lenses on the frigate's optical viewers would
allow a detailed look at another spaceship at a range of several thousand kilometers, and as they drew into that distance,
they fastened on the mysterious hulk.

"It's the *Pangaea*, sir!" reported the mate who had discovered the magnetic anomaly. "She's dark and cold, but it's definitely her."

The frigate set up a matching orbit barely a thousand
klicks away from the motionless civilian ship, which was
drifting in a high orbit above the huge planet. Remaining in
position for a number of hours, they watched and observed
and took care not to draw attention to themselves.

They noted a supply ship, a nondescript civilian vessel
from a large, apparently industrial station orbiting Darius III.
The smaller ship decelerated as it came up to the *Pangaea*
and docked at one of the great ship's four shuttle ports on the
exterior of the hull. It departed an hour later, and four hours
after that another, similar ship approached. When the third
supply ship made a visit, Carstairs had the inklings of a plan.

"When that supply ship leaves, I want to follow it home,"
he said. "Still running as quiet and dark as we can."

They did so, and the captain was not surprised to see the
ship making for the same massive industrial space station
from which the other supply ships had departed. The installation was in the same orbit as the Bazaar, where Jackson
and his Teammates had gone to seek the prisoners, though

there were tens of thousands of kilometers of distance between the two artificial moons. The *Pegasus* took up an orbit matching the station, barely fifty kilometers away, and still was drifting there when Olin Parvik hailed him over the intership communicator.

"I'm coming back with the *Starguard II,* Captain, in case you find it useful," the Assarn pilot announced. "Request permission to come aboard."

"Granted," Carstairs replied immediately, unable to hide his relief at word from at least one of the missing actors in this galactic dance.

An hour later the Assarn pilot, dressed in a clean uniform and with his long blond hair braided down his back, boarded the frigate and met with Sanders and Captain Carstairs.

"Lieutenant Jackson was working on a lead when I left him at the Bazaar," Parvik explained. "He thinks he's located at least some of the missing humans and was looking for a means of establishing contact with them. In the meantime, I think I've picked up some information about your ship, the *Pangaea,* though judging from your orbital position here, I'm guessing that you've found her already."

"Yes, a matter of hours ago. We're still observing. She looks dark and cold, but there's some activity going on."

"Yes. That would be Tezlac Catal's men," Parvik said, spitting the savant's name angrily.

"We've seen a steady stream of shuttles coming and going. They seem to be carrying some cargo up to the ship or else bringing every stick of furniture off. It's not like she was carrying anything other than a lot of people," the captain said.

"No, I think they're loading her up—with what, I don't know," the Assarn said. "She's quite a prize with those Shamani drives and the unique touches you humans added. For all we know, he intends to use her in his own fleet."

"But she's really only outfitted for carrying passengers," Sanders said. "Why would he use her for cargo hauling?"

Parvik looked at the lieutenant, his expression dour. "You remember one of Catal's major trading commodities, don't you?" he asked.

"Slaves!" Carstairs said at once. "She'd be perfect for hauling lots of people across the galaxy—lots of life support capacity, more than a thousand berths. That son of a bitch!"

The conference was interrupted by a radio operator from the CIC. "Captain!" she called urgently. "I have Lieutenant Jackson calling for you!"

The three hastily made their way from the wardroom into the combat information center, where Carstairs took the mike and the other two men crowded close. "Stonewall!" he said. "Damn, it's good to hear from you."

"Good to be able to report, sir. We've made some progress here on the Bazaar." He described briefly the infiltration that had led them to the captive delegates and Admiral Ballard. "The admiral guessed there are about a hundred captives from the ship aboard the station. He thinks, and I hope, that the rest of them are still aboard the *Pangaea*."

"That's our thinking, too," Carstairs replied. He told the SEALS officer about their discovery of the hijacked ship. "Olin Parvik is back here and suggests that Tezlac Catal might want to use her as a slaver. Why not, when he has nine hundred captives already aboard?"

"Damn," Jackson snapped. "But at least you've found her. Now we have to figure out a way to get her back."

"We're working on that up here," the captain replied. "But what about getting the hostages out of their cages down on the Bazaar? I wonder if I should make a request through channels?"

"With all respect, sir," Jackson replied, "these bastards don't give a shit for channels. We'll have to break 'em out the old-fashioned way. But we'll need a ride. Sandy, are you there?"

"Right here, LT," Sanders replied.

"I'm going to work up a jailbreak down here. I think it's going to be up to you to take the Team aboard the *Pangaea.* and get control of the ship away from the Eluoi."

"Roger that, skipper," the junior lieutenant replied. He knew better than to ask how but also knew enough to wonder about that very important question.

Fortunately, there were other officers in the conversation, and a few of them had some creative ideas.

Once again it was Olin Parvik who provided transportation for the SEALS, carrying them toward the industrial station where the supply ships departed, one about every five hours, for the nearby *Pangaea.* Unlike the four-man mission to the diplomatic station, the Teammates in Sanders's party were all in uniform, each man carrying a full complement of weapons and ammunition.

The Assarn pilot guided the *Starguard II* into the industrial station's vast docking bay. With a little deft negotiation—Sanders suspected that credits changed hands—Parvik was able to lock on to a port just two bays over from the supply ship that recently had returned from the *Pangaea.*

The station seemed to be a vast warehouse conglomerate in space. It was about six klicks across, and unlike the diplomatic station where the human hostages were held, there was no rotation-generated gravity effect. Essentially it was a great disk orbiting the planet Darius III that had numerous hatches in its "upper" surface, that is, the side of the disk opposite the planet. Those hatches were massive, ranging in size from one to five hundred meters across, and were opened to allow the entry and exit of ships.

When a ship was in the dock, the hatch was closed so that the whole hangar could be pressurized. Each berth was separated from the others by solid walls so that some docks could be pressurized while others were exposed to the hard vacuum of space.

The *Starguard II* hooked up to a docking berth, similar to an airport jetway, connecting to the vessel's main air lock and leading into the central passages of the station.

"Don't you think we'll attract a lot of attention, moving through the station with our suits and weapons?" Jackson asked as they reviewed the plans.

"Ha!" the Assarn pilot snorted. "If you didn't have weapons, you'd attract more attention, most of it undesirable, I assure you. This is a place where everyone is expected to take care of themselves and nobody asks too many questions. It's used by vessels of all three empires, but it's sort of a no-man's-land. None of the governments hold sway here, and everything is more or less ruled by the almighty credit."

"Isn't that how you described the Bazaar?" Sanders asked skeptically.

Parvik flashed him a shrewd smile. "You're catching on," he said, "though the level of violence here is a lot higher than you'd find on that commercial station. Here, pirates have been known to charge right through an air lock to steal a ship. Which, now that I mention it, is pretty much what you're planning to do, isn't it?"

"I'm not a goddamn pirate!" Sanders snapped, revealing more of his nerves than he cared to display. But the truth was, his stomach was in a knot, and he had to admit that the plan he was currently in charge of was pretty much of an intent to commit an act of piracy, at least as far as the opinions of the locals might go. Not that they would care, apparently.

"Let's go ashore, then," the officer added, wanting to get the plan moving. He'd already spent too much time thinking about it.

Parvik led them through the entry passage, each man

pulling himself along by using the numerous handles and railings on the side. Drifting weightlessly, they soon emerged into a crowded passageway where individuals moved in all dimensions and a number of small air-powered carts and tractors hauled cargo through the crowds. The floating "pedestrians" were expected to yield to the vehicles; Sanders discovered that immediately as an angry honk caused him to pull himself out of the way of a cruising cargo train. It consisted of a single man driving a device that looked more like a flying snowmobile than anything else; attached to the rear of the machine was a string of about a dozen cylindrical containers. The trailing containers were weightless but seemed to possess considerable mass, judging by the way the little tractor had to work when it slowed and turned into one of the nearby docking ports.

The SEALS drifted along among the crowd, with no one seeming to take notice of them. They saw burly crewmen from freighters and combat ships, many roaming in large gangs, some of them drinking and some of them going to get drunk in one of the many taverns and bars that seemed to line the whole concourse.

Soon they approached the jetway leading up to the ship they planned to steal. A pair of Eluoi commandos, each carrying the battery pack and plasma guns that they first had encountered the year before, floated before the entrance to the tube leading to their ship. There was no door across the hatch, and the SEALS watched as another of the cargo trains, this one manned by two commandos and carrying six cylinders of cargo, pulled up before the two guards.

One looked over a manifest while the other watched the passing crowd; clearly, these men took their duties seriously. Sanders led his team right past the entrance, the men pulling themselves along, taking care not to appear interested in the Eluoi supply ship.

"That's our target, men," the junior lieutenant said when they had floated down to the balcony of a crowded tavern a couple of dozen meters away. "We need to take out those two guards and then get into the ship in a hurry."

His Teammates nodded. Sanchez and Marannis started out, using the air jets of their suits to ease down to the main concourse level, darting through the crowd toward the entry to the access tunnel. Sanders, Schroeder, Dobson, Robinson, and Keast came next, drifting near the upper bulkhead of the compartment, some ten meters above the two scouts. For the time being, LaRue, Falco, Rodale, and Chief Harris waited at the outside shelf of the tavern across the way, where they could keep an eye on things and react as necessary. They were the follow-up force.

Although each man wore his personal carbine on its strap, for form's sake Rodale and LaRue had placed their heavy weapons in soft duffel bags, since even Parvik had allowed that the sight of something like Baby or the M76 Wasp rocket launcher might attract undue attention from the rough crowd in the industrial station. It seemed that there was at least one inviolate station rule, as Parvik informed them: Use a weapon large enough to put a hole in the outer hull and everyone in the place would drop what he was doing and try to kill you. Even G-Man found that an acceptable reason to leave Baby in her wraps.

The two scouts drifted past the guards at the mouth of the docking tunnel, moving within about six meters of the two Eluoi. The green-eyed sentries watched the SEALS move on; Marannis and Sanchez displayed no interest in the guards.

"Hey!" Sanders cried loudly, addressing the two Eluoi from his position near the ceiling of the wide concourse. "What the hell do you think you're doing down there?"

The outburst drew the attention of many of the occupants

of the station, including the two guards, who looked up and fingered their guns, watching the officer and his men suspiciously.

That was their last mistake. Marannis and Sanchez moved like striking snakes, reversing course with the aid of their suits' directional jets. Each scout had a knifc in his hand, and the two blades slipped almost simultaneously up through the side of the sentries' necks and into their brain cases. In the same movement the scouts pulled the Eluoi corpses, neither of which leaked so much as a drop of blood from the fatal puncture wounds, still plugged by the knife blades, into the entryway of the air lock leading to the target.

The rest of the SEALS swiftly joined them, Sanders and his men swooping into the docking tunnel with the aid of their maneuver jets while Chief Harris led the backup party from the balcony toward the objective. The scouts already were stashing the two bodies in a storage locker just around the corner, out of sight of the main concourse, as Sanders shot into the passageway.

Even before they had completed that grisly task, the rest of the Team had moved up, flying up the long, curving tunnel that had reminded Sanders of an airport jetway. They came around another right-angle corner where the passageway curled up to merge with the air lock in the belly of the large cargo shuttle.

There they encountered one of the zero-G trains they had observed in the station concourse. Piloted by a single driver, the jet-powered tractor hauled a string of floating cylinders that swayed freely as the fellow made the turn into the tunnel. From the easy movement, Sanders guessed that they were empty.

"Hey!" shouted the driver, uttering his last word as a suppressed burst of three rounds from Keast's G15 hit him in the chest. He flopped backward, held in his seat by a belt, and the uncontrolled tractor careered down the tunnel toward the SEALS.

"Chief Harris!" Sanders barked into his communicator as the jet-powered tractor carried its trailing cars past him. "We got a runaway train coming your way. Stop it before it gets away!"

"Roger, sir," the chief replied, as if this was nothing more than he'd expected.

Trusting that the matter was under control, Sanders burst upward through the air lock and into the hold of the cargo shuttle. He spotted two soldiers, Eluoi ray guns in their hands, watching a half dozen crewmen secure a series of long crates along one wall of the hold. Here, too, the element of surprise was complete; the two armed hostiles were taken out with suppressed bursts, and the terrified crewmen were herded into one corner of the hold. Robinson and Keast covered them while the rest of the Team continued through the ship.

A large air lock, currently open, connected the main hold to smaller holds toward the bow and the stern. Sanders, Dobson, and Robinson swept into the after compartment to find the hold nearly full of the same crates that the crew had been storing in the main hold. A quick inspection failed to reveal any hostiles lurking there, so they quickly shot back through the belly of the vessel.

"Bit of a train wreck in the jetway, sir," Harris reported laconically, rising through the hatch. "But it's not going anywhere from there. Might make a nice redoubt if they send a party after us, though," he allowed.

"Nice work," Sanders replied. "But I intend to be out of here before they can even think about a rescue."

LaRue, Falco, and Rodale already were moving into the forward hold. Sanders came after them just in time to hear the lethal whisper of a suppressed G15. Another of the Eluoi soldiers, his gun floating from his lifeless hands, drifted slowly across the compartment. Beyond the dead man Sanders could see the hatch leading up from the hold to, presumably, the crew quarters and the bridge. He propelled himself toward the aperture, fearing at any second that he would see the hatch close in his face.

"Stay open, you bastard!" he hissed. Although it wouldn't necessarily be disastrous to have to force their way through a hatch, he desperately needed to capture this ship in working order, and that meant that the number of explosions caused by the attack would have to be held to an absolute minimum.

Here, at least, no explosive would be necessary. He pushed through the hatch into a narrow shaft extending perhaps four meters upward, with another open hatch at the opposite terminus. He came up through that point of egress with his G15 cradled in both hands. Falco came right behind him, oriented to face the other direction when he emerged. One after the other the two SEALS burst into the shuttle's flight deck, where they found a very startled pilot and co-pilot. Neither Eluoi was armed, and they quickly hoisted their hands over their heads, so the officer allowed them to live.

While they were covered by Falco and several more Teammates who quickly joined them, Sanders settled into the pilot's chair. He didn't even try to read the array of alien dials and instruments before him. Instead, he activated his communicator.

"Captain Parvik," he called. "Do you copy?"

"Right here, Lieutenant," the pilot came back.

"We have captured a shuttle. What say you come aboard and fly it out of here for us."

In another ten minutes the Assarn had joined them. He contacted the station controls, which seemed only too happy to do whatever he asked. The docking bay was depressurized, and shortly thereafter the upper door slid back to reveal a vista of stars. The shuttle's engines thrummed, and with Olin Parvik at the controls, the captured ship moved out of the station and into the crowded space over Darius III.

"All the way out to *Pangaea*?" the Assarn pilot asked.

"Negative," Sanders replied. "I'd like to stop by the *Pegasus* first and pick up some reinforcements."

Twenty-one: Reclaiming the Mother Ship

The stop at the frigate lasted barely twenty minutes, and then the little cargo shuttle was off toward the big starship. It was less than an hour later when, with Olin Parvik at the controls, the shuttle slid smoothly up to one of the *Pangaea*'s docking bays. At the same time, another shuttle departed from the next dock over, a burst of engines firing as soon as it had drifted away from the big Earth ship. With the fading of those rockets, the departing shuttle began the return trip to the industrial station. The SEALS on their stolen ship waited for the command.

The *Pangaea* had four docking berths on the outside of her hull, and the shuttle was affixed to the first one of them, the air lock closest to the bow. Even so, they would be a good two hundred meters from the ship's bridge when they emerged. Neither Sanders nor any of his men had been aboard the massive spaceship before, but they had the advantage of detailed deck plans that had been downloaded from the *Pegasus*.

After a thorough briefing, they knew that they would emerge into a large pressurized docking area inside the air lock. The chamber extended along the hull for a hundred meters and included the air locks for all four docking ports. The shape was roughly cylindrical, and it led to three passages into the interior of the ship: a forward transport passage for personnel, a larger middle passage for personnel and sup-

plies, and the after hatch, which was the largest of all—some
four meters in diameter—and was used primarily to carry
supplies from shuttles into the great ship's hold and operating areas. By docking the shuttle at the most forward of the
four ports, Parvik ensured that the SEALS would be as close
as possible to the bridge, which was their initial objective,
when they emerged.

Lieutenant (j.g.) Sanders took a breath. His last communication from Jackson had wished him well, but he was acutely
conscious that he was on his own, responsible not just for the
ten SEALS under his command but for Lieutenant Wesling's
twenty hastily trained navy troops and, beyond that, the
whole contingent of passengers, crew, and diplomats from
the *Pangaea* herself. It was a crushing load of responsibility,
but once the air locks had snapped together, locking the shuttle to the big spaceship, he forced it from his mind and
turned to the task at hand.

The Team and the sailors had gone over the plan in such
detail that there was no need for talking. Some of the sailors
seemed to take comfort in the quiet professionalism of the
SEALS and tried to copy them. Wesling's men were to remain in the docking bay, holding it against any Eluoi counterattack and acting as a reserve should the SEALS need
help. Sanders would lead his reduced platoon—reinforced
squad, he kept telling himself—directly to the bridge of the
big ship. Using the element of surprise for as long as it lasted
and then continuing with aggressive tactics once they were
discovered, he would attempt to wrest control of the ship
from the Eluoi raiders who had taken her over. Because of
the weightless condition of the ship, each of the SEALS was
armed with recoilless rocket rounds for his G15; the navy
complement of the group would have to make do with the
standard 6.8-mm caseless ammunition that, though low in
recoil, could send a shooter tumbling unless he or she was
well braced.

"We're secure against the docking air lock," Parvik reported from the shuttle's bridge, using the little ship's secure communicator. "So far as they know, we're just a humble supply ship bringing them another shipment of food or whatever else they're taking aboard."

"Let's delay their understanding as long as possible," Sanders replied to his men over the same medium. "Once we're out of the hatch, observe radio silence—and move fast."

Marannis and Sanchez were waiting beside the air lock. Sanders and Schroeder moved up behind them while the rest of the Team formed up in pairs to follow: Rodale and Dobson, then Robinson and Keast, followed by LaRue and Falco. Chief Harris would bring up the rear. The light above the hatch flashed green, signaling that all ports were secure, so Sanders unplugged the secure communicator and waved "Go!" to the two scouts.

The wheel of the air lock hatch spun easily as it was manipulated from the outside. As soon as it came free, the scouts, bracing themselves by gripping handles inside the shuttle, kicked it hard, smashing it open and knocking the cargo handlers on the other side of the hatch away from the portal. The two SEALS propelled themselves through the suddenly opened hatch and into the large docking bay; Sanders wasted no time pulling himself after them.

The compartment held some dozen men, but a quick glance showed that all but two of them were unarmed workers waiting to unload the cargo of the stolen shuttle. None of the Eluoi wore pressure suits, though the pair who were armed also wore helmets and body armor. Marannis and Sanchez went after those two immediately, Sanchez with a knife and Marannis with his heavy, sharp, breaching tool. The soldiers, taken by surprise, tried to raise their weapons, but the scouts were on them before they could shoot or get off an alarm. Sanchez plunged his knife into the first soldier's throat just above his body armor, and Marannis brought the axlike breaching tool down hard, splitting the man's helmet and the skull underneath it.

By then all eleven SEALS had shot out of the air lock. Waving a menacing display of firepower in the faces of the terrified cargo handlers, they shepherded the group into the shuttle. There Lieutenant Wesling took charge of them, locking them in the small after hold of the supply ship. His navy troops spilled out of the air lock to secure the docking bay and hold it against counterattack while the SEALS used their maneuver jets to propel themselves to the forward end of the large compartment.

Rodale manipulated the hatch into the ship's interior as Dobson floated beside him, his G15 at the ready. The porthole popped open and proved to be unguarded, so the Team, in shooter pairs, started along the passageway toward the bridge. Sanders cast one glance back to see that the navy personnel already were spreading through the docking bay, with Grafton's small detachment moving to cover the large cargo hatch at the rear of the compartment. Lieutenant Wesling gave the SEALS officer a thumbs-up, which Sanders returned, before following his men through the hatch. Two U.S. Navy sailors already were approaching, and he knew they would close and secure it behind the Team.

Speed and surprise were crucial, so the SEALS used the full power of their maneuver jets, each man streaking straight along the tubelike passage toward the bow of the ship. Four ladders ran along the walls of this corridor, which would be a vertical shaft whenever the ship was under acceleration- or deceleration-induced gravity. Hatches interrupted the interior wall periodically, and Sanders knew they led to many of the most luxurious passenger decks in the big spaceship. As with the *Pegasus,* those decks were aligned at right angles to the length of the hull, so as the SEALS flew along, they essentially were passing ascending decks, as if they were flying up an elevator shaft. Each man kept an eye on those hatches, but they all remained closed as the Team raced for the ship's bow. Each hatch had an external mechanical lock, and one of the SEALS engaged that lock for each access door they passed. The locks wouldn't stop a really determined adversary from breaking through the hatch, but they might serve to delay someone who was trying to come after them in a hurry.

They passed only one hatch on the exterior wall of the shaft, and Sanders remembered from the deck plan that it provided access to one of the three large domed viewing compartments that extended outside of the ship's long hull. This hatch, too, they secured with the mechanical lock.

Finally they reached the terminus of the transport shaft, which was at the bridge level, or B Deck, of the large spaceship. The A Deck, the only level forward of the bridge, was a massive viewing dome and cocktail lounge. When the ship was under way and generating artificial gravity, first-class passengers could while away the hours there, enjoying very expensive drinks and looking "up" through the Plexiglas dome at the vast darkness of space.

The SEALS collected at the hatch and just below it, as always in pairs, with Harris at the tail of the column. Every man knew it had to be a surgical attack: If they regained control of the *Pangaea* but knocked out all of her control systems in the battle, it would be a hollow victory indeed. Sanders waited until every man was in position, each SEALS holding his carbine in one hand and a handle, rung, or railing with the other. Only then did he wave the scouts forward.

Sanchez spun the wheel of the hatch and pushed it open, and Marannis shot past him onto the ship's large bridge. Sanchez followed his partner, each man again armed with a blade for the initial attack. Sanders and Schroeder came next to see Sanchez grappling with a big Eluoi soldier who had been posted just inside the door. Marannis glided past the melee and sank his breaching tool into the skull of an Eluoi in gold braid who was trying frantically to unstrap himself from a seat at the large navigation console just inside the hatch.

In all, there were some two dozen Eluoi on the bridge, which was a circular compartment about twenty meters in diameter. About half of them were armed soldiers; the rest were uniformed officers and crewmen seated at the various controls around the large room. Many banks of equipment, including screens, monitors, keyboards, and mechanical controls, were bolted to the deck. None of them extended all the way to the overhead bulkhead, so the SEALS could see all the way across the bridge, but there were many obstacles behind which an adversary could take cover.

The SEALS came in shooting fast, sending vicious controlled bursts while quickly spreading out to command the entire compartment. Sanders fired the first three rounds, taking out a sentry near the main computer bank. The rocket rounds sizzled through the air and caught the target in the chest and shoulder, sending him spinning away while his ray gun floated out of his hands and drifted nearby, attached only by the heavy battery cord.

Robinson and Keast rocketed up to the "ceiling" and shot across the bridge, snapping off short bursts at a pair of Eluoi troops who were bringing their guns around to the hatch. Marannis pulled his breaching tool from the ghastly wound in the helmsman's head, leaving a trail of blood and brain droplets drifting in the air as he pushed off toward the next seat. Another officer, wearing even more braid than the first, held up his hands in stark terror, and the scout loomed above him but didn't strike.

"I got one prisoner here, Lieutenant," he said, his eyes never leaving the terrified captive's face.

Rodale, Dobson, and Schroeder also fired at the armed troops. One of the Eluoi got off a burst from his assault rifle;

the rounds punched into Dobson's chest and belly, knocking him back against a computer console. The lanky Alabaman grunted as the wind was knocked out of him, but his armor absorbed the impact of the shots, leaving him bruised but unbloodied.

The Eluoi who had been seated at the controls faced a significant disadvantage in that each of them had been strapped in to his seat, whereas their armed protectors had been drifting about the bridge. The last of the soldiers died in a cross fire from LaRue and Schroeder while the seated hostiles were still snapping open their strap buckles. One bounced upward, a pistol in his hand, and Sanders shot him with a double burst, knocking the gun free and sending the corpse tumbling backward through the weightless cabin.

Another officer spun away from his chair and dived across a wide console. Schroeder killed him with a single shot to the temple, but even as he died, the man's hand came down on a red button. Immediately a warning siren started to wail.

But that was the last act of any of the bridge's defenders. In ten seconds it was over, with every one of the Eluoi complement killed except the officer who still cowered under Marannis's menacing glare. All the while, the siren continued to blare and the lights flashed on and off in a clear visual warning.

"Falco, LaRue," Sanders snapped. "Check A Deck!"

Immediately the two men shot through the hatch in the center of the upper bulkhead, emerging into the domed lounge that formed the prow of the *Pangaea*. They found several Eluoi soldiers diving for the hatch, presumably in response to the alarm, which was honking there as loudly as on the bridge. The hostiles were carrying their guns at the ready, but even so they were unprepared for the sudden death that came shooting up through the hatch. The two SEALS snapped off a couple of bursts each, killing all four hostiles before the Eluoi could get off a shot. A few of the lightweight rocket rounds missed the targets, but the slugs spattered against the sturdy Plexiglas of the dome without causing so much as a dimple. Moments later the two SEALS floated back down to the bridge to report that A Deck was secure.

"How many troops do you have aboard?" Sanders demanded, confronting the lone prisoner.

For a second the man looked defiant, his green eyes darkening almost to black. Marannis hoisted his breaching tool, the ax blade still gory from the residue of his first kill, and the captive reconsidered.

"Sixty!" he said at once.

"Where are they?" the junior lieutenant pressed.

"Mostly in the living cabins, J and K Decks. Some will be in the after hold," he said.

"And officers?"

"Just us, those you found here. Please, don't kill me!"

"Maybe I won't," Sanders said calmly. "If you continue to cooperate." He gestured to Marannis and Sanchez. "Tie him up and keep an eye on him."

The rest of the men were moving through the bridge, turning on the equipment and checking for information about the ship's status. Falco, Keast, and Schroeder were the most tech-savvy of the group, and they sat at the main consoles, bringing up screens and consulting pages of data.

"I got the internal cameras here, sir," Keast reported from one bank of computers. Sanders floated over to him and saw some twenty small viewing screens, each with an image of a different section of the ship. Keast twisted some dials, looking into the after hold, where several agitated soldiers were ordering a dozen workers to clear away from the hatch. Then he scanned through the interior halls. The alarm klaxon, accompanied by flashing lights, was sounding on every deck of the big ship.

"Here's trouble, Lieutenant," Keast reported suddenly. He

had come upon an image of the ship's main gallery, the wide deck that served as a grand ballroom and extended as a single huge compartment across the midpoint of the ship's hull. A number of Eluoi, at least a couple of dozen, were gathering there.

"That hatch, there," Kcast said, indicating the port that was clearly the soldiers' objective. "That leads right into the docking bay, where our navy friends are watching our backs."

"Damn!" Sanders snapped. He switched his communicator to full power. "Wes!" he barked urgently.

"What is it, Sandy?" replied Lieutenant Wesling in the hold.

"Get your people ready. You're about to have some unwelcome visitors."

Coxswain Grafton listened to the chatter over his helmet's communicator, deciding that the SEALS were damned terse when they were busy. He heard a few requests for support, an urgent suggestion that someone watch his back, and a warning that a closed hatchway might conceal some hidden and very unpleasant surprise. Most of all, however, he heard nothing as the serious men of the elite unit went about their business with quiet, grim competence. The distance to the bridge from the docking bay and the low power of the transmissions conspired to make it hard to hear exactly what was being said.

His own little party, he knew, lacked nearly all of the training and a lot of the equipment of the SEALS. Still, he was proud of the contribution they were making and was determined to do whatever he could to live up to the standards of the men of the SEALS Team, the first human military unit trained specifically to function on a battlefield in space.

"Damn, I'm thinking too much," he told himself aloud, trying to focus again on the matter at hand. His orders were clear, his task specific: He and the four sailors who had

crewed the drop boats were to watch the stern access portal
to the docking bay. They had positioned themselves behind
bulwarks and docking shelves where each man could see the
large hatch leading to the *Pangaea*'s stern section.

Grafton held his G15 comfortably in his hands, the butt
cradled against his shoulder and the muzzle generally
aligned toward the stern hatchway. He saw Roberts nearby
and returned the young gunner's mate's thumbs-up. He was
just a kid, the petty officer thought, a round-faced youngster
from some small town in Wisconsin. And now he was carrying a ray gun that could cut an enemy—or a slab of plate
steel—in half with a single burst. Christ, did the guy even
shave yet?

Then came the warning from Lieutenant Sanders to
Grafton's immediate commander, Wesling. Broadcast on full
power, the urgent call to watch out for unwelcome visitors
echoed long in the coxswain's ears.

The hissing of the big hatch was a subtle sound, but his
external microphone picked it up at once. "Look sharp!" he
hissed into his communicator, watching as the wheel on the
large air lock continued to spin. In another second it stopped,
and Grafton's fingers tightened around the stock and the trigger of his carbine.

When the explosion came, it was a sudden flash of light
and pressure that almost cost the petty officer his life. The
hatch was blasted inward by the force of a charge that had
been set to explode after the hatch's lock had been released.
Grafton, his head a little too high above the bulwark that was
providing him with cover, tumbled backward, the force of
the blast smashing into his face, wrenching his neck with
whiplash force. In the weightless space he didn't come down
but instead continued into a second somersault, drifting
away from the hull and into the utterly exposed space in the
middle of the docking bay.

It was Gunner's Mate Roberts who saved his life. The boyish sailor somehow had managed to hold on to his perch even as the more experienced petty officer had been careless. Now a stream of hostiles, at least a dozen Eluoi commandos in pressure suits, burst through the hatch into the docking bay. Roberts activated his ray gun, and sent the searing beam of energy sweeping back and forth through the haphazard formation of attackers. Wherever the beam touched a suit, it cut through the material and, inevitably, the flesh underneath.

At the same time, the rest of Grafton's little detachment opened up, as did the attackers. One of his men caught a burst in the face, the rounds exploding his helmet and scattering bits of blood droplets into the air. Still drifting in the bay, Grafton shot into the attacking file, cursing as the recoil sent him rolling backward. He activated a maneuver jet on his suit and shot toward the outer hull, where he was able to grasp a handle and pull himself around.

In that instant he saw that the center hatch into the docking bay also had been breached, and an even larger company of hostiles was pouring into the compartment. Wesling's sailors, including the small complement at the forward hatch, caught this group in a cross fire, but the veteran Eluoi troopers moved smoothly past the bodies of their own dead, firing volleys at the sailors and forcing the defenders back into the very mouth of the air lock around the shuttle's dock.

Grafton braced his feet between the rungs of a ladder and shot another series of controlled bursts, remembering to aim after each three-round series. Another one of his men went down, nearly cut in half by the blast of a plasma ray, and Roberts squeezed off another beam from his ray gun, the fiery energy beam tearing through the torso of the shooter. Unlike the impact of bullets, the ray didn't push the target or the shooter away, but it rendered him just as dead as a bullet to the brain.

There were just too many of the sons of bitches. A third sailor grunted and died, blood seeping out of the holes in the front and back of his suit as he was punctured by an extended burst. More rounds spattered against the metal hull beside Grafton's head, and he shot reflexively, almost surprised as his hasty burst caught the Eluoi full in the chest. The hostiles were floating to all sides now, and the coxswain saw Roberts rise up, sweeping the beam of his ray gun through the attackers, hitting at least three of them.

Many of the survivors turned toward the shooter, and Grafton sprang from his ladder, grabbing Roberts by the arm. He pulled the young sailor behind a hull bulwark as the rounds zinged and ricocheted from the metal barrier.

"In here, son," Grafton said, realizing that they were right at the door to an open storage locker. The two sailors ducked inside as another barrage of rounds spattered home. The locker was large enough to hold the two of them, giving each one some shelter beside the entrance. Each ducked to one side of the hatch, leaning out to return fire and then pulling back to avoid the enemy's shots.

But there was no denying the fact that they were utterly, hopelessly trapped.

Sanders left Keast, Marannis, and Sanchez to control the bridge while he led his remaining seven men into the lift of the central transport shaft. The car zoomed quickly, and in twenty seconds the eight SEALS emerged into the grand ballroom, the large open compartment in the very middle of the ship. They burst from the car as soon as the door opened, carbines at the ready, but the compartment that previously had been occupied by two dozen armed Eluoi was empty.

"There's the hatch, sir," Dobson declared, pointing to the large access door connecting the gallery and ballroom to the shuttle docking bay. Even from twenty meters away they could hear shots banging off the superstructure of the hull and see the smoke of the firefight that drifted through the entryway.

"Let's move!" Sanders barked, quickly activating his maneuver jets. The other SEALS followed suit, and in moments they burst through the hatch into the docking bay.

The officer's first impression was that the carnage had been terrible. Dozens of bodies, many of them trailing blood that still trickled into the weightless atmosphere, drifted here and there. Some wore the white uniforms of the Eluoi soldiers, but all too many wore dark blue U.S. Navy pressure suits.

But there were survivors on both sides. The Eluoi had trapped the surviving sailors in the air lock of the shuttle and closed in from three dimensions, moving around the flanks and along the upper and lower surfaces of the hull. Many bulwarks and supporting brackets gave them cover from Wesling's people, who were putting up a snappy fight.

The Eluoi never saw the SEALS coming up behind them. Immediately the Teammates started shooting, picking targets, hitting them with the recoilless rounds, and moving on. The hostiles, protected by their cover from the sailors, were completely exposed to the attackers coming at them from behind. In seconds, the last of the enemy had been dispatched, their bodies added to the floating graveyard of the docking bay.

Only at the rear of the bay did the firing continue, as Sanders saw that a couple of men had sought shelter in a storage locker and were holding a half dozen hostiles at bay. One of the navy men blasted out of the door with a ray gun while the other shot short, disciplined bursts from his G15. The Eluoi had them cornered and were closing in from above and below as well as to the right and left.

The SEALS moved after them with ruthless determination. The Eluoi, surprised at the reinforcement, tried to turn their weapons against Sanders and his men, but the Teammates had the drop on them. A deadly web of rocket rounds burst from the G15s, slicing through the air and through the bodies of any Eluoi unfortunate enough to be in the way. Because of the accuracy of the volley, that was most of them.

And then the beam of the ray gun shot from the storage locker and cut the last three hostiles in half. Coxswain Grafton and the young sailor Roberts floated out of their redoubt and looked around in some amazement, as if they were surprised to be alive.

"Sanders to Parvik," the officer said, breathing very hard in the aftermath of the battle. "Do you copy?"

"Come in, Lieutenant," the pilot said from the flight deck of the docked shuttle.

"The *Pangaea* is secured," Sanders reported. His whole body was shaking, but somehow his voice sounded smooth, confident, even commanding.

Twenty-two:
Unwelcome Interference

Jackson flipped off his communicator in disgust. He had been trying for more than four hours to raise Captain Carstairs on the *Pegasus* but had been rewarded only by a whole galaxy's worth of static. The range was too great or the power of his personal comlink too limited for the connection to be established. Whatever the reason, a previously reliable means of contact was failing him when he most needed to make a coordinated plan.

The SEALS lieutenant was becoming increasingly frustrated with his isolation. He had located the VIP prisoners being held hostage and was progressing with a plan to effect their rescue. But all his preparations would come to nothing if he led the hundred humans to the docking bay of the Bazaar only to have no way to get them off the station and quickly out of the Darius system. He had a feeling that Tezlac Catal would not take the escape of his VIP prisoners well, and Jackson wanted to be far away—far measured in light-years—before the savant came around for an accounting.

His last contact with exterior forces had been after Olin Parvik had departed in a large shuttle. In a brief conversation with Carstairs, Jackson had learned that the missing passenger ship had been located and that Sanders was going to make an attempt to retake the vessel. How that dangerous mission had fared, the LT had no idea. Dammit! He shrugged and decided that he had to proceed as if the attack had been successful. If it failed, everything was pretty much down the drain, anyway.

The officer currently was sitting by himself in one of the small shops just off the main avenue traversing the third midlevel of the Bazaar. It might have been a street in some crowded city on Earth except for the steel roof over his head and the alien spices and foods being served on all sides. He was sipping a bitter drink that was the closest approximation to tea he'd been able to discover on the whole bustling station, waiting for his three men to join him.

The first to arrive was Baxter, who slid into the seat across from the LT with a look of quiet satisfaction. "How'd it go, Fritz?" Jackson asked. "I could use a little good news."

"Well, maybe I have that, sir," he said. The electrician's mate waited as a seductive Shamani waitress brought him a cup of the bitter infusion and then he placed two circular cloths on the table between them. Each was white in color but woven through with a weblike pattern of copper wires. "I was able to rent a booth in one of these commercial workshops. I used the card, just like Mr. Parvik suggested, and there were no questions asked. I made these to your specifications. I only had time to do two of them, though."

"Thanks, Fritz. That might just be enough."

Baxter pointed to a pair of slender wires, each tipped with an alligator clip, that trailed from each of the cloths. "You just have to fasten these to a power source, like the battery pack of a Mark IV suit." The electrician's mate shook his head and looked at the officer skeptically. "Are you sure they'll do what you want them to?"

"Not at all," Jackson replied, wishing he could be more cheerful. "But this is the best idea I've been able to come up with. Nice work." The LT picked up one of the cloths, folding it and tucking it into the pocket of his coveralls. "I'll give the other one to Master Chief Ruiz when he gets back."

As if on cue, the other two members of the detachment

came up to join them. "I think we found a place that'll work, LT," the master chief said. "There's an empty storage locker about twenty meters away from the door to the prisoners' quarters. Harry was able to pick the lock, and it's just big enough for our needs."

"All right," the officer said, glad for the chance to do something. He nodded at the small duffel bag Ruiz was carrying. "And that?"

The Puerto Rican smiled tightly. "Two Eluoi uniforms, sir, carefully sized to fit Teal and Baxter. Their original owners, um, don't have any further need for clothing."

Jackson nodded; he didn't need to hear any more details to know that his men had accomplished the task he had asked them to do.

"Any luck on getting through to the frigate, sir?" the master chief asked.

Jackson only shook his head in disgust. Then he handed the cloth, with its weave of copper wires, across the table. "But here; Baxter made this. I've got one, too. We'll put them on when we get into our pressure suits."

If they made it that far in the plan, he thought disgustedly. "Dammit, this is a helluva time for my comlink to fail!"

"We found something that might be useful," Ruiz said. "They have a communications center, a commercial one, about half a klick from here. You go in and pay your credits, and then you have access to a high-power radio, kind of like a phone booth to the rest of the star system."

"Well, that might be worth checking out," the LT said. He was reluctant to trust a commercial circuit with his military communication but was forced to face the fact that his personal comlink didn't seem to have the power he needed. "I'll keep it in mind. For now, let's get started with Operation Dry Cleaner."

The name was only partially humorous, he reflected, as the four SEALS, still disguised in the maintenance coveralls they had been wearing all around the Bazaar, made their way to the service center where they had spotted the technician's garage and laundry service on their first reconnaissance. As usual, the outer door was open, with workers in laundry whites and denim coveralls continually moving in and out. One of the laundry trains was just returning, the small tractor cart pulling a series of five trailers heaped with dirty linens.

Jackson and his SEALS boldly followed that train as it turned into the steamy corridor of the laundry installation. A dozen workers were tending large machines. They were folding a variety of cleaned products, including sheets, blankets, and many maintenance and service personnel uniforms, and maneuvering a second train out of the way while the newly arriving vehicles moved up to a large table. There several women, female Eluoi, to judge by the coarse hair and greenish eyes, waited to unload them.

The LT was holding a small gauge in his hand and made a prominent display of watching the dial.

"Hold it!" he barked in a tone that invited no argument. "We have a potential radiation hazard here!" He gestured to the pile of laundry that had just come in. "Don't panic, but clear out of here until we give the all-clear. Let's see if there's any real danger."

The workers didn't need to be asked twice; every one of them ran toward the exit at the front or back of the laundry section. Within thirty seconds, the four SEALS were alone.

Moving quickly, the Teammates put the plan into action. Ruiz disconnected all but one of the cars being hauled by the tractor pulling the empty carts. Then he hopped into the driver's seat, and started over toward the disbursement table while Teal and Baxter went behind the barrier to the stacks of clean laundry. In a few seconds they located piles of white coveralls, the same garments worn by the laundry and other service personnel throughout this level of the Bazaar, and started to throw them into the carts behind Ruiz's tractor.

Jackson, in the meantime, ostentatiously studied his meter but also kept an eye on the entrance as he stalked back and forth beside the stacks of dirty laundry. His men kept count, collecting some 150 of the coveralls to be on the safe side, and then signaled to him when they were done.

Ruiz started the tractor forward with Teal riding beside him. Jackson jogged along next to the train, and Baxter came behind. The master chief drove his stolen vehicle right out the front of the service center, where they came upon several of the workers who had evacuated upon Jackson's alarm.

"It's all clear now," the LT explained breezily. He gestured at the cart being towed behind the tractor. "There was some contamination, but we got it all cleaned up. You can go back to work."

In part because he was towing only one car, Ruiz was able to make his way easily through the traffic bustling both ways along the thoroughfare. In five minutes they pulled up to a door that was just across the way from the entry to the prisoners' quarters. Teal hopped off the passenger's seat and manipulated the door by punching a couple of buttons. The portal slid smoothly open, and the four SEALS and their stolen stacks of laundry drove inside and closed the door.

"Nice work, men," the LT said. They had enough uniforms for all the human prisoners on the Bazaar. Even so, that was only a first step, and a lot of other things needed to go right. For a moment, he considered his next move and quickly decided what to do.

"Fritz, Harry, I want you two to wait here. Rafe, show me where this commercial radio center is. I guess it's time I made a phone call."

*　　　*　　　*

Sanders and his men wasted no time locating and freeing the large number of humans imprisoned in their cabins and berths aboard the *Pangaea*. Of the original complement of some 1,000 individuals, 900 remained aboard the ship. Though Captain Pickens and his highest-ranking officers had been included in the hostages taken aboard the Bazaar, there were enough junior officers and crewmen to operate the big starship. The reactors and then the engines had been powered up, and the communication and detection systems were engaged. The ship was almost ready to move.

He appointed Senior Lieutenant Brown as acting captain and asked him to get the big craft up and running. Lieutenant Wesling took charge of the passengers, most of whom were lower-level functionaries who had come along as assistants to the diplomats and brass-encrusted military people who had been assigned as delegates to the now-defunct conference. Those folks went to work cleaning up the detritus of the recent battle.

The fight had been costly. Though the SEALS had emerged with only a few bumps and bruises, ten of the navy personnel, including three of Grafton's drop boat crew, had made the ultimate sacrifice. Their bodies were set aside, frozen for later services, while the slain Eluoi were jettisoned into space.

Olin Parvik found the young SEALS lieutenant on the bridge as Sanders was finishing the final operation intended to restore the great ship to operability. "Have you gotten in touch with Captain Carstairs yet?" the Assarn pilot asked.

"I'm just about to do that," Sanders replied. "Care to listen in? I suspect we could use a little more help from you, if you're willing."

"I'm in favor of anything that's going to get under Tezlac Catal's skin," Parvik replied with a rather nasty smile. "Let's see what the good captain has to say."

With a veteran radio operator manning the console on the *Pangaea*'s bridge, it took only a few minutes to raise Carstairs in the CIC of the *Pegasus*. Sanders gave a concise account of the action aboard the big starship, confirming that the vessel had been restored to human control and that all systems were fully operational.

"Excellent work, Sandy." The captain's praise crackled through the earphones, and the young lieutenant couldn't help feeling a flush of pride. "So you'll be getting under way soon?"

"They tell me it'll be any minute now, sir. I confess, I'm looking forward to feeling some gravity again."

"I hear you. Mark a course for the frigate. My helmsman will give yours the coordinates. We'll link up and stand off about a thousand klicks from the Bazaar."

"Very good, sir. Has there been any word from Lieutenant Jackson?" the SEALS officer asked.

"He'd been out of touch for some time, but he came through not ten minutes ago," the captain replied, to Sanders's considerable relief. "He says that he's found the prisoners on the Bazaar, and has a plan to get them out of confinement. But we'll need to coordinate a pickup or they'll be standing around at the docking bay and won't have much of a chance."

"Roger that, sir. Olin Parvik is here. Do you want to bring him in on this?"

"By all means. Parvik? Thanks for all your help already. I'm going to put you in for an auxiliary medal of some kind or other. Can you do one more thing for us?"

"I already told Sandy that I'd be happy to help," the pilot replied.

"Excellent. For the time being, put your feet up and enjoy the ride back to the *Pegasus*. Once we get into formation, I'm going to ask you to take that shuttle right up to the dock of the space station. If all goes well, Stonewall Jackson will

meet you there with a group of passengers who will be looking for a ride home."

It was twelve minutes later when Jackson emerged from
the communications booth for the second time, having just
gotten off the line with Carstairs. Ruiz, Teal, and Baxter met
him in the avenue of the Bazaar's midlevel, and he immediately gave them the thumbs-up. "We're good to go," he explained. "Parvik is on his way to the station with a shuttle
and should be docking within the next hour. By that time our
radios should be capable of local communication with him,
so we'll know exactly where to go."

Since his initial meeting with Admiral Ballard in the prisoners' compartments, Jackson had resisted the urge to bluff
his way past the guard at the door again. It had seemed too
risky, and there really hadn't been anything to say. Now,
however, it was time to throw caution to the wind. They
needed action, and they needed it fast. Walking purposefully
along the always bustling avenue of the Bazaar, they came to
the room where they had stored the stolen cart and trailer full
of coveralls. Once again the lock Baxter had reprogrammed
worked smoothly, opening the door to give the four SEALS
access.

Quickly Teal and Baxter shucked off their maintenance
coveralls and donned the two Eluoi uniforms they had acquired earlier. Jackson made sure that the two pressure suits,
together with a pair of G15s equipped with noise suppressors, were stowed safely in the laundry hamper underneath
the stacks of white coveralls. He and Ruiz still carried the
two cloth devices webbed with wiring that Baxter had made
to the LT's specifications.

Jackson wasn't going to carry a firearm openly in the orderly civilian station, but he made sure that his sheath knife
was readily accessible, attached to his forearm where he

could wear it under the maintenance coverall. Ruiz, he noted, did the same with his knife.

"All right, men. Good luck. Let's move out," he said tersely.

Once again Baxter opened the door. Ruiz drove the tractor with Jackson sitting in the passenger seat. The two enlisted SEALS in their Eluoi uniforms trailed along a few steps behind. The little procession made its way up to the door to the prisoners' compartments, where the usual two guards stood at ease, watching the stream of people moving past on the bustling avenue.

Jackson eased himself out of the seat and approached the first guard while Ruiz swiveled to ease his legs out of the driving compartment. He was only about two meters away from the second guard.

"What's that?" the guard demanded, pointing to the single trailer. "We're not due for new linens yet."

The officer took a quick step closer, dropping the knife into his palm and pressing the tip against the guard's solar plexus. "You're coming with me or you're dying right here, right now," Jackson said grimly. "Make up your mind— quickly!"

Out of the corner of his eye he saw that Ruiz was confronting the second guard. The two Eluoi exchanged frightened looks as the SEALS put their hands on the weapons slung from each man's shoulder. The outcome was predictable: Each guard gave up his gun and backed up to the wall right behind him.

"Open the door," Jackson ordered as Teal and Baxter smoothly stepped up to take the weapons. The frightened guard punched in the code numbers, and the door to the prisoners' compartment slid open. The SEALS officer prodded both Eluoi through the door while his two men, now armed and uniformed like the guards, took up position in the corridor outside. Ruiz drove the tractor in right behind them.

Once the door was closed, Jackson reached into the laundry cart and pulled out their two G15s with the suppressors attached. He handed one to Ruiz, who waved it menacingly toward the two guards. Jackson quickly bound the prisoners together, and the SEALS started jogging down the corridor he had explored cautiously several hours before. Now, however, he knew where he was going.

They halted at the first corner, the master chief and the LT silently making eye contact, remembering the guard station with the four soldiers that had been right around this bend. Both SEALS went around the corner together, their suppressed G15s set for fully automatic fire. The Eluoi sentries looked up in shock and died before they could reach for their weapons, much less raise an alarm.

Jackson took off at a run, and in less than a minute he came to halt outside Admiral Ballard's room. He knocked sharply on the door.

"Come!" came the immediate reply. A push of the button slid the panel smoothly to the side, and Jackson found himself once again staring into the fearsome visage of Ball-Breaker Ballard.

"Jackson!" the admiral declared. "What's the word?"

"We're going to try to get you out of here, sir. I have enough coveralls to disguise all the prisoners, and there's a shuttle arriving at the docking bay to fly us out of here—if we get that far."

"What about the *Pangaea*?" the admiral asked, though he didn't let the question stop him from moving toward the door.

"Recaptured, sir, by the SEALS and a complement of navy commandos. She's standing by with the *Pegasus*, ready to get us out of here."

"Nice work," the admiral said gruffly. "Let's spread the word."

Ballard quickly roused the two generals in the neighboring cabins, and Jackson sprinted into the other wing of the prisoners' compartments. Fortunately, their captors had left the humans pretty much to their own devices, so none of the individual quarters were locked. Each prisoner released passed the word, and in a matter of minutes the captives had filled the corridors of their prisoner compartment. They were men and women ranging in age from mature adults to the elderly, and they represented the spectrum of races and cultures of planet Earth. They were universally eager to catch a ride back home.

Ruiz tossed stacks of the coveralls to the prisoners, who quickly doffed their black, pajama-like attire in favor of the white workers' uniforms. Jackson and Ruiz, in the meantime, donned their pressure suits. Before attaching the helmets, each of the two SEALS placed one of Baxter's copper-weave handkerchiefs over his scalp, attaching the alligator clips to the power source of the suit's battery pack. The LT felt a small tingle along his close-cropped hair, but the sensation was not unpleasant or distracting.

Although a group of a hundred service personnel might be a little unusual on the Bazaar's avenue, Jackson had observed enough of the place's laissez-faire attitude to feel fairly confident that no one would accost them on that basis. He was more worried about officious Eluoi, but that was a chance they'd have to take.

He was beginning to worry about all the things that could go wrong when he was encouraged by a crackle in his earpiece. "Stonewall? How goes it?"

"Parvik! Excellent, now that you're here. You *are* here, aren't you?"

"Parked, with the air lock connected, and fully fueled. We're in dock number seven six six zero, right in the hub of the Bazaar. How long are you going to keep me waiting?"

"No more than ten minutes if I can help it. Can you stay put that long?"

"Certainly. We'll fire up the engines just as soon as your people are on board. Over, for now."

"Thanks, Olin. Out." The LT signed off and looked over the situation inside the door.

The two original Eluoi guards had been bound securely with strips of torn uniform material. They laid the pair off to the side and, when the last of the prisoners had donned the white coveralls, made ready to leave.

"Everyone move casually," Jackson said, conscious that some of the people receiving his orders outranked him by about twelve grades. Admiral Ballard seemed to set the standard as he showed his willingness to comply with this SEALS officer's commands, at least on a tactical basis. "Don't run and don't stay too closely packed. Just follow the two soldiers outside the door. They're dressed like the Eluoi, but they're my men in disguise."

With that, he opened the door. Teal and Baxter immediately started sauntering toward the lift to the hub-positioned docking bay. The prisoners, true to Jackson's plan, moved casually along behind them.

None of the merchants or pedestrians seemed to pay them any mind as the white-clad humans made their way down the midlevel's crowded avenue. The did a good job of moving in small groups so that they didn't look like some kind of column formation but like random bands of workers who presumably had just finished their shifts of work. The route appeared to curve upward in front of and behind them, because they were walking along the inside of a circular ring. Yet despite the illusion of climbing, at every spot along the ring the deck underneath felt like it was straight down and the ceiling overhead appeared to be straight up.

Jackson, in his pressure suit, ambled along beside the file of prisoners, trying to look nonchalant. He could see the entrance to the transport shaft up ahead. He knew that even the big lift cars of the Bazaar would be able to carry only half the prisoners at a time. His greatest fear was that something would disrupt the escape attempt while half the humans still were standing around waiting for the elevator.

The screech that suddenly penetrated the street of the Bazaar was not so much a sound as a subsonic wave. It came from an unseen source and struck like a physical attack. The prisoners staggered and, to the last man and woman, tumbled to the deck. Many of the civilians and merchants on either side of the avenue also were knocked off their feet, and those who were still standing bolted from their stalls, vanishing into the depths of the station.

Jackson, too, was lying on the deck. He recognized that sensation from his first meeting with Tezlac Catal and was not surprised to see an approaching phalanx of Eluoi commandos.

In the middle of the formation stood the savant himself.

Tezlac Catal was there.

Twenty-three:
The Lazarus Plan

Jackson recognized that hawklike visage with the beaked nose, high cheekbones, and terrifyingly dark eyes that looked black but, if one dared to stare into them, proved to be a very sinister shade of green. Tezlac Catal stalked toward the escaping prisoners, all of whom still lay prone where they had been felled by the sheer power of his unnatural voice. The savant's face was contorted by rage, and he shouted again, the excruciating power of his mind spearing into his listeners' skulls, turning muscles to jelly and paralyzing minds with unreasoning fear.

Catal was accompanied by the same wiry little man the SEALS had observed earlier, the fellow with an ornate series of gold braids gracing the shoulders and arms of his tunic. This was the mijar, the LT remembered: a lackey who spoke for the savant, because the sound of the great leader's voice was excruciatingly painful to friend and foe alike. Both of the leaders, in their immaculate white uniforms, were surrounded by rank upon rank of elite Eluoi commandos, every one of them armed with a plasma cutter, marching in lockstep as the savant ordered them forward. They wore armored helmets with closed facial visors, and alone among those on this level of the station they seemed unaffected by Catal's psychic power.

Others of the Eluoi emerged from the far end of the street, and Jackson realized that the whole complement of humans had walked right into a trap. Apparently, the savant or his agents had been watching the prisoners with unseen monitoring gear. As soon as the escape had begun, the leader of the Eluoi had been able to set the encirclement into motion.

"Foolish humans!" the mijar squawked in a high-pitched, nasal voice. "You dare to challenge the might of an Eluoi savant! You dare to challenge the authority of Tezlac Catal! For this you will feel his wrath!"

"This is the sound of my wrath!" the savant roared, his words a physical assault on the humans on the ground. Some of the prisoners cried out in pain, and others sobbed softly. The sound of Catal's voice was, as Jackson once had described it, like spikes being driven into one's brain. Those who suffered from its effects could neither move nor speak.

"Did you think you could flee us?" It was the mijar, thankfully, who spoke next, his words a taunt. "You are indeed fools! You have been brought here from your ship because you are useful bargaining chips for the Eluoi Empire. The savant in his wisdom determined that your worth is greater than that of your miserable companions aboard the starship that brought you all here. Those who remain aboard the ship are destined for the slave markets, but you, exalted humans, have more worth than that!

"And this is how you return my master's beneficence?" The mijar gestured to Jackson, who lay on his back at the edge of the column of immobilized prisoners. "By letting this ragged soldier, this saboteur, thug, and assassin, lead you in a foolish escape attempt?"

The mijar stalked toward the SEALS officer, with the savant looming just behind. They came to a stop several meters away, and Jackson felt Catal's powerful eyes burning into him. He stared straight up, concentrating but unwilling to meet that terrible gaze.

"You, soldier," the mijar said to the LT. "You now face a future of almost unimaginable suffering. Do you realize what your vandalism cost my lord on the world of Batuu? You destroyed more than a billion credits' worth of property! You killed hundreds of loyal Eluoi soldiers! You caused thousands of slaves to be released, most of whom were recaptured only at considerable cost."

"Billions!" the savant screeched, in that voice that froze the will and liquefied the guts of the terrified humans cowering on the floor. He took a step forward, standing beside his mijar, still two meters away from the prone SEALS lieutenant. An Eluoi captain stood right behind them, his plasma gun held at the ready.

"Can you imagine the tortures that lie in your future?" the mijar asked mockingly. "We have masters of pain who can bring you to the point of death over a matter of days, and then, when you believe your life is ended and you are freed from the agony of the flesh, they can restore you to complete health only so that you can die again more slowly!"

He laughed, a nasty cackle of sound. "The cycle can be sustained for more than a year in some cases. I believe that you are one who might survive very well, indeed, to be killed a very great number of times. My master, the savant, is eager to find out."

The savant took another step so that he was looming over Jackson, staring down at him through the faceplate on his helmet.

"You will suffer!" he said quietly, and even that low volume paralyzed the nerves of the nearby humans, sending shivers of pure agony coursing down their spines.

Jackson lashed out with his foot—a very much unparalyzed foot—bringing his boot around in a sideways kick that caught Tezlac Catal in the knee, dislocating the joint and dropping the savant with a shriek of pain.

In the next second, the LT's G15 was in his hand. The assault rifle spit a single round through the suppressor, the 6.8-mm slug punching a neat hole through the nearby commando's forehead, sending the lieutenant flying backward. The Eluoi was dead even before his body hit the floor.

Jackson was twisting around even as he fired the shot and punched the barrel of his assault rifle none too gently under the savant's chin. Catal's eyes, a green so dark that they were almost black, were wide but for the first time ever filled with unadulterated fear. His mouth opened, tongue extended, spittle flying from his lips.

"Be quiet!" the LT snapped. "Don't make a sound unless you want to feel the brains blown out the top of your head. You'd better believe it would give me a great deal of pleasure to kill you."

By then Ruiz had sprung to his feet and was holding his pistol to the back of the mijar's head. That lackey was sputtering in disbelief, glancing wide-eyed back and forth between the two SEALS.

Admiral Ballard, nearby, groaned and tried to sit up. His head flopped back to the deck, and he shivered like a man suffering a mild seizure. "Don't try to move, sir. The effect of this SOB's voice takes a little while to wear off."

"But you?" the mijar stammered. "How can you move? How can you speak?"

"Trade secret," Jackson snapped. He gestured to the Eluoi commandos, dozens of whom surrounded them with weapons poised to shoot. None dared to move, not while their lord and master was at the mercy of this mad human soldier, the one the savant himself had called a saboteur, assassin, and thug. "Now, call off your dogs. Get them out of here!"

Catal groaned, his leg twitching, the knee twisted at an awkward angle. "It hurts, doesn't it?" Jackson asked conversationally. He addressed the mijar again. "Get rid of those troops or I'll break his other knee. Do it now!"

The mijar recoiled from the force of the command. He might have been a high-ranking leader, Jackson thought contemptuously, but his power flowed from the savant. He had no stomach for leadership on his own.

With a meek nod, the mijar waved to the Eluoi troops. "Move back," he ordered. "Do nothing that will endanger the savant!"

Reluctantly, the elite soldiers backed away, putting up their weapons and moving down the avenue in both directions. When they were a hundred meters away, Jackson spoke to the savant and the mijar together.

"This is what's going to happen now. You and your boss here are going to come with us. We're going to take the transport shaft up to the docking hub, and we're all going for a ride in a nice shuttle. When we humans are safely delivered to our ship, we're going to let you and Mr. Catal here go. Of course, if anyone tries to stop us, the two of you are going to be the first ones to die."

"Corpsman Teal," the LT called. "Can you come over here?"

The SEALS medic stood shakily, still trying to shrug off the effects of the savant's paralyzing voice. Unlike Ruiz and Jackson, he had suffered the full fury of the psychic onslaught. He glowered at the prisoner as he stumbled toward Jackson. With each step, he appeared to grow stronger, until he was able to stand at attention when he reached his CO. "Please get a hypodermic ready," the officer said. "I think the savant is going to take a little nap."

The mijar looked at Catal, who mutely communicated something to his lackey. It was the mijar who then spoke to Jackson. "How do we know we can trust you?" he asked.

Jackson smiled, but it was an expression totally devoid of humor.

"You don't," he said.

Three hours later, the shuttle, with Olin Parvik at the controls, four SEALS and three Eluoi captives on the flight deck, and a hundred rescued prisoners in the hold, eased up to the docking bay of the *Pangaea*. Tezlac Catal was unconscious, still slumbering from the effects of Harry Teal's syringe. The mijar and one unarmed Eluoi pilot who had been brought along to take them back to the Bazaar, watched suspiciously as the humans debarked from the shuttle.

Instead of removing himself immediately, however, Admiral Ballard came up to the flight deck to talk to Jackson. "Do you mind filling me in on the rest of the plan, Lieutenant?" He phrased the words as a question, but the LT recognized the order, and now that they were almost away, he was ready and willing to return to the normal hierarchy of command.

"Not at all, sir. I figured we would let the savant and his officer go as soon as the *Pangaea* is ready to accelerate toward a jumping point. They'll be in this shuttle, chugging back to the Bazaar, so if any Eluoi ship makes a move to interfere with us, we'll be able to blow up their Most Precious Leader in retaliation. They'll let us go, sir, because they won't dare let any harm come to him."

"What about taking the screechy son of a bitch with us, all the way back to Earth?" Ballard asked, scowling at the unconscious Tezlac Catal.

Jackson shrugged. "I would do that if ordered, sir, but I suspect it would be tantamount to a declaration of war. This—well, sir—this is a just a rescue mission."

Ballard nodded, appraising the lieutenant with narrowed eyes. "That's some good strategic thinking, Lieutenant. Nice job, Bravo Zulu. Carry on."

"Yes, sir! Thank you, sir," Jackson replied. In spite of himself, he was warmed by the praise. *Damn, the old Ball-Breaker just gave me a compliment.*

"Oh, and one more thing, Lieutenant," Ballard said before he departed through the hatch. "That SOB's voice just about knocked me out, and it had the same effect on everyone else.

How is it that you and your master chief were able to ignore it?"

Jackson grinned and unsnapped his helmet. He pulled the
headgear off to reveal the handkerchief with its web of ionizing wires wrapped around his skull.

"My very gifted electrician's mate Baxter came up with
the idea after he did some reading about the savant while we
were on that ice moon. In fact, your own observation—that
you could swear you saw the lights flicker when the savant
spoke—helped cement the hypothesis. He realized that
Catal's power is rooted in the projection of an electrical field.
The consul, Char-Kane, told me that they had determined
that a savant's power is based on a powerfully negative electrical charge. Baxter came up with this. I guess you could
call it a polarized skullcap, kind of a Faraday cage, to neu-
tralize the charge. Worked like a charm, too."

The admiral chuckled heartily, then ducked through the
hatch to make his way aboard the starship.

Once aboard the *Pangaea,* Jackson, Teal, Ruiz, and Baxter
were greeted warmly by Sanders and the rest of the Team.
The men went off to one of the lounges—Admiral Ballard
himself authorized them to enjoy some shore leave, including alcohol privileges—while the two officers went to the
bridge for a radio conference with Captain Carstairs.

"We're going to make a jump to an intermediate star, Sirius," the captain informed them. "There we'll rendezvous
and return Consul Char-Kane to another Shamani ship. She
seems pretty interested in making sure she gets that shield
driver back."

"Damn," Jackson said, only half joking. "I was hoping we
might get to hang on to that."

"Don't worry," the captain replied. "I have my whole engi-
neering team going over it right now on a full-time basis. By
the time we have to give it back, we'll have a pretty good idea
of what makes it tick."

"Nice!" Jackson replied enthusiastically.

"I thought you'd approve," the captain replied. "And it would be a shame to let all your hard work go to waste."

"I couldn't agree more, sir!"

"Anyway, Stonewall, as soon as we get back to SAT-STAR1 or some watering hole down on planet Earth, I want to buy you a drink."

"The pleasure would be mine, sir, but you have to let me repay the favor. We'd still be stranded down on that station if you hadn't been able to work things out with the *Pangaea*."

"All right, we'll say it's mutual. Good work, any way you shake it! Over and out."

Finally the ship was ready to start accelerating. The shuttle with the Eluoi mijar and pilot and the still groggy savant was released and allowed to start on its return voyage to the Bazaar. As a precaution, the SEALS had disabled the little vessel's radio so that the enemy leaders wouldn't be able to communicate with their subordinates for a number of hours. In the meantime, the *Pangaea* and the *Pegasus,* side by side, would be traveling much, much faster in the opposite direction. By the time the savant returned to the station, the two human ships would be almost in position to make the jump to Sirius.

In the meantime, Jackson found himself at loose ends. Sanders had made the acquaintance of many junior officers on the big spaceship, and he seemed sincere when he invited Jackson to join him in the forward lounge, watching the stars as the ship accelerated toward the jumping point. But somehow the LT felt like he'd be the older sibling crashing his kid brother's high school reunion and didn't feel like playing that role.

Instead, he wandered down to the stern lounge, looking through the clear deck at his feet toward the star that already was starting to dwindle into the distance. It was there that

Doctor Sulati found him, coming up from behind and taking his hand in hers.

"Hey, sailor," she said, a twinkle in her eye.

It felt very good to pull her close to him.

"You know, I've been saving that bottle of wine," she told him.

They left the lounge behind in favor of her small but comfortable cabin. Sulati was important enough to warrant a porthole in her quarters through which they could take in the vista of the galaxy as they clinked a toast to their reunion. The stars gleamed with exceptional brilliance, and the deepness of space yawned darker than any ocean blue.

The bottle was only half empty when the stars twinkled and, in a flash of momentary weightlessness, the *Pangaea* jumped out of the Darius system on the path toward home.